Some Distant Shore

ALSO BY DAVE CREEK

A Glimpse of Splendor

The Human Equations

The Silent Sentinels

Some Distant Shore

By

Dave Creek

Copyright © 2015 by Dave Creek
All rights reserved.

This book or any portion thereof
may not be reproduced or used in any manner whatsoever
without the express written permission of the publisher
except for the use of brief quotations in a book review.

This is a work of fiction. Names, characters, businesses,
places, events and incidents are either the products of the
author's imagination or used in a fictitious manner. Any
resemblance to actual persons, living or dead, or actual
events is purely coincidental.

Printed in the United States of America

ISBN: 1-942212-16-X
ISBN-13: 978-1-942212-16-4

Second Edition

Cover art by David A.Hardy

Author photo by Tim Waggoner

Hydra Publications
1310 Meadowridge Trail
Goshen, KY 40026

www.hydrapublications.com

Dedication

To Roy and Alma Shepherd
Beloved grandparents

Some Distant Shore

CHAPTER ONE

Afterward, watching the debris of two star systems go their separate ways, Mike didn't think of the stupendous forces he'd witnessed as much as he thought of the dead. *Even planetary collisions*, he thought, *don't affect the soul as profoundly as watching a loved one die*.

*****

Four months earlier:

Mike Christopher quickened his pace down a broad corridor within Urhaven Station, with Linna Maurishka and Luther Kindred right behind him. The place smelled of piss and ozone and smoke. Sickly green pipes resembling tentacles thrust chaotically through featureless, dingy yellow walls.

"Why in space we're meeting a Unity ambassador here is beyond me," Mike said.

Linna said, "It would've been nice to come up with a plan before we ran out hell-bent for who-knows-what." She was his shipmate, though circumstances kept them from sharing quarters most of the time. She had a round face, pert nose, brown eyes. Mike had included her in this because she was an empath -- a handy skill in a volatile situation. Linna asked, "Where are we headed, anyway?"

"A tavern called The Accretion Disk," Mike said. He pushed aside his concerns about Linna; now wasn't the time. Ambassador Song had arrived here early, then for some unknown reason left her courier ship and started across the station toward the *Asaph Hall*'s dock, without any security.

Luther was along because of his genetically engineered strength -- his broad, solid shoulders, and hands that looked as if they could crush a bulkhead. "Why'd she stop there?"

"No idea. I had the impression her trip across Urhaven didn't go so well." Mike was an artificial Human, his features a sampling of Human heritage, his skin light brown, dark brown hair lightly curled, eyes a bright blue but with epicanthic folds. He was also second-in-command of the Earth Unity exploratory starcraft *Asaph Hall*, but neither distinction counted for much in a fight. And a fight was likely. Station security had laughed when he'd asked for an escort.

They were close to the Disk. Mike touched his wrist sensor. "Eight inside. Five Humans. Two Arols. One Kanandra." He pulled his stunner. "Let's go."

Mike pushed through the Disk's swinging doors and was disoriented for an instant; gas giants spun sedately overhead and comets arced across an inky starfield. Holograms. "The Disk lives in a busy galaxy," he muttered.

Every being in the tavern peered at the three Humans. The tripedal Kanandran sat at a table near the door. The two leather-skinned Arols sat at the bar. Two of the five Humans stood behind the bar -- the men were apparently twins. A third man sat at the bar ordering a drink.

Rockhopper, Mike thought. This man's idea of freedom and independence would involve jaunting from one asteroid to the next hoping to find one rich in iron, nickel, or even water, and bartering the rights to it for whatever they needed to survive. *An anachronism*, Mike thought, *but it's not my place to judge*.

Toward the rear of the room, Ambassador Song sat at a table with two more rockhoppers. By the looks of their dirty, greasy clothing and long, stringy hair, they'd not had much luck lately. One of the men was leaning toward Song and repeatedly stabbing his finger at her.

The ambassador cowered. She looked to be in her early thirties and held a personal bag clutched tightly to her chest. Her long black hair was disheveled, but she didn't appear to have been harmed -- not yet. Then she saw Mike and stood up -- and she was clearly about four months pregnant.

Great, Mike thought. *Just another complication. This is the turning point. I know I can count on Luther. I only hope Linna's up to this.*

I can only hope I am, as well.

The two rockhoppers stood and stared at Mike, Linna, and Luther with open contempt. Then the third one, at the bar, said, "You must've come here for your woman."

Mike said, "She's no more mine than yours. But she *is* going with us."

The man eased his hand from his drink as Luther took strong strides past him, toward the ambassador. A kaleidoscope of light from the gas giant over his head played across his broad shoulders.

Linna said, "Luther, behind you!"

It was *after* Linna spoke up that the rockhopper at the bar pulled a disruptor. Luther turned and rammed both his fists into the man's belly. The man collapsed. So did the two Arols, whose species could not stand to witness violence.

More softly, Linna told Mike, "The closer barkeep."

Mike aimed his stunner and fired. The bartender, who hadn't even moved yet, also collapsed and his twin rushed to break his fall. The man glared up at Mike as he cradled his brother's head in his lap, face silhouetted against the light from several comets. "Bastard," he said.

"Not possible," Mike told him. "I'll know if anyone else tries to hurt us. Just let us go."

No one said a word. Mike nodded toward Luther, who took Ambassador Song by the arm and led her out. Linna followed, then Mike backed out slowly, leaving the tavern's busy galaxy.

Then he took the ambassador's other arm and he and Luther pulled her down that smelly yellow corridor so quickly her feet barely brushed the deck.

*****

Mike stood with folded arms and Linna and Luther stared in wonderment as they waited in the *Asaph Hall's* embarkation corridor with Ambassador Song. *Thank goodness that's over*, he thought. *I knew Luther would come through, but I was worried about Linna, in her condition.*

All of them, except the ambassador, were trying to catch their breath after that sprint from the Accretion Disk. Mike asked, "Pardon me, Ambassador, but what the *hell* possessed you to go into that bar?"

"Urhaven Station is not a civilized place, do you know that? I left the courier, minding my own business, when those three men accosted me."

"Ambassador, they wanted you as their sporting girl!"

"Their what?"

"Their lady of pleasure, fancy woman, you know."

"Their *whore*?"

"I was trying not to put it so bluntly to a Unity ambassador, but yes, just that!"

"Me? I'm not that kind...and I'm pregnant!"

Captain Rosa Sandage's voice came over the P.A.: "Everyone to duty stations. Clearing moorings in two minutes."

"Uh, oh," Linna said. Mike's heart sank; he *had* to talk things out with Linna soon, but who knew when he'd get the chance?

"What's going on?" Ambassador Song asked.

Mike said, "We're leaving quicker than we thought."

"No doubt your friends back in the bar are making more trouble."

"Not *my* friends, Ambassador. I'll bring Captain Sandage to see you in your quarters after we get underway. Luther, can you show the ambassador there?"

"Can do. Ambassador?"

Song picked up her bag and followed Luther into the main corridor. When she was gone, Linna said, "What was *that* all about?"

"We can't worry about that now," Mike said. "Let's secure the tube and get upstairs."

*****

As he and Linna headed toward the *Asaph Hall*'s bridge, Mike was disappointed that he'd not had a chance to speak with her in private. They were shipmates -- a couple who remained faithful whenever they were aboard the *Hall*. It was a relationship more than lovers, less than spouses. Linna had to spend much of each day alone, to avoid "burning out" on the constant flood of emotional radiation from Mike and everyone else on the ship.

It seems Humans aren't meant to have empathic powers and remain happy, Mike thought. An empath who lived around the same people constantly felt the flow of emotions from them more intensely over time -- like a stream eroding a deeper, straighter channel through rock. And that stream could not be slowed.

The genetic engineering techniques that had made Linna and a handful of other Humans into empaths or telepaths had been abandoned decades ago -- too many had gone mad, some committing suicide.

Linna was one of the more stable ones. One of the luckier ones.

By the time Mike and Linna reached the bridge, the starcraft was already backing away from Urhaven Station. Captain Rosa Sandage, sitting at the command chair, looked up as they entered. She was tall, red-haired, Martian-born. "Great job getting our ambassador out," she said.

Mike said, "Thanks." He nodded toward the main viewscreen, where Urhaven Station became smaller by the instant. Beyond was boundless beauty that Mike remembered from a previous journey to this system; Urhaven Station orbited twin stars at the center of Leavitt's System. Those stars orbited so closely to one another that their outer edges touched, and in their embrace they'd transformed from globes into egg shapes. "I suppose we wore out our welcome."

"To say the least. Even though Unity security wasn't willing to lend a hand, they said don't come back. So, no more vacations on Urhaven."

Mike smiled. Then Rosa said, "Well, give me a sense of the ambassador?" Mike's smile faded. Rosa's shoulders slumped. "Don't tell me. Some bureaucrat with a rod up her -- "

"No," Mike said, keeping his voice low, aware of other crewmembers' presence on the bridge. "She's not a bureaucrat."

Linna said, "We're still waiting for word on the rod."

Rosa said, "Well, then -- let's get to it." She led the way off the bridge.

*****

Mike pressed the chime at the quarters Ambassador Song had been assigned. No response came for a few seconds, and he was about to press it again when he heard, "Come in."

Mike let Rosa and Linna enter first. Ambassador Song's quarters were little larger than anyone else's on the ship -- a living room with just enough space for everyone to sit, a small bedroom, a bath. Her bag was in one corner, unopened.

The ambassador stepped forward, expression very proper and formal, to shake Rosa's hand. "Captain Sandage. A pleasure. Earth Unity Ambassador Teresa Song. Won't everyone sit?"

Everyone sat. Mike waited for Rosa to speak first. And he suspected Linna would remain content to listen, to "read" their guest.

Rosa said, "So, Ambassador."

"Please, Captain, call me Teresa unless we're at formal occasions." She glanced at Mike and Linna. "I'm including all of you, of course."

Rosa said, "You were a late addition to our journey. I'd been told we wouldn't carry an ambassador."

Teresa crossed her legs, hands cupping over one knee. "The Unity obviously changed its mind."

"How much do you know about where we're going -- and who we're going with?"

"I know we're headed toward the Moruteb system. And that a rogue star, Neska, and its two planets will pass close to it, in not quite...five months, is it?"

"That's right," Rosa said. "But it's taken so long to organize this mission that we won't have a lot of time to explore. Both systems are likely to see planets disrupted by the encounter. We're to explore as many worlds as we can before that happens. And we're to record the encounter as it occurs. Fortunately, we don't believe any of the planets in either system have intelligences on them." She glanced at Mike.

He picked up the hint. "We'll be part of a small fleet. A Cetronen raider, the *Cerenam*, will be the military component, in case that's needed. Although the Cetronen will supply their share of explorers, too. And a Drodusarel ship, the *Dirat*."

Teresa said, "Presumably, that's why I'm here, to deal with them."

Rosa said, "This mission is as much cultural and political as scientific. Each of us will send crewmembers over to the other ships, to learn more about one another. If I may ask, Ambassador -- how much experience have you had with such matters?"

"Inter-species relations? Only a little."

Rosa said, "I'll speak frankly. The courier ship arrives at Urhaven Station, and you start for us before I have a chance to send anyone to escort you. That hardly seems prudent. I have to be concerned about your judgment."

"I expected someone with the courier to come with me. They told me it was too dangerous. I reasoned, how dangerous could a Unity-affiliated station be?"

Mike said, "You reasoned wrong, and almost became a ship's whore."

"That's my business."

Rosa said, "Not when you're a Unity ambassador. And not when my people have to rescue you, and we get banned from Urhaven, even though it's not a fun place. You have larger responsibilities. Including, it seems, a child sometime before this mission is over."

"I've...stabilized...my pregnancy, Captain. It won't go any further until I want it to."

Mike said, "We're going to be together for the better part of a year."

This time Teresa didn't even look at Mike, but continued to address Rosa. "I demand that your crewmembers treat me with the respect due my position."

Rosa stood up, and Mike and Linna quickly followed suit. Rosa said, "I intend to treat...your *position* with exactly that respect. Good day." Rosa turned on one heel and headed for the door, Mike and Linna following close behind.

At the end of the corridor, they all paused at the grav tube to the bridge. Rosa looked at Mike. "She seems to like you about as much as a fart in an airlock. Did you say or do something back there -- "

Linna spoke up before Mike could. "He was great back there, Rosa. There's nothing she could be upset about." She turned to Mike. "She has a visceral response to you. Like someone who hates spiders and finds one in her bed."

"Could it be because I'm artificial?" Mike had been grown from genetic material created in a laboratory. He'd developed within an artificial womb.

"That occurred to me. I have the impression she's trying to hide something, and that could be it. But a Unity diplomat having such a prejudice? That doesn't make any sense."

Rosa said, "This very long trip just got longer. And a lot less fun." Then she stepped into the grav tube and rose up toward the bridge.

Linna was about to follow, but Mike touched her arm. He knew he didn't have to tell Linna what he was feeling.

Linna, though, wouldn't meet his gaze. "Not yet," she said. And she stepped into the tube and was gone.

*****

As Mike was returning to his quarters, Georges Remy approached him in the corridor. He was a short, balding man, the *Asaph Hall*'s communications and ecology specialist and a maintenance engineer. "Tell me this mission isn't being canceled."

Mike said, "The mission's not being canceled."

Georges let out a long sigh. "Thank goodness. I've already been frustrated that we're running late. The Cetronen must be beside themselves just waiting for us."

Mike couldn't help chuckling. "They're paired symbionts. They're always beside themselves."

Georges rolled his eyes. "I'm just glad this mission is still happening. Just think, a rogue star, worlds colliding -- it's our own Hero's Journey."

"Excuse me -- what kind of journey?"

"Like something out of mythology. The hero faces a challenge he doesn't want to accept, but he's forced to. Just when everything looks to be going straight to hell, he triumphs."

Mike said, "And the hero's you."

"Each of us, really. But yeah, mostly me."

"But this isn't the same kind of challenge. We're accepting it. Doesn't your idea fall apart?"

"Don't worry, Mike," Georges said. "Something will come up to create the right kind of challenge. Especially as we spend the better part of a year trying to get along with Cetronen and Drodusarel." Georges threw Mike a casual wave and continued down the corridor. Mike was left to concede the man was probably right.

*****

Once in his quarters, Mike called up a wall holo of the Moruteb system and the rogue star, Neska. *How many times have I viewed this?* he wondered. *Doesn't matter. I'll look at it a hundred times more before we arrive.*

The Cetronen had made the initial discovery that the two systems would have this catastrophic encounter, and they'd named both stars and all the worlds. Their scientists had named Moruteb after a celebrated explorer -- Mike wondered what his exploits had included. Humanity still had some pretty big gaps in its knowledge of Cetronen history.

Moruteb was about the same size as Sol, .98 its mass, but was older, having formed nearly seven billion years previously. By all accounts, it should have been halfway through its lifetime, a healthy, mature star, loyal guardian of its four planets and countless smaller worlds.

Cetronen historians had named Neska for a mythical creature that ate unworthy or careless children. It carried along two planets, believed to be the only survivors among several other worlds that would've been destroyed or spun away into space when Neska began its wild journey. One planet, Pantor, was named for Neska's mate. The other, Lasira, was named after Neska and Pantor's child. All three were bearing down upon Moruteb.

No one knew how Neska had been set on such an unusual course through this part of the galaxy. Perhaps it had burst out of a star-forming nebula ages ago, or had been one component of a double-star that spun apart. Whatever its origins, within five months it and its two planets that remained would pass within 30 A.U. of the Moruteb system -- an A.U. being the distance from Sol to Earth. Moruteb and its four planets could see effects ranging from disruption of orbits to worlds from the two systems colliding.

Mike watched the display of stars and planets without really seeing it. Humans had never witnessed such an event.

Merely to consider its magnitude, Mike thought, *is to feel humbled, and to consider how precious life is. Would any of this -- massive suns, entire worlds colliding like billiard balls -- would any of it mean anything without sentience to observe it, to measure it, to stand in awe of it?*

Does that idea also run in the opposite direction? This event will run with clockwork precision, all encounters among suns and worlds predetermined, yet far beyond Human capacity to forecast in meaningful detail.

Mike went to the small bay window at one end of the main room of his quarters. Usually it was a comfort to look out at the stars. With the lights dimmed, he saw one that shone with the azure of blue skies back on Earth, another a jem-like emerald, yet another a bloody crimson. And on and on, by the hundreds, the thousands, the millions and billions, each one shining strong and steady.

And just how far do they go? Mike wondered. Forever? How is that possible? How could we ever find out in a single lifetime?

Without such wonders to let us revel in our Humanity, would we be fully Human?

I can't know that. I only know...that no matter how much I try to distract myself, even with an astronomical event nearly beyond imagining, I can't stop thinking of Linna.

CHAPTER TWO

Two days later, it was time to rendezvous with the other starcraft in their small fleet. Mike arrived on the *Asaph Hall*'s bridge even as the kaleidoscopic swirl of the stardrive field was fading from the main viewscreen. He'd had dealings with both Cetronen and Drodusarel before, and Rosa wanted him here in his role as Chief Contact Officer to lend advice if needed. He sat in the seat to the left of Rosa's command chair. Behind her stood the ship's exobiologist Rishona Kwan. As she was an expert on Cetronen biology and psychology, and even spoke some of that species' dominant language, no doubt Rosa wanted to take advantage of her insights.

The seat to Rosa's right was empty. Mike leaned in close and asked, "Didn't you invite Ambassador Song to be here?"

Rosa spared Mike only the briefest of glances. "I did," she said, then returned her attention to the main screen.

The image of the Cetronen military starcraft *Cerenam* dominated that screen, with the Drodusarel craft to one side. The Cetronen ship was vaguely mushroom-shaped, a hundred meters tall, with blue-and-black mottling. Most Cetronen cargo or passenger craft featured similar designs, but this craft's hull bristled with sensor pods, shield generators, and disruptor ports, revealing its identity as a raider-class warcraft.

Each species represented in the exploratory fleet had agreed weeks earlier on this rendezvous point, light-years away from any inhabited worlds. *That way*, Mike thought, *we know that any unknown ship that approaches us is a potential hostile.*

A small holo of *Cerenam*'s commander, Codari, appeared before Rosa's command chair.

Cetronen were paired symbionts. The larger of the two, called the major, was about two and a half meters tall, with reddish fur, and represented the pair's physical strength. He held the smaller minor in his arms. A hump on the major's belly served as a seat, and the major's thick muscular tail helped counterbalance the minor's weight. Majors rarely initiated actions and generally followed their minors' unspoken commands.

Minors were smaller, thinner, and represented the pair's brains. "Greetings, Captain Rosa Sandage," the Codari minor said. Mike heard the translation over his implanted datalink. The minor's words were cordial enough, but Mike could tell he was barely keeping his impatience in check. His wide pointed ears waggled back and forth and the protective membranes in his nostrils opened and closed rhythmically. Those nostrils were flat against Codari's face; Cetronen had no noses, and their eyes were deep-set beneath a jutting brow. "You are late."

Rosa said, "I apologize. We had to pick up our ambassador."

"I was not assessing blame. I was merely stating fact. I had thought to greet your ambassador. Is she not there?"

Poor Rosa, Mike thought. *She can't even scrape her feet against the ground while looking toward the sky and whistling.*

"Captain Codari, I've asked her to be present for the entrance into stardrive. But I -- "

From behind him, Mike heard, "I'm here!"

Teresa stood just inside the doorway. Rosa cast Mike an about-time look, then told Codari, "This is Earth Unity Ambassador Teresa Song. Ambassador, Captain Codari of the Cetronen raider *Cerenam*."

Teresa stepped briskly to the middle of the bridge next to Rosa and said, "A pleasure, Captain. I apologize that I made us late. It was not Captain Sandage's fault."

The Codari minor's nostrils were really going now. "Once again -- I was not assessing blame. I greet you in return. Now, Captain Rosa Sandage -- prepare for stardrive jump within an hour." The holo faded out.

Teresa appeared perplexed. "That's *it*?"

Rishona spoke up, her tone that of a teacher to a not-very-bright child. "The Cetronen are known for focusing laser-like on one topic, then moving on just as quickly."

Which is something a Unity ambassador should know already, Mike thought. He glanced at Rishona, who shrugged behind Teresa's back. Mike told the ambassador, "The Drodusarel captain should be next. You'll find him mighty talky, I expect."

The Drodusarel starcraft *Dirat* was a silvery oblong as smooth as the Cetronen ship was rough-edged. Like every other Drodusarel craft Humans had encountered, its form gave no hint of its function. Drodusarel military ships looked the same as cargo craft which looked the same as passenger vessels. Mike had seen what their military craft were capable of; five years earlier, he'd gone on a mission to a space station that ended with Mike witnessing a Drodusarel craft firing weaponry that broke the station apart, then dissolved it.

What's more, each of their craft reflected the nature of Drodusarel technology -- they employed the biological sciences with as much skill as other Galactic species used the physical sciences; the *Dirat*, for instance, would have been grown, not constructed. That was generally felt to be the consequence of the Drodusarel having developed as sentient beings within an atmosphere rather than on a planetary surface.

Now a holo of the *Dirat*'s captain, Dresk, appeared. Drodusarel were methane breathers, resembling nothing so much as jellyfish to a Human eye. Dresk's body was oval-shaped, his skin a robin's-egg blue. A dozen tentacles kept him suspended in the sluggish minus-150 methane atmosphere aboard *Dirat*. Mike felt an uncomfortable tingling at the back of his neck; he always wondered whether a Drodusarel he was meeting for the first time knew he'd been the first Human to make contact with their species -- if you counted a Drodusarel starcraft taking a potshot at him as he was searching for a lost friend "contact."

Dresk spoke, and the translation through Mike's datalink was, "Greeting the Humans! I wish you well. Hive mind reserves judgment. Watching with studious eye on Mike Christopher."

Dresk's image faded. Rosa gave Mike a resigned look. "So they know about you."

Mike shook his head slowly. "They always do."

He watched with amusement as Teresa shook her head as if trying to clear it of a mental fog. She glared at Mike. "'Talky,' indeed. A bunch of nonsense! Who knows what it meant?"

Mike said, "*I* do."

Teresa's expression left no doubt she didn't believe him. It was Rosa's expression that caught his eye next -- those raised eyebrows and tilted head telling him *be careful.*

Mike understood. *No matter how I feel about her competence, or lack of same*, he thought, *it's not a good idea to bad-mouth a Unity ambassador to her face, especially in front of the crew.* "Dresk's greetings were sincere. As individuals, Drodusarel can be easy to get along with."

"But methane breathers!" Teresa said.

Mike told her, "The laws of physics are the same for both species. And they're curious, just as we are. That's mostly what we have in common."

"But what did it say about...the hive mind?"

"Drodusarel have a bit of a hive mentality. Not as severe as the Buruden or Jenregar, but effective all the same. Unfortunately, the hive mind can come to very different conclusions about something than individuals do. Dresk may think you or I or Rosa are great company, but the hive could decide the *Asaph Hall* needs blowing up."

"And these," Teresa said, "are our *allies*?"

Mike said, "Much better than having them as enemies."

*****

When the chime sounded in Mike's quarters, he didn't dare hope Linna was waiting for him on the other side of the door. *It's got to be Rosa*, he thought, *wanting to discuss something about the mission in private, now that we're safely in stardrive and on our way. Or maybe even our ambassador, looking to start over on the right foot this time.*

He pressed the door control and the door slid open.

Linna.

"It's time," she said.

Mike held his breath an instant before he told her, "Yeah. Com'on in."

They sat together on the couch in Mike's main room, as they had countless times before. They'd planned countless missions here, examined who-knew-how-many holos of mysterious worlds or astronomical anomalies. They'd sat quietly, reading, and held each other and cried, and made some damn fine love right here more times than Mike could recall.

"So," he said.

Linna sat, hands folded in her lap. She stared at the floor. "Yeah, *so*."

Mike knew Linna well enough to know it was best to wait for her to talk. She couldn't turn off her empathic resources. He knew she was reading every subtlety of his emotions, every frustration and anxiety, every bit of his concern for her.

"I'm sorry," she said.

"Sorry? Why?"

"It's been difficult being around you. I'd hoped it wouldn't come to this."

Mike's voice nearly caught in his throat. "To...what?"

"We're becoming...you might say, 'in tune' because we've been together so long.

"What's that mean?"

"It means it's more and more difficult to be around you." She scooted closer, took his hands in hers and gazed into his eyes. "Not because I care about you any less. But I feel it *all*."

"Such as?"

"Every time you glanced at me in the Accretion Disk you were...worried."

"Well, of course I was," Mike said. "We were all in danger."

"No, it's not that. You didn't feel confident in me. Not like you did toward Luther." When Mike started to protest she took her hands from his. "I know I've not been performing as well as I used to. I'm not saying you shouldn't have felt that way. But it hurt."

Mike sat straighter. "If I hadn't thought you could handle yourself, I wouldn't have brought you. And you must've felt how proud I was of you afterwards."

"I *know* that. But it's everything else, every moment. You're worried about me right now, and that used to be reassuring, even charming."

"But now?"

Linna said, "I can barely stand it."

"So I shouldn't be worried about you?"

"Don't take it that way."

"Aren't positive emotions more intense, too?"

"They are. But they're also more rare. It's not just you, Mike. It's everyone on the ship. Outwardly, there's the smiles, the jokes, the idea of being up to any task required of them. But underneath, we're all a mass of anxieties. Feeling unloved, or incompetent. I can feel them holding back anger and saying the 'right' thing instead. Or not daring to tell someone how they really feel about them. They *ache*."

Mike settled back into the couch. "I don't know what to say. Except what you've never allowed me to say."

That got a smile from Linna, one Mike eagerly returned. It was an old exchange between them, that Linna never wanted Mike to say he loved her. "You know what I always tell you," she said.

"Yeah." She would remind him that to an empath such a statement was either a lie or redundant.

"I *do* want to be with you, Mike. That's always. But wanting...and being able to bear it...." Linna's expression was stricken. "That, I may not be able to do."

Hearing that, it was Mike who ached now, even as he knew that only added to the intensity of Linna's emotions. *What must it be like*, he wondered, *to deal with this doubling of emotions whenever you and a loved one dealt with the same sorrows, the same grief? I've been Linna's shipmate for nine years, and considered that question over and over. And never found a good answer.*

Mike's reverie ended when Linna cupped her hand on the back of his neck and pulled him close. She kissed him, her lips barely touching his, then again, more firmly this time. When they started pulling clothes off, though, Linna said, "Not on the damn couch again. To the bed!"

So. To the bed. Linna pulled Mike on top of her. He asked, "You don't want to navigate?"

"You figure out something I'll like."

He looked into Linna's eyes. Her arms went around his neck and her heels to the backs of his knees. They moved slowly at first, with the rhythm of years of familiarity, then more quickly and confidently. Linna's pleasure was assured at the same moment as Mike's, thanks to her empathic powers that allowed her to feel his orgasm.

Afterward, Mike held Linna close and said, "I wish we could stay like this all night."

"We can't," Linna said. "At least, *I* can't. It all moves on. Everything changes."

"That's a lesson we'll learn all over again at the Moruteb system," Mike said. He was just starting to feel the chill of perspiration drying on his body.

*****

Like the rest of the *Asaph Hall* crew, Mike kept busy as the journey stretched into weeks, then months. As an artificial Human, designed from scratch, Mike had grown up an only child. "As 'only' as you can get," he would tell people. Most of his childhood had been spent in institutions; foster homes never worked out for long. He'd learned to cope, and those skills worked well for him on long starcraft journeys -- he spent a lot of time in his quarters catching up on his reading, or immersing himself in a virt, or in listening to music -- Shostakovich, Anderson-Howe, and Lopez were particular favorites.

Sometimes he just sat and missed Linna. She came to him in those brief periods when she could handle exposure to his emotions. Mostly she remained alone in her room, unable to bear the intensity of emotion around her, yet unable to ignore it.

At first Linna would visit him about three times a week. Sometimes they'd make love. Sometimes just talk. Mike would suggest a book or a virt for her and she'd take it back to her quarters.

Then her visits dwindled to once a week. Then about every ten days. Mike remembered what she'd said about those around her, that they ached. He knew she ached every bit as much.

*****

One night Codari agreed, at Rosa's request, and to Mike's puzzlement, to transmit a lecture on Cetronen political and trade alliances with other Galactic species through the centuries.

Mike sat in the commons with Rosa, Assistant Medical Officer Althea Canady, Operations Chief Alice Nicolson, Pilot and Nav specialist Darwin Haidar, and Chief Engineer Molly Hakata. On a desk before them, a small cube display of Codari pontificated. The major, of course, stood as passively as usual, while the minor droned on: "We Cetronen always desire to make alliances with other species. This very mission is such an alliance with Humans and Drodusarel. We've even occasionally had alliances with the Sobrenians. I'm sure you know the challenges there, as they are an aggressive species. But what can you expect of a people for whom weapons technology is its highest art form?"

That only led Mike to wonder why the Sobrenians hadn't been invited on this trip -- or if they had been and it hadn't worked out. *After all,* he thought, *the Cetronen and Drodusarel fought a pretty bitter war over a decade ago, but now they're cooperating. I'd think having the Sobrenians along as well would be quite a coup.*

Those musings were quickly lost within continued droning-on from Codari: "You may wonder why we love creating such alliances. We have ourselves pondered the question. But you know how difficult it can be for a species to examine its own motives. We take too much for granted, we are too close to our own motivations."

Codari actually paused for a moment, and Mike found himself in a blissful state, one in which the Cetronen commander was about to wrap up his remarks.

But it wasn't to be. Codari continued: "Many of our psychologists believe our natural state -- that is, our status as paired beings -- brings about this desire for alliances. After all, each of us is two beings -- different, yet complementary. And we look for such relationships in our dealings with other Galactic species."

Mike shifted in his chair as the soporific effects of Codari's speech threatened to overwhelm him.

Then his colleagues were clapping politely, the cube of Codari was fading away, and the dreary event was over. Mike could've sworn he'd been asleep with his eyes open. In fact, Rosa was smiling at him and saying, "You'll have to teach me how to do that sometime."

Everyone scattered. *Looks like no one's eager to discuss what we heard*, Mike thought. *Can't say as I blame them.*

Except -- as Mike was headed down a corridor to his quarters, he thought of *Asaph Hall* exobiologist Rishona Kwan. *She's supposed to be an expert on the Cetronen*, he thought. Why wasn't she there? He went past the door to his quarters and buzzed at Rishona's.

"Yes?" came a voice from inside.

"It's Mike. Care for a visitor?"

The door opened and Rishona said, "I'm not up to anything. Com'on in. Care for some green tea?"

It wasn't Mike's favorite beverage, but to be polite, he said, "Sure." Rishona went to her small kitchen area and pulled out cups. She picked up a teapot and began to pour. "I just made this. Not replicated, you know. I realize some people say they can't tell the difference, but I can."

Mike stood in the middle of Rishona's living room and took a look around. The patterns of her many rugs were a geometric latticework. Silken wall hangings depicted fruit and flowers. And over a small wooden table hovered a holographic image of a gray-haired old man with an expressive, lined face.

"For goodness sake, sit down," Rishona said as she handed him a cup of tea. He did, in a plush chair across from hers. "So, what brings you here?"

"Questions about the Cetronen."

"Oh, God, you didn't go to that awful lecture, did you?"

"Sure did. Sorta had to, you know."

"Exactly why I don't aspire to your high status."

Mike smiled and sipped the tea. Slightly sweet, and not at all bitter, it was a revelation. He looked up at Rishona in surprise.

"Better than what you've usually had?" she asked.

"Much."

"There's just a little bit of milk in there. And the real secret is brewing just when the water's about to hit the boil."

Mike took another sip. "Sounds like that could be the motto for this trip."

"Especially with the Cetronen in charge."

"Meaning what?"

Rishona sat back in thought as she sipped her tea. "Meaning I'm sure Captain Codari told you everything about Cetronen psychology -- that business of making alliances because they're pairs, and all that."

Mike let go a deep sigh. "That he did. At great length."

"And it's all bullshit."

"How's that?"

"Bullshit. Being pairs doesn't make them seek out other Galactic species because they love to commune with them, or anything like that. There's one reason behind these alliances, behind their involvement in this very mission. The Cetronen suffer from a tremendous insecurity."

Mike paused in mid-sip, said, "That's a rather sweeping generalization about an entire species, isn't it?"

"Com'on, Mike, we all make these comparisons. And each Galactic species uses itself as the base line. We think of Sobrenians as being a violent species. That doesn't mean Humanity isn't. Just that the tendency is even more pronounced in them. And it doesn't mean every Sobrenian is more violent than every Human. Assume that they are, and you've got something closer to race prejudice than noticing general trends."

Mike held up a hand. "I get the point."

"Sorry. Don't want to be as tedious as Codari. But consider the Cetronen. Compared to Humans, they're more insecure -- in general. Captain Codari helps prove the point."

"Yet he's commanding this mission."

Rishona said, "None of this means he isn't competent. Remember, it's all relative. He could be having this same conversation about how overconfident Humans are. And compared to most Cetronen, he'd be right."

"Any idea what causes that insecurity?"

"They've never encountered another intelligent paired Galactic species."

Mike sat holding his teacup in his lap. "That means so much to them?"

"They don't like to admit it, but it does. Imagine if the only other Galactics we encountered were methane-breathers like the Drodusarel. Or if we were the only species that wasn't paired."

"I don't think I'd care that much."

"But you've spent all your life as an outsider."

"An artificial."

"That's right. You've gotten used to it. The Cetronen, as a species, have not. Does that help?"

"I think it does," Mike said as he got up and placed his teacup on the kitchen counter. "But I think I might not know how much until later."

Rishona said, "Then let me know after the fact."

"You'll be among the first," Mike said, and left for his quarters.

*****

Later that week Teresa sat down across from Mike in the ship's commons. His hands paused with his sub sandwich in midair. His mouth stopped in mid-chew. Teresa just stared.

Mike used his tongue to push a mass of half-chewed food to one side of his mouth. "Umbass'dr?"

"I have an idea," Teresa said. "A joint dinner."

It was all Mike could do to keep from rolling his eyes. A couple quick chews, a painful swallow, and he said, "A dinner?"

"Yes. Humans and Cetronen. Together. We could start with a nice Vietnamese soup, with vegetables and herbs and either rice or vermicelli noodles. Then *sole ala meunière*."

"My datalink isn't programmed for French."

"Sautéed fish. And for dessert, cream puffs filled with banana cream, and drizzled with chocolate sauce."

Mike put down his sandwich. "Drizzled, huh?"

Teresa sat back in her chair, one hand rubbing her still-four-month-pregnant belly. "That's right."

"All the best a replicator can create. That's not a good idea."

Teresa frowned at him. "That's as much as I expected from you. Just because it's my idea -- "

"It's not that it's *your* idea. It's that it's a *bad* idea."

"What's so bad about it?"

"Have..." He leaned forward to speak more quietly. "Have you ever seen Cetronen eat?"

"What does that have to do with it? I wouldn't expect them to eat Human food."

"Are you prepared to watch them sitting here consuming unreplicated meat, from actual dead animals? The major holds the slab in front of the minor as the minor takes his share. No utensils, by the way. They pick off chunks of meat with their fingers. And there's lots of lip-smacking and loud swallowing."

"Well -- we have to be open-minded about such matters."

"They don't like Human habits any better. We only eat replicated meat, which they find unnatural. We eat liquid food such as soup. They find that disgusting. And what about the Drodusarel?"

"What about them?"

"We can't have a social event with the Cetronen and not include the Drodusarel. Diplomatically, that's a *faux pas*. But could you stand having a dinner date with methane-breathers?"

Teresa stared wide-eyed at Mike for a long moment. Finally, she said, "Well, I guess the commons here isn't really equipped for it, anyway." Teresa appeared to be suddenly chilled, whether at the thought of the Cetronen eating sounds or of sharing a table with the Drodusarel. She left without another word. *Too bad*, Mike thought. *I'd never actually seen Human flesh turn green before.*

CHAPTER THREE

Mike went to Linna's quarters. He buzzed at her door, and her muffled voice replied, "Mike, I'm sorry, but you have to go away."

That set him back -- she'd never turned him away so abruptly before, even on earlier occasions when her empathic powers led her to seek solitude. "Linna, please, just see me for a minute."

"No. Please leave."

"Is something wrong?"

"I just need...to be alone."

An emotion he was unaccustomed to feeling around Linna rose up within him -- *suspicion*. "Why won't you open the door, just for -- ?"

The door opened. Linna stood there. Her eyes were puffy and her cheeks were red and she looked as if she could barely keep on her feet, as if she hadn't slept for days. "*There*. Satisfied? There's no one else here."

"I wasn't thinking *that*. I was worried about you."

Linna closed her eyes for a moment, then opened them again and said, "I know you were. But everything else was there, too -- suspicion, jealousy."

Mike stepped forward hoping to take Linna into his arms, to reassure her -- but she stepped away. "You can't, Mike. You can't help me. *That*'s the problem."

Linna's door slid closed. Mike knew the best thing he could do would be to leave as quickly as possible.

*****

The *Asaph Hall*'s alert klaxon sounded in the middle of the night. Mike sat straight up in bed -- a glance at the time: 4:37 a.m. He rolled out of bed, dressed himself in shorts, pullover shirt, and slip-on shoes, and started for the bridge.

The run down the corridor to the grav tube took just long enough for him to imagine any number of deadly scenarios -- a massive equipment failure here on the *Hall*, some disagreement between the Cetronen and Drodusarel, even a Sobrenian attack.

Then, up the grav tube, hop out, down another short corridor. Even as the door to the bridge slid aside, the klaxon stopped. Mike saw normal space on the viewscreen and realized the ship had dropped out of stardrive -- something he hadn't even perceived on his way here.

Rosa was already there, standing in the middle of the bridge, asking for everyone to be calm. Alice Nicolson was standing at a sensor console shaking her head and pointing at the readout before her. "I don't *understand*," she said. "I really don't see the same thing Codari says he did."

The viewscreen showed both the mushroom shape of the *Cerenam* and the organic, silvery oblong of *Dirat*. Rosa sat in her command chair. "Everyone dropping out of stardrive -- it's just another delay, exactly what Codari didn't want -- but it looks like he caused it."

Mike approached her, kept his voice low, and asked, "What the hell happened?"

Rosa was calling up records of recent scans. "Codari called the alert from *Cerenam*. Said he detected several unknown starcraft headed right for us."

"Which I assume wasn't the case."

"As far as we can tell."

Alice said, "This might be an interesting system to look at sometime, though. I'm detecting one Earth-like planet."

"Log it for now," Rosa said. "Maybe it's something we can check out on the way back. Oh, here's Codari." The Cetronen's image stared at them from a holo to one side of Rosa's chair. The *Cerenam* captain's minor was sitting in the usual embrace of his major, his wide pointed ears waggling again, his nictating membranes opening and closing, opening and closing. "Captain Rosa Sandage. I must apologize. I called the alert. We can now find no trace of the unknown craft we believed we detected. It may have been a grouping of comets. We will continue now." And, in typical Cetronen fashion, with no further apologies or elaboration, Codari's image faded away.

It was immediately replaced by that of the Drodusarel captain, Dresk. "Greet the Humans," Dresk said. "Fewer stops. More progress! Watching with studious eye on Mike Christopher."

Dresk's image faded. Rosa gave Mike a resigned look. "Masters of the non-sequitor."

*****

Mike was sitting alone in the commons that night, sipping a glass of orange juice, when Georges Remy found him. The man's face was starkly pale and when he sat down next to him, Mike saw that Georges' hands shook. "What's wrong?"

Georges was clearly fighting back tears. "I just got a message. From Earth. We were still barely in range...the power boosting the signal...tremendous. Anyway, it's from my brother Renaud, back in Lyon."

"He's all right, isn't he?"

"He is. It's our mother. She...died." And now the tears flowed, unashamedly.

Mike didn't know what to say -- he knew what it was like to lose a loved one, but the extreme emotions brought on by the death of a close relative -- or any relative, for that matter -- were foreign to him. "I'm sorry," he said, as much to fill the silence as any other reason.

"She was visiting friends on Ptolomy," Georges said. "It was a heart attack. So sudden. She was only eighty-eight." Georges' eyes were haunted. "I've got to go back."

Mike cleared a sudden lump in his throat. "What?"

"Go *back*. To Earth."

"You...can't."

"I will."

"You...can't."

Georges wiped tears from his face. He gave Mike a stricken look. "I know."

"We're so far out, a shuttle would never make it. And..."

"I *know*."

"I can't blame you for asking."

"It's just...Arnaud, he's all alone. He's got to head to Ptolomy...get Mama's body...make all the arrangements."

"It would take months to get back to Earth -- back to him -- as it is. If he's anything like you, he's strong. He can get through this."

"I'm his brother..." Another sentiment that held no emotional resonance for Mike. "...I should be there. You have to understand. This isn't just grief -- it's guilt."

"Guilt? Why?"

"Arnaud and I...we've not spoken for some time. I was always enamored of space travel. He and Mother and Father always had a strong sense of family continuity."

Mike said, "I'm not sure what that means."

Georges wiped at his eyes with thumb and forefinger and said, "Our family deals in antiques. We have our own shop in Avignon, and we take part in the antique fairs there in February and September. You see? My family celebrates the past, tradition -- the known. But I embraced the new, the unknown. It's made things difficult."

"If Renaud was here instead of you -- would you understand?"

One corner of Georges' mouth turned up. "He'd never be here." When Mike started to speak, he held up his hand. "I see your point, though. Of course I'd understand."

"Then he'll do the same for you."

Georges managed a sad, knowing smile. "Because he's my brother."

Maybe, Mike thought, *I'm starting to understand families more than I realized.*

*****

Three months out from Urhaven Station, Mike was pulling an overnight shift with Alice Nicolson on sensors and nav and Darwin Haidar at the pilot's position.

Suddenly Alice's voice rang out: "Sobrenian starcraft straight ahead!"

Mike, without thinking, looked toward the main viewscreen, though that was a useless gesture -- he only saw the swirling colors of the annihilation of old-space before *Asaph Hall*. He punched the comm channel to Rosa's quarters. "Captain to the bridge. Sobrenian contact." To Darwin, he said, "Exit stardrive." The Alcubierre drive wound down and the *Hall* fell back into normal space. He knew already-established protocols would have the other two ships of their fleet following suit.

The Sobrenian ship filled the main screen. *One of their new designs*, Mike thought. It was dark green and roughly the shape of a water drop turned on its side, with the rounded part being the stern and the narrower, sharp-tipped part being the bow. It wasn't nearly as smooth as a water drop, though, being festooned with any number of blisters and projections that would be everything from sensors to the Sobrenians' adored weaponry.

As Mike expected, both the Cetronen ship, the *Cerenam*, and the Drodusarel one, the *Dirat*, were also visible.

Rosa entered the bridge just as a holo appeared before the command chair -- but it wasn't the Sobrenian captain -- instead it was the Cetronen, Codari. Mike stood and let Rosa have the command chair.

Codari's image said: "Your crew has done well in leading us out of stardrive. I, however, will make the initial contact."

"Understood," Rosa said.

"You're welcome to it," Mike muttered.

Rosa raised eyebrows at him. "*Shush.*"

The door at the rear of the bridge slid open again. Unity Ambassador Teresa Song wore a cloth robe over a flimsy nightgown that didn't at all suit her eternal four-month-pregnant condition. Mike couldn't help thinking, *That's something you wear when you want to get pregnant.*

A second holo appeared next to Codari's. *This* was the Sobrenian captain. His head had a blunt snout rather than a nose. His skin was slightly green-tinted, rough rather than scaly. Mike had dealt often enough with Sobrenians that he no longer found their eyes swinging independently in their sockets disconcerting. *But I have to wonder*, he thought, *what Teresa thinks of him.*

"I am Syradok, commander of the Sobrenian starcraft *Meradeus*." Syradok wore the usual elaborate robes that signified military rank. Mike peered closely at the holographic image and saw that he must be of high rank, indeed -- lines of green, red, and gold laced through the basic blue of the robe's fabric.

Codari asked, "What is your reason for intercepting us?"

Syradok replied, "We wish to join your small fleet."

Mike mused that watching the holos of the Cetronen and Sobrenian confront one another was like watching a live performance of a two-character play. *Except*, he thought, *a tragic climax will have more than artistic interest.*

"Why," Codari asked, "do the Sobrenians take such a sudden interest in exploration?"

Syradok said, "We changed our mind."

So the Cetronen did try to invite the Sobrenians along, Mike thought.

Codari asked, "Do you agree to place yourself and the *Meradeus* under Cetronen command?"

Mike had never seen a Sobrenian's eyes swing around so violently -- Syradok pointed a thick finger outward and said, "I do *not*."

"Then you may not join this fleet."

"I will not leave."

"Then you are welcome to follow us back to familiar space." Codari's image faded away.

Mike watched as Rosa pressed a finger behind her left ear. *A private datalink message*, he realized. Then Rosa said, "Codari meant what he said. We're to turn back."

Mike said, "After coming all this way? Three months into a four-month trip and we turn around just like that?"

Teresa said, "I...agree, Captain Sandage. You have to find a reason to convince them both to keep going."

Mike wanted to blurt out that Teresa was the ambassador, why didn't *she* come up with a reason, but he restrained himself

Rosa turned around in her command chair to face the ambassador. "Just what would you have us do, Ambassador?

Codari *is* heading back. The Drodusarel will follow him. Would you have us continue on, with only the Sobrenians for company?"

Teresa didn't have a comeback for that. Rosa spun her chair forward again and told Darwin, "Prepare for stardrive jump to match the *Cerenam*."

Moments later, as the *Asaph Hall* made the jump, Teresa left the bridge without another word. Mike couldn't help letting out a relieved sigh. He leaned in close to Rosa and kept his voice low. "The Unity can't be this desperate for ambassadors."

"None of that matters now. I'm sorry, Mike. This was going to be the highlight of my career. I couldn't wait to watch you and Linna and Georges and all the others heading out to explore those worlds."

"Yeah."

"You OK?"

"Just thinking," Mike said.

"About what?"

"Just...worlds colliding like billiard balls. Being there to observe it. Standing in awe, that kind of thing. And if you thought the trip so far became a lot longer and a lot less fun, just imagine what the trip back is gonna be like."

CHAPTER FOUR

Three hours later, his shift over, Mike grabbed a quick sandwich in the ship's commons, intending to sit just a moment, then grab a nap. Then hands began rubbing his shoulders. He recognized the touch, the scent.

Linna.

He put down his sandwich and let himself relax into the chair as she worked her way across his shoulders and down his upper back. "Oh, that's great."

Lips brushed the back of his neck, and Linna whispered into his ear. "This afternoon. Sixteen-hundred."

"What if -- "

"What if, nothin'. Do you realize how long I've had to avoid everyone on this ship to work up to spending a night with one person?"

"How long?"

"None of your business. Don't forget that person is you, by the way. Make it sixteen-oh-one and I'm going with the first good offer."

"I'll, uh...be there."

"Good boy." Her hands left his shoulders and her scent, her wonderful scent, dissipated.

*****

Georges Remy sidelined Mike in a corridor on the way to his quarters. "Tell me it isn't true."

"It is," Mike said. "We're headed back."

Georges' voice gained an angry edge. "This can't be. This is the worst of everything. I missed my mother's funeral. I'd started looking at the trip to Moruteb as a...a tribute to her."

"That's a good attitude. You're an explorer. That's what we do."

"But what kind of life do we have out here? I wouldn't want to raise a family on an exploratory craft -- it's too dangerous, and children need to grow up beneath sky and clouds, and in the rain and snow."

Mike was relieved when Georges clasped Mike's arm and told him, "Thank you for listening, anyway." As Georges started back the way he had come, Mike felt a twinge of guilt that his thoughts turned so suddenly to the nap he expected to be taking within about three minutes.

Just the kind of thing Linna would pick up on, he thought. *Maybe I understand her better than I thought*, too.

*****

As important as the nap was to Mike, he wasn't about to oversleep. Before crashing into bed, he told his datalink to awaken him at fifteen-hundred. He tossed and turned through a restless sleep, in which he dreamed of diving toward the Earth in a lifepod only to burn up in its atmosphere. When the link awoke him, it took a moment for Mike to sort out the subjective reality of his dream -- the flames had seemed *so* hot! -- from the everyday reality of his bed, his quarters, the fact that he was aboard *Asaph Hall*.

And Linna. She was the most important reality for him just now. A quick sonno-shower, an even quicker rush to the commons for another snack, then the briefest of checks with Rosa to make sure no emergencies were pending, and Mike was on his way to Linna's quarters.

Arrival time: 15:59:30, based on his wrist readout. He waited thirty seconds and rang for Linna. The door slid open and she waved him inside. When he started to speak, she covered his mouth with her hand. "Not yet." And she led him to her bedroom.

Linna was as responsive as ever as they undressed and embraced -- how could she not be, when she felt Mike's building excitement along with her own? But her lovemaking -- this time she did "navigate" -- held an urgency Mike had seldom experienced with her. It reminded him so much of the first time they'd been together that he couldn't help wondering if it could be the last.

When they were done, Linna collapsed onto the bed next to him, her back to him, and said, in a tense whisper, "Hold me, while I can still stand it."

Mike cuddled against her. "It's getting that much worse, is it?"

"I wonder how I can stand to stay on this ship."

"It's been home for you for eleven years."

"That's just it, Mike. I realized I should tell you when I heard we were headed back...."

Mike's stomach clenched. His mouth went dry. "Don't tell me...."

"I'm going to leave."

Mike held her tighter. "What can I do? How can I make things better for you?"

"You can't. And you can't go with me, either. I need to be alone."

"This goes beyond me, beyond the *Asaph Hall*. Will you have to...go into exile?"

"I've thought about it," Linna said. "But no, I couldn't do that. Maybe somewhere quiet back home near Kyoto. Somewhere I can mostly be alone. Maybe have a dog. Don't you miss having a dog?"

"Never had one. I lived in institutions, sometimes foster homes, then became a spacer -- never had the chance."

"Poor thing."

"If you did go to Earth -- maybe, eventually, you'd have a visitor?"

Even in the darkness, Mike could sense Linna smiling. "Yeah -- you, on Earth? Now *that* would be worth the wait."

"I'll go back someday." He kissed the back of Linna's neck. "I'd always hoped to go with you."

"How long since you've been there?"

"I left, let's see...over twenty-two years ago. Never looked back."

"Maybe things have changed there. Maybe they're ready to accept an artificial Human."

Mike mulled that over a moment. "Or maybe it's gotten worse."

"I know it was tough...the foster homes...."

"The beatings. Nearly getting *killed* more than once."

"It *is* time, then. To see what it's really like."

"Let's not get too far ahead of ourselves. We're still out here, for now. A *damn* good many light-years away."

"And still together," Linna said.

"Yeah. Still together." Mike kissed Linna's shoulder, then her neck again. She moved against him and as they embraced Mike didn't say anything else, didn't even consider telling Linna he loved her.

*****

The next morning Mike arrived back in his quarters and called up the display of the Moruteb system. He'd just realized he was viewing without absorbing when Rosa's voice came over his datalink: "Get up here right away."

Mike touched behind his left ear. "What is it?"

"We're turning around. Again."

Within a couple of minutes, Mike was on the *Asaph Hall*'s bridge. The holographic two-character play had added an unexpected act. Mike stood behind the captain's chair and watched over Rosa's shoulder as it continued:

The Codari minor, sitting as usual on his major's hump, said, "Captain Syradok has an announcement to make to the fleet."

That's when, behind Mike, the door to the main corridor slid open and Teresa said, "So is this rumor true? When are we -
- "

"Ambassador," Mike said, as he held his finger to his lips.

Teresa looked mortally offended. But she felt silent.

Meanwhile, Syradok was saying, "Just as we Sobrenians earlier changed our mind regarding the exploration of the Moruteb system, now we have altered our position on the command of this fleet."

Those words must be about to choke him, Mike thought. He knew, though, that Sobrenians could force their heart rates to slow, and halt the flow of their equivalent of adrenaline, forcing calm. Syradok concluded, "I am at your service, Captain Codari."

Codari's minor replied, "And I accept that service." The holos of both Sobrenian and Cetronen faded.

Mike said, "Just that simple, huh?"

Rosa grinned. "I wonder how many coded messages went back and forth before Codari squeezed that concession out of the Sobrenian."

Teresa walked up to Mike. "Of all the rudest -- "

Mike interrupted. "You were speaking out of turn, Ambassador. They can see and hear us just as we see and hear them."

That silenced Teresa, and Mike stood there and watched as conflicting emotions played across the ambassador's face -- indignation, anger, a bit of fear, then a grudging acceptance. Finally she said, "You were right, then. I apologize."

Mike was just starting to comprehend what Teresa had said when Darwin Haidar spoke up from the pilot's position: "Captain, it's the Drodusarel -- *Dirat*'s firing up its stardrive!"

Mike went to the nearest sensor console. "Confirming that. Comm chatter between *Cerenam* and *Dirat* tells me this is a surprise to Codari, too."

"Put as much distance between us and *Dirat* as you can," Rosa told Darwin. "We don't want to be caught in their new-space wake." Stardrives created "new-space" behind a craft while annihilating "old-space" before it. The localized curvature through space-time sent a starcraft on its way as surely as a thumb and forefinger squeezing on a pumpkin seed.

Sure enough, the Drodusarel craft was there one moment, and in the next a cocoon of light surrounded it and it was gone.

Rosa said, "Message from Codari...we're to power up as quickly as possible -- he wants us on *Dirat*'s trail."

"Working on it," Darwin said. "I'll match *Cerenam* into stardrive without a problem."

"This has to be frustrating for Codari. *Cerenam*'s faster than *Dirat*. But we're slower, and so are the Sobrenians."

On the viewscreen, *Cerenam* entered stardrive. "*Go*," Rosa said. Darwin worked his pilot's console, and the same cocoon of swirling light surrounded *Asaph Hall* and it burst into stardrive. Darwin said, "We're matched successfully. And the Sobrenians are right behind."

"It seems," Mike said, "That we've traded the Drodusarel for the Sobrenians."

Rosa said, "I just wish I knew what that meant."

Mike watched the flowing colors of stardrive as if he could discern patterns within them. "Can't be anything good."

*****

Just as Mike was about to go to bed, Linna called on his datalink. "I wasn't going to tell you what I decided until after we left Moruteb. Then we started back...."

Mike sat up on the edge of his bed. "Everything happened pretty fast."

"I'm staying alone as much as I can. 'Saving up,' you might say. Mostly for ship duties. But also to be with you. At least a few times before...."

I don't have any words, Mike thought. He sat with his hands folded in his lap.

"Mike?"

"I'm here."

"I'm sorry how this is turning out."

"So am I."

Silence for a long moment. Then Linna asked, "Are you angry with me?"

"Not with you. Never with you. Only the circumstances."

Linna's voice was tentative. "All right."

"I guess you're so used to -- "

"Reading you -- that *is* what I'm used to."

Mike said, "Talking like this might've been good for us all along."

Linna said, "It's like saying we'd get along better if you were blind or deaf."

Mike considered that. "I suppose you're right."

A pause. "Sleep tight."

"'Night," Mike said, and crawled into bed for a restless night's sleep.

CHAPTER FIVE

When THE day arrived, Mike made sure to show up on *Asaph Hall*'s bridge early. Rosa sat quietly in her command chair, but he couldn't stay still. Finally Rosa said, "Will you stop pacing?" She patted the seat of the chair to her right. "Sit."

Mike did what he was told. *So help me*, he thought, *if she says*, "Good boy...."

She didn't. Mike asked, "What do you think we'll find when we come out of stardrive?"

"If we knew that, it wouldn't be exploring."

Mike folded his arms, exasperated, growing more so by the minute as he caught Rosa's grin out of the corner of his eye.

Today Katarina Diop was at the pilot's position. She was an eastern European woman in her thirties, with black hair and olive skin. She reported, "Less than a minute from exiting stardrive."

Mike felt Rosa's hand on his shoulder. He stared up at her and found her beaming as he'd seldom seen before. "Let's hope we have the chance to savor this," she told him.

Mike returned Rosa's smile and didn't dare bring up his fears -- that the Drodusarel had rushed ahead of them and gotten into trouble, that the Sobrenians could pick this very moment to start misbehaving.

Alice Nicolson, from her post at nav and sensors next to Katarina, said, "Exiting stardrive in five seconds."

The cocoon of light faded away on the main viewscreen, and *Asaph Hall* was in normal space. On the main screen, the mushroom shape of the Cetronen raider was visible just ahead.

Mike glanced at Rosa as she tilted her head slightly, apparently listening to reports over her datalink. "Codari says

Cerenam exited stardrive without any problems. So did the Sobrenians -- *Meradeus*. Wait...*Meradeus* isn't wasting any time. It's releasing thousands -- no, tens of thousands of nanoprobes."

Please, Mike thought, *don't be weapons.*

Alice checked readouts and holos. "No sign of *Dirat* yet."

Rosa reported, "Codari's telling me the Drodusarel won't respond to his comm."

Mike said, "They could've gotten here a few days ahead of us. I wonder what they're up to."

Rosa stared straight ahead. "I just hope they haven't gotten into some kind of trouble."

Mike called up a holo of the relative positions of the Moruteb system and the oncoming Neska system. Sure enough, Neska and its two planets were still about a month away from drawing close enough for their gravitation to affect Moruteb and the four worlds that orbited it. "We made it within a few hours of when we intended," he told Rosa.

"All well and good," she said. "But I don't like this business with the Drodusarel. They shouldn't have left us behind. We have to make sure they're here and safe before we start exploring."

Mike switched his holo to a display of Moruteb's four planets. The *Hall* was entering the system slightly above the plane of the ecliptic, which gave him a real-time view that allowed him to take in the whole system at a glance.

Jilan was a vaguely Mars-type world just over one A.U. distant from the primary. Calculations showed its orbit around Moruteb would be altered, but most likely the primary would be able to hold on to it. Jilan, however, might lose one or two of its three moons.

Heuri, a gas giant, was 8 A.U. out. One of Neska's planets, another Jovian named Lasira, was expected to collide with Heuri, destroying both. The remnants of the two worlds would probably form a ring around Moruteb eventually.

At 41 A.U. was Itherin, a smaller gas giant, and 44 A.U. distant was an icy world, Risula. Itherin had probably helped draw Risula into orbit around Moruteb. In turn, Neska would probably rip Risula away and destroy it.

Mike pointed to the image of the large gas giant, Heuri, named for the Cetronen's first world leader. "That's where we should look. Heuri's a gas giant similar to the Drodusarel homeworld. And it has an extensive series of rings, again, just like their homeworld."

Rosa asked, "Are the rings important?"

"Primitive life -- the equivalent of the first algae on Earth -- arose in the Drodusarel system's rings. They, in turn, seeded the planet."

"How the hell did *that* happen?"

"No one knows. Correction -- no *Human* knows. However it happened, the Drodusarel would be drawn to that type of planet the way Humans would be drawn to a terrestrial world with large oceans."

"Codari needs to know this." Rosa touched behind her left ear and spoke to the Cetronen commander, summarizing their findings. Rosa signed off, then told Katarina, "We're following *Cerenam* again."

"Heuri?" Mike asked.

"Codari hopes your hunch is a good one."

Mike held up his hands in frustration. "I guess I'd better hope it is, too."

"You know what they say -- hell hath no fury like a pissed Cetronen."

"Who says that?"

Rosa shrugged. "Maybe someone will start."

On the viewscreen, Mike saw *Cerenam* make a brief stardrive jump. *Always a bit risky in-system*, Mike thought, *but I don't blame Codari at all.*

Asaph Hall followed, the light distortion indicating the creation of new-space and annihilation of old-space lasting only for an instant.

Then they were on the other side of the jump, only a few million K from Heuri, close enough that Mike could call up a finely detailed holo giving the planet's vitals -- a year nearly 24 Earth years long, a day of not quite nine hours, the typical bands of clouds, and an extensive ring system.

But as usual with such a world, the stats weren't as impressive as the sheer power of the imagery.

The cloud bands covering Heuri ranged from tan to brown to red, dotted with dozens of storm systems. Those clouds were mostly hydrogen and helium, with minor components being ammonia, methane, and water.

Heuri's ring system wasn't as magnificent as Saturn's, but neither was it as tenuous as Jupiter's; Mike could make out at least four broad segments, and the system as a whole, though it was only a few hundred meters thick, still made a magnificent sight as the *Hall* drew closer.

Magnificent perhaps, but also doomed, once Lasira drew close enough to Heuri for the two worlds to be drawn together gravitationally and collide.

But that was weeks away at the earliest. For now: "There!" Mike said. He switched the output of his personal holo to the main screen. The smooth silver surface of the *Dirat* was easily visible against a couple of the darker bands of Heuri's clouds. Its orbital path was a couple of hundred K lower than *Asaph Hall*'s. Soon it would pass below them and move ahead.

Rosa said, "Codari says they're still not responding. What the hell are they *doing* here?"

Alice was also calling up holos and other readouts. "I've got Drodusarel shuttles coming up through Heuri's atmosphere."

Mike switched over to Alice's readouts and magnified. "I bet they're taking samples, probably inserting probes."

Alice glanced back at Mike. "Just what we would do." When she brought her attention back to the readout, though, she said, "Wait a minute. Look at these lifeform readouts."

Mike took a good look, then asked Rosa, "What's the complement of the *Dirat*?"

"Twenty-three," Rosa said. "That's the traditional number...something going back to Drodusarel mythology."

Mike said, "They've got thirty-two lifeforms aboard."

He could hear the breath catch in Rosa's throat. She said, "With some of their crewmembers accounted for aboard those shuttles."

"They've been down to the planet. Or, I should say, in its atmosphere."

Rosa nodded. "This probably isn't the shuttles' first trip. They went down there before we got here, and brought lifeforms up from Heuri."

Alice spoke up again. "I thought this system didn't have any lifeforms."

Mike said, "No *intelligences*, at least as far as we knew. These lifeforms may not be intelligent. But I'd bet they're similar to the Drodusarel."

Rosa said, "I wonder if they knew Heuri contained life before they started on this mission. Could they be mounting a rescue effort?"

"It's a pretty poor one if they are. They'd have brought a lot more ships to take off a significant portion of a planetary population. That's a damn big undertaking. I know that much from working on Splendor." The planet Splendor was a world under a death sentence from the gas nebula of a nearby star that had exploded. The process of evacuating its two intelligent species had already taken several years, and would last years or decades more.

Rosa leaned forward, hands on knees, and stared at the *Dirat*, which was starting to receive its shuttles. Mike saw her close her eyes in concentration. "Codari says they're still not responding."

Mike said, "I'd like to take a shuttle over there. Try to find out what they're up to."

"Do you think that's a good idea?"

"Dresk seemed pretty reasonable until he went ahead of the fleet. Even now, he's only risking his own ship, no one else's."

Rosa leaned back and folded her arms, and stared straight ahead for a long time. Finally she sat up, touched behind her ear to activate her datalink, and spoke quietly. Then she said, "Codari approves. Take *Cosmic Egg*. And Linna. Keep in mind that I'm maintaining the *Hall* in this higher orbit. That means we'll keep falling behind."

Mike said, "You don't want to be too provocative, I take it."

"Exactly right. So be careful. Oh, and I think it'd be a good idea if you took our ambassador, too."

Mike managed not to groan, but his expression must have turned downcast, because Rosa said, "Think of it as on-the-job training."

Mike groaned again, and muttered: "She was supposed to be trained before she got here."

"Now, now. Who trained you for Splendor? Or first contact with the Jenregar? Or surviving on the Station of the Lost?"

Mike's shoulders slumped and he bowed his head slightly. "No one, I guess."

"Damn right. We're stuck with her. Let's at least bring her back a little more seasoned than when she left."

"Fine," Mike said. He left the bridge to fetch Linna and Teresa and make the *Cosmic Egg* ready to lift.

*****

Mike found his fingers pounding at the shuttle *Cosmic Egg*'s controls as he performed preflight checks, and he made himself slow down and take things easier. He was in the pilot's position, with Linna to his right as co-pilot of the smooth-skinned, silvery craft. "Why are we always waiting on this woman?" he asked.

Linna said, "She's not done any of this before. And she *is* four months pregnant."

"She's been four months pregnant *for* four months. She should be used to it by now."

"What she should be is eight months pregnant, and about to be over her misery."

Mike paused in his preflight checklist. "I wonder who the father is."

"*Shh.* Here she comes."

Mike went to the open airlock and extended his hand to Teresa. There were two steps from the hangar deck into the shuttle, and he thought she might need an assist.

Teresa just stared for a moment that was probably not nearly as long as it seemed to Mike. Then she extended her own hand to Mike's and stepped into the *Egg*. "Thanks," she said, without inflection, and sat behind Linna's position.

Moments later, Mike was guiding the *Egg* off the *Asaph Hall*'s hangar deck and toward the Drodusarel craft *Dirat*. Linna checked sensors and said, "*Dirat* still has a couple of shuttles out."

Mike opened a comm channel to the *Dirat*. "Captain Dresk, this is Mike Christopher aboard the *Asaph Hall* shuttle *Cosmic Egg*. Please respond."

Mike waited, but no one answered. "Captain Dresk, I and my crew stand ready to help with any rescue operations you may be undertaking."

Dresk's response was audio-only. "Not greeting the Human ones! Inappropriate curiosity. I *and* hive-mind disapprove." Then the connection was cut.

"That's it," Mike said, and boosted the *Egg* into a higher orbit and started working on a trajectory back toward the *Asaph Hall*.

"Wait a minute," Teresa said. "What do you mean, 'that's it?' We just turn around without the Drodusarel even asking us to leave?"

"Don't you understand? They *did* ask us to leave. They did more than ask, in fact. They demanded we leave and threatened us if we didn't."

"It's that business with the hive mind, isn't it?"

"You bet it is," Mike said. "And unless you want to be at the center of the biggest cluster event you've ever experienced, you'll be happy we're heading back."

Teresa touched Linna's shoulder. Mike was impressed with Linna for not flinching, but couldn't help but notice the cool stare she gave that hand.

Teresa either didn't notice or didn't care. "Is what this...man...is saying true, Linna?"

Linna turned to face Teresa. "First of all, this *is* a man, in every sense you might care to name. Secondly, I've trusted him with my life any number of times and no doubt will again. Any more questions?"

Teresa's voice was frosty. "I suppose not."

Mike had never been more grateful to notice an incoming transmission. He thought it might be Rosa, but when he accepted it the green-skinned, blunt-snouted image of the

Sobrenian starcraft captain, Syradok of the *Meradeus*, formed before him. "Mike Christopher. Linna Maurishka. And Ambassador Teresa Song. It's unfortunate that the Drodusarel are such poor colleagues. I will state my purpose plainly. I wish to upstage them. Will you visit the *Meradeus*?"

Mike's finger reached out nearly without conscious thought as he prepared to agree, but then he paused. "Ambassador, this is really your call."

Teresa cast Mike a disapproving eye. "Hmmph. Now, all of a sudden, it's *my* decision. For the first time in four months."

"You have to understand the meaning of this offer. The Sobrenians so seldom reach out to Humans, or anyone else. And their entire reason for grafting themselves on to this mission is unknown."

Teresa considered that for a long moment, longer than Mike wished. Finally, she said, "We came out here for one visit. We can certainly make another instead."

Mike asked, "Rosa? Do you copy that?"

"Yes, and I agree," Rosa replied over the datalink. "And while you're making that visit, I'll be talking to Codari."

"Understood." He said to Linna, "Well, the Drodusarel were one Galactic species whose motives in being here I was wondering about. Maybe we can add the Sobrenians to that list."

He altered *Cosmic Egg*'s course yet again, this time toward the *Meradeus*.

*****

To Mike, the interior of a Sobrenian starcraft was a familiar place -- more dimly lit than most Human craft, warmer, and more humid. As he, Linna, and Teresa stepped out of the airlock into the *Meradeus*'s main corridor, Mike couldn't help but be amused as Teresa wrinkled her nose in distaste. He'd anticipated the musty and organic smell common to a Sobrenian craft, but Teresa obviously hadn't.

Syradok was there to greet them, with another Sobrenian at his side. A female, by the look of her -- slightly shorter than her captain, shoulders not as broad, snout shorter.

As Mike expected, the *Meradeus* commander was wearing his blue robes with their lines of green, red, and gold running through them. The top of Syradok's head came about to Mike's shoulders. As was typical of his species, he wore no footwear, and his tough feet slapped the cold metal deck as he approached.

But something was missing, and Mike realized what it was.

Syradok didn't have a Garotethan with him as an "ancillary."

The tiny Garotethans were a species that by all accounts had willingly acceded to Sobrenian domination of their homeworld. *Normally*, Mike thought, *you see a Sobrenian starcraft commander, you see a Garotethan. Something tells me Garotethans don't get vacations. I wonder where Syradok's slave is. A question for another time, I suppose.*

Syradok's eyes rolled independently in their sockets as they looked down his snout at the three Humans, obviously taking their measure. "Is this not a better greeting than the one from our Drodusarel friends?"

Mike kept his lips pressed tightly together as he waited for Teresa to speak. For an instant, *no one* spoke, but then Mike heard a gasp from Teresa, as if she realized she really was the ambassador here. "This is a most welcome greeting, Captain."

Syradok raised a rough, green-skinned hand to present the other Sobrenian. "I must introduce you to my second-in-command, Govanek. She is also an explorer -- a geologist."

Mike stared at Govanek with a sudden respect. *Exploration isn't normally the Sobrenian way*, he thought. *For this Govanek, to be an explorer, to advance to being Syradok's second, is impressive. But the lines of fabric running through her robes are only a single color, red. That puts her social status at odds with her status aboard this ship.*

Govanek said, "I would like to accompany you, Mike Christopher, on one of your explorations."

Mike blinked. "Really? May I ask why?"

Syradok spoke up. "This mission was decided upon at the last moment. The *Meradeus* is not an exploratory vessel, although we did bring our many nanoprobes to help us gain a swift viewpoint of the system. I would consider it a favor to me to take her along sometime."

What I'd like to ask, Mike thought, *is whether the Sobrenians even have any exploratory craft. Something else for other time.* "I'd be honored, Captain," he said.

"Excellent," Syradok said.

Govanek said, "I'm especially interested in the world Jilan." That was another of Moruteb's planets, the Mars-like, dry and cold, low-grav world.

"Then Jilan it is," Mike said. "Of course, I'll have to clear it with Captain Sandage, and probably Captain Codari, but I don't foresee any problems."

After a few more pleasantries, it was clear that no refreshments or an offer to tour the *Meradeus* were forthcoming. *We've taken all of about five steps out of the airlock*, Mike thought.

Obviously Linna had the same thoughts, because she gave Teresa a "gentle" nudge in the ribs to get her to beg the Sobrenians' forgiveness, that they had to get back to *Asaph Hall*.

Then it was back through the *Meradeus* airlock and Mike undocked the *Cosmic Egg* and headed for home. He told Linna and Teresa, "Well, I was right. That makes *two* Galactic species whose motives I'm wondering about."

Linna said, "Both Syradok and Govanek seemed sincere, especially Govanek. She's legitimately excited about the idea of exploring with us.

Teresa asked, "How well can you perceive Sobrenian emotions?"

"About as well as a Human's or anyone else's. It's the cultural subtext that can be the tricky part. Knowing what emotional responses are appropriate in their particular culture. I *did* perceive that Syradok looks upon Govanek with...let's say, amusement."

Mike said, "That would fit Sobrenian culture. They're usually so focused on weaponry as an art form, and on conflict, that someone who's curious might seem a little strange."

Linna asked, "Did you notice Syradok didn't have a Garotethan with him?"

"I *did*! I wondered what it meant. Or even if it meant anything at all."

Teresa pointed out, "This *is* supposed to be a mission in which each species discovers things about one another as well as Moruteb and Neska."

"That's what I'm worried about," Mike said. "Just what we might discover."

Teresa cried out, and so did Linna. Mike saw Teresa doubled over in pain. He touched Linna's arm. "You're not the one who's hurt, are you?"

"No," Linna said through gritted teeth. "I'm reacting to *her*."

Teresa held her hands tightly to her belly and said, "I need to see a doctor *now*."

The baby, Mike realized. "*Asaph Hall*, this is *Cosmic Egg* calling with a medical emergency. ETA..." He checked the shuttle's controls. "Seven minutes. Lauren to the hangar bay."

*****

Mike guided the *Cosmic Egg* through the energy shield that protected the *Asaph Hall*'s hangar bay from the vacuum and cold of space. As he settled the shuttle down to the deck he saw the *Hall*'s Chief Medical Officer Lauren Takahashi and her assistant Althea Canady standing by with a smart-gurney.

The *Egg* was still rocking back and forth slightly from its touchdown when Linna punched the control to open the airlock doors. The gurney, guided toward Teresa by a previously provided DNA sample, raised itself on multi-socketed legs and walked through the airlock. It opened up its bubble top, embraced Teresa with tentacle-like arms, scooped her up and placed her within itself and closed the bubble top.

The gurney exited the airlock and waited as Lauren checked the initial sensor readings on the gurney's side. She nodded toward Althea, who pressed a control that sent the gurney across the hangar bay, bound for the *Hall*'s infirmary. Althea followed close behind, making further checks on Teresa's condition with a portable sensorpac.

As Mike stepped down onto the hangar deck, Lauren paused just long enough to say, "I'll let you know how she is. If we're lucky, I may just need to tweak the stabilization process."

"Hell of a 'tweak,'" was all Mike could manage to say. But he said it to Lauren's back; the doctor was already halfway across the hangar bay trotting to catch up to the gurney.

Linna told Mike, "I'm impressed with your reaction back there."

"Huh?"

"You were legitimately concerned for Teresa. Oh, you still dislike her -- that's plain. But your concern for her overrode all your other emotions."

"Hmm. Thanks, I think."

Rishona Kwan entered the hangar bay, her gait purposeful enough that Mike thought, *This can't be good.*

"Don't get too comfortable," Rishona told him. "Linna, you get to stay here to help look after the ambassador."

Linna grinned, and Mike's heart leapt at the sight. Linna said, "Who'd I piss off?"

"Lauren wants to see you, too -- she knows how you must've reacted with Teresa in so much pain so near you."

Linna gave a mock salute to Rishona, and asked Mike, "You coming?"

Rishona spoke up. "Mike and I are taking the *Egg* right back out. Rosa's orders."

Mike asked, "*Now* where to?"

"That's why I'm going along, as the resident Cetronen expert. *Cerenam.* Time to visit Codari."

"I've made four trips today -- or at least three and a partial -- and haven't traveled more than fifty K total." He caught Linna's eye, squeezed her hand, then watched as she left the hangar bay. He started back toward the *Egg*, telling Rishona, "Let's see what Codari wants."

CHAPTER SIX

As Mike guided the *Cosmic Egg* out of the *Asaph Hall*'s hangar deck again, he asked Rishona, "So what are you expecting when we get over there?"

"No way of knowing," she said. "Though I suspect he wants to firm up this alliance between Humanity and the Cetronen."

"Why would he think it needs firming up?"

"It's all a matter of maintaining the actual alliance or at least the appearance of one. No doubt he'll want to deepen the relationship between our two species."

"Should be interesting," Mike said. Less than half an hour later, the *Egg* docked with the mushroom-shaped Cetronen craft. A *Cerenam* crewmember named Natai greeted Mike and Rishona. Both the major and minor of this paired symbiont were shorter than most Cetronen, the major standing little taller than Mike. Natai escorted them down corridors that were wider than those within most Human starcraft -- they had to be, to accommodate the bulkier Cetronen form. Then they arrived at Codari's quarters, deep within the ship.

"Captain Codari will arrive shortly," Natai's minor said as he stood aside to allow Mike and Rishona to enter. "Please allow yourself to enjoy your surroundings as you wait. It's a pleasure to meet you. I am also an explorer. I hope to share a journey with Humans someday."

Mike started to express a similar sentiment to Natai, but he (they?) was (were?) gone.

And there they stood, waiting for Codari's arrival. Standing, because the room held no furniture.

Mike took the opportunity to gain some insight into the fleet commander by examining the holos of the Cetronen homeworld that decorated the walls. One depicted a mountain range more extensive than anything on Earth, with one summit after another peeking out from a cloudscape that seemed eternal.

"Beautiful," Mike said.

Rishona was staring at another holo depicting a parched plain, looking as much like a symbolic representation of desolation as it did a real place. "I've heard of this feature, but I've never seen it. I'll have to ask when Codari -- "

That's when Codari entered, the two-and-a-half-meter tall major carrying the smaller, thinner minor in his arms.

After introductions all around the minor said, "I apologize for your wait."

Mike said, "It's Captain Sandage who apologizes. She didn't feel she could leave the *Asaph Hall*."

Codari's minor stared at Mike with those eyes, deep-set within his noseless face. "I understand. A captain's place is with her ship."

Rishona said, "We were admiring your holos."

The Codari major carried the minor over to the holo of the mountain range. "The Sorrowful Mountains. Named such because of the many Cetronen who died trying to reach their summits. They reach fourteen thousand meters into our skies."

"And this other one?" Mike asked, pointing at the desert holo.

"The Plain of Itherin. It's the desert where Cetronen mythology says the god Itherin split us in two -- making us more than mere animals. We named that world in this system after him."

"I've always found it interesting," Rishona said, "that animals are all 'singletons' on your homeworld?"

Codari's minor said, "And of course that informs our outlook on other lifeforms we encounter."

Mike couldn't help thinking, *The Cetronen are the only Galactic species we know of that isn't a singleton species. Do they sometimes slip, and think of other species...think of Humans...as animals? Is that why they're so eager to create alliances, to remind themselves to look beyond that basic mindset so they can function in Galactic society?*

The minor's pointed ears waggled. "The Sobrenians just made a proposal to you -- cooperation."

Mike asked, "How do you know that?"

"Not all of my discoveries are astronomical. Some are political. I also know that moments earlier, the Drodusarel had a very different proposal -- that you boost as far away from them as you could, as quickly as you could."

Mike smiled. "That's a clever way of putting it."

"Cleverness is not my goal, only understanding. This time is unique for all our species. We will observe and record an astronomical event, the nature of which none of us has seen before."

Mike warmed to this part of the conversation. "To witness something like this -- besides the knowledge we'll all gain, it'll be a time of much wonder. It's why I became an explorer."

"Each Galactic species has its own motivations for being here. Not all are as pure as your own. I presume Cetronen and Human motives are the closest. We explore these colliding systems physically and intellectually. And the other Galactic species culturally and, perhaps, philosophically."

"I would agree with that."

"Four species here. We're far from the area of the galaxy where we predominate. Far from our superiors. Here is where our true natures are revealed."

"Perhaps," Mike suggested, "that's our most important discovery."

"And potentially, the most dangerous. I urge you to accept the Sobrenian invitation. In fact, I would like all the crews to trade personnel during their many exploratory missions to these worlds."

"I want to. Though I don't want to be considered a spy."

Codari said, "You are an explorer. You see and hear things. You learn. All I ask is that you continue to do so."

"I think I understand," Mike said, though he knew he would never report anything to Codari unless it might save lives.

"The Sobrenians' attitudes are still molded by their disaster of many generations ago."   Mike understood the reference -- a comet strike in the Earth year 1862 had nearly rendered the Sobrenian species extinct. The survivors believed that only the strongest of them survived the desperate struggle afterwards.

It was also why the Sobrenians often looked down on other Galactic species. Mike had been called a "pre-sentient" by individuals of that species more than once.

Well, he thought, *if I don't ask now, I'll wonder why I didn't.* "If I may, Captain Codari -- is there a reason the Sobrenians didn't want to be part of this fleet from the beginning?"

The Codari major shifted the minor in his arms for a better grip.   The minor said, "Cetronen-Sobrenian alliances constantly shift. Currently they do not favor us."

Rishona said, "But you'd like that to change."

"With your help, yes."

Mike told Codari, "We'll be honored, Captain."

"Very good. Now, about the Drodusarel. As we speak here, they're moving on from Heuri to the smaller gas giant, Itherin, which I mentioned a moment ago."

"I have to wonder what they found at Heuri," Mike said.

"You may never know unless you travel there yourself. I'd like you to take Natai -- you just met him -- to Heuri after your jaunt with the Sobrenian to Jilan."

"I'll be pleased to."

"You understand the potential danger the Drodusarel represent. After all, you made Humanity's first contact with them."

"In a sense," Mike said.

"I know it was unexpected, and violent. Always remember that, no matter how many times they 'Greet the Human ones,' or some such phrase. They either enjoy playing the buffoon or do not realize how their translations sound. Either way, one can easily forget how different they are from oxygen-breathers."

"I'll remember."

"We are finished here," Codari's minor said, and with his "laser-like" focus having moved on to the next topic, the Cetronen commander's major, without further formalities, carried the minor away and left Mike and Rishona alone in his quarters again.

Soon Natai arrived to escort them back to the *Egg*. The minor said, "Captain Codari was to ask whether I may accompany you on a mission to Heuri."

"He did. And I agreed."

"That is wonderful, Mike Christopher."

"We'll go soon," Mike reassured Natai, and he and Rishona excused themselves and returned to their shuttle. Mike couldn't help noticing that the Cetronen stood at a viewport and watched the whole time Mike was easing *Cosmic Egg* out of *Cerenam*'s hangar deck.

Mike wondered if he should add the Cetronen to his list of Galactic species whose motives he should be concerned about. *And*, he thought, *putting Humanity on there wouldn't be a bad idea.*

He asked Rishona, "What'd you think about Codari?"

"An impressive individual. Especially his attitude toward exploration."

"I thought maybe you'd just consider him a typical Cetronen, concerned with alliances and his own insecurities."

Rishona said, "Tendencies aren't destiny. All of us can transcend who we are as a species. Codari's potentially a great example of that."

"And what are our Human tendencies? What do we have to transcend?"

Rishona shrugged. "We're no more insightful about ourselves than the Cetronen are. That's a question I expect to spend my whole life answering."

*****

Once he and Rishona made it back to *Asaph Hall*, Mike went immediately to the infirmary to check on Teresa. He found her sitting up in bed, laughing uproariously with Lauren. He didn't know whether to be concerned that Linna wasn't there. "Well," he said, "it looks like everyone's feeling better."

Lauren told Mike, "Everyone *is*. All four of us, I hope, including yourself."

"Was it a good joke?"

"It was, but none of *your* business. Girl talk."

Mike rolled his eyes in mock exasperation, then, more seriously, asked Teresa, "You're feeling better, though?"

Teresa maintained her grin, but still spoke warily: "I am. Thank you for getting me back here so quickly."

"Just a 'tweak,' exactly as I told you," Lauren said. "Hormone imbalance. The child is fine, and Mom's in a much better mood."

"Glad to hear it."

Teresa said, "Mike -- I have to apologize. I've treated you unfairly. You've shown me every courtesy, even after I -- "

"You're part of the crew. That's all I need to know."

"But I've treated you so poorly..."

"I don't define myself by how others treat me."

"You still don't like me, do you?"

Mike considered. "I'm starting to respect you. I'll work on liking you. For now, I'll accept your apology."

Teresa pressed her lips tightly together for a moment. Then she said, "That's all I can expect, I suppose." To Lauren, she said, "Can I go now?"

"Straight to your quarters, and right to bed. At least eight hours."

Teresa left. When Mike looked toward Lauren, the doctor returned an exaggerated smile.

Mike asked, "How's Linna?"

Lauren's smile faded. "I sent her on to her quarters. She'll be better once she has some more time alone." She gave Mike a stern stare and said, "That includes you. Actually, *especially* you."

Mike, in turn, gave Lauren a mock-disgusted look and said, "Girl talk, huh? What *was* that about?"

Lauren chuckled. "You'll never know."

"I'm making a list of Galactic species whose motives I should question. You just confirmed I'm adding Humans to it."

"Question away, my friend," Lauren said. "But you may never get an answer."

"Story of my life," Mike said, and left the infirmary. The sound of Lauren's chuckling followed him most of the way to the grav tube.

*****

A few days later, *Asaph Hall* took up an orbit around Jilan, which circled 1.2 A.U. from Moruteb. Soon Mike was piloting the *Cosmic Egg* down toward the planet, with Georges next to him in the co-pilot's position. The Sobrenian geologist, Govanek, sat behind Georges. She asked, "Did you know the planet's named for a Cetronen singer and instrumentalist?"

"I'd wondered," Mike said. "I knew the Cetronen got to pick the names."

"You can imagine," Govanek said, "with the symbionts' consciousness so tied together, how wonderfully they can perform. At least two instruments, and marvelous harmonies."

"Wait a minute," Georges said. "I thought the majors didn't speak."

Mike, remembering a violent encounter five years earlier with a Cetronen major, said, "They do. But it's rare, and you probably don't want to be nearby."

Govanek said, "They sing when the minor prompts them."

On the way toward Jilan, their trajectory took them within a few thousand K of one of Jilan's moons, Reulo. They flashed past it within a few moments, catching only a glimpse of a small, pockmarked, and barren world, just a few hundred kilometers across. Mike knew it barely appeared as a perceptible disk from Jilan's surface. The planet's other moons, Nilanu and Tyaila, just as small, were on the opposite side of the globe.

Just before the *Egg* began to enter Jilan's thin atmosphere, Mike launched a horde of nano-bots designed to map and holograph the planet, take air and soil samples, and generally gather as much information as they could in the little time available.

For now, though, Mike had to concentrate on getting down to Jilan safely. He could sense the first stirrings of Jilan's atmosphere against the *Egg*'s skin. "Let's stay focused on this world for now. Neska's pull here will represent about ten times the force it'll assert against Heuri. It'll probably disrupt Jilan's orbit."

Govanek said, "Then we have so much more work ahead of us, and so little time to perform it." The Sobrenian had requested a landing next to deeply furrowed cliffs on the side of a mountain near Jilan's equator. With the nano-probes gathering as broad a picture of the planet as they could, Govanek insisted upon seeing that specific feature for herself.

Cosmic Egg broke beneath the cloud cover. Below them, mountains and low ridges alike cast broad shadows across the lightening plain -- Mike had timed the *Egg*'s landing for local dawn. He said, "It looks as if a lot more water once existed here than does now."

Govanek said, "You speak correctly. See those riverbanks -- their rivers barely fill them. Once, though, rapidly flowing waters often rushed over those banks. And those seas in the far distance once filled those mostly dry basins."

Mike said, "Govanek, this reminds me of a planet in Earth system, named Mars. It's where Captain Sandage is from. It has even less water than Jilan -- no oceans or even seas, but it had a greater quantity of water long ago."

The *Cosmic Egg* descended toward the foot of the mountain, which stood nine hundred meters tall. To the west, it rolled lazily down toward a heavily vegetated plain. Its eastern side, however, made a precipitous drop toward a dusty, barren valley.

Time to find a landing site, Mike thought. *We've got some pretty rough terrain down there in some spots. It looks like the face of an old, grizzled man.*

Mike brought the shuttle down slowly and steadily, hovering over a potential landing spot. "That looks like...marble," he said.

"More evidence of water," Govanek said. "A turbulent stream creates these channels and holes in the hard surface."

Govanek's enthusiasm is infectious, Mike thought. *And she's obviously knowledgeable.*

Under Mike's guidance, the *Egg* settled down onto the hard, rough ground. Mike cut its gravitics and inertials, and Jilan's lighter grav of .65 Earth asserted itself.

Govanek stood and took off her robes. Mike felt vaguely embarrassed but wondered why -- nudity taboos certainly had little reason for existence among different Galactic species. Govanek stowed those robes, pulled out her spacesuit, which was the same blue as her robes, and started putting it on.

Mike and Georges had an easier process -- touch the left middle finger into the palm, and a nanotech action code instantly formed a lifesuit around their bodies, including a bubble helmet protecting their heads.

Humans and Sobrenian cycled through the *Egg*'s airlock. Mike made the first step onto Jilan's surface, easing gingerly onto the edge of one of those dark rocky ridges. Here, examining those furrows more closely, Mike thought they resembled not so much an old man's wizened face as his gnarled hands, reaching with gray fingers across a smooth black landscape.

He checked his wrist sensor. Temperature just below freezing, but things would warm up as the day went on. The atmosphere was too thin and not nearly rich enough in oxygen to be breathable to Human or Sobrenian. He stood under purple skies that would ease toward a reddish blue close to noon.

Before them rose the mountain that so interested the Sobrenian. Moruteb, just barely over the horizon behind them, shone full upon it. Mike looked up at the nine-hundred-K tall cliffside. The deep furrows running vertically down the cliff face looked almost too regular to be natural. He asked Govanek, "Just what's so interesting about this mountain?"

The Sobrenian said, "According to detailed sensor scans I performed aboard the *Meradeus* before coming here -- *life*, and several examples of it."

"What! You didn't tell us..."

"You're very excitable, Mike. Not intelligent life."

"Oh."

"Small animals we call -- *squraulek*."

"Excuse me? Failure to translate."

"Perhaps a problem of slang terms. You might call them...cliff-dwellers."

Not terribly evocative, Mike thought, *but it'll have to do.*

Govanek continued: "They live about halfway up. They have marvelous abilities to climb, and their tough shells protect them from predators. Their young live in chambers they dig within those furrows."

"But they don't create the furrows?"

"They're natural," Govanek said. "The result of thin streams of water flowing down rock which dissolves easily."

Georges said, "The same thing happens on Earth. China, Hawaii, you name it. Basalt, limestone -- we see it everywhere."

Govanek continued: "With rain relatively rare here, it takes years for those furrows to form. And they do not erode away quickly."

Mike said, "I suppose you want a closer look at the cliff-dwellers," and started to take a step forward.

Govanek said, "If you would, Mike...walk very carefully."

"That's right," Georges said. "This looks pretty slick underfoot."

Govanek gestured toward the rocky, ridged ground. "You must forgive me. This is part of Sobrenian mythology -- not scientific, but still very powerful in our thoughts. We once revered such formations as sacred."

Mike said, "I never knew any of that. Does that concept relate to the ideas of the Giver and the Shaper?"

"It relates very much to the Giver, our moral god -- which I follow."

"And the reason you want me to walk carefully?"

"Simple respect for the Creation. I realize to the scientific mind, it may seem foolish. But I'd like us to tread lightly here."

"All right," Mike said. "I certainly will," and started to take another step.

"And -- " Mike stopped short again.

Govanek, continued, "Georges is also correct. The ground appears very slick."

Mike could only take a slow, deep breath before he said, "Thank you. We'll proceed carefully."

"One last thing."

Fortunately, Mike hadn't even begun to take a step this time. It was a fight, though, to keep exasperation out of his voice, even though a datalink wouldn't communicate it. "Yes, Govanek?"

"Your lifesuits harden into armor if you're attacked, don't they?"

"Uh...yes, they do."

"Good," the Sobrenian said, and walked off with exaggerated steps across the dark slippery surface.

*****

Mike, Georges, and Govanek neared the broad expanse of the cliff base. Mike noticed his stride kicking up dust, and asked the Sobrenian, "What happened to the marble?"

"It's still there," Govanek said. "Just buried."

Georges said, "Is that due to runoff from the top of the mountain?"

"Yes." Govanek spread her hands wide. "Water runs off in either direction, and feeds small streams. But only intermittently. This is a dry period. I suspect running water will never appear here again before this planet dies."

That observation left Mike strangely sobered. *Why does that affect me so?* he wondered. *There's no sentient life here. No intelligences will die. It's just rocks, vegetation, and some primitive lifeforms. Just....*

His hand moved, without thought, to his lifesuit's wrist sensor. Its results made his heart beat faster, gave him a shot of adrenaline.

Life. Beneath his feet.

He kneeled and started digging the loose top layer of dirt with his gloved hands, ignoring Georges' and Govanek's silent stares.

The object he sought lay only a few centimeters down. A nearly perfect sphere, about nine centimeters across. He examined the thin striping of blue and gold that made the object resemble a tiny model of a planet. *Perhaps it looks like Itherin,* he thought. *One of the many odd synchronicities of nature, and proof that the simplest things can exalt us.*

Georges apparently couldn't hold his curiosity in any longer. "So, are you going to tell us what you've found, or not?"

Mike's mouth formed a wide grin. "It's a fish."

George's features revealed amazement. "A fish? Here? How?"

Mike laid the small creature onto the dirt and took a more detailed sensor reading. "This outer sphere is its shell. It's made up of overlapping pieces that let it contain a reservoir of water. In fact, most of the sphere's interior is water. The creature inside is quite small."

Georges took his own reading. "And it's hibernating."

"Looks like. It lives off the oxygen and nutrients in the water it's retaining and waits for the next flow of water off the cliffs."

Govanek said, "That water would represent a rich chemical environment -- more so than many standing bodies of water."

"All the same," Mike said, "they must have a high mortality rate."

Georges looked up from another sensor scan. "They're buried all around here. Hundreds of them. They must reproduce like crazy."

Mike used two fingers to dig a hole for the spherical fish, then placed it within and smoothed dirt over it. *I'm not sure why I'm concerning myself with this single fish, when we're going to take plenty samples of others, killing them in the process. Not to mention, the whole planet's about to be vaporized.*

He did it all the same. And when he stood up, he saw Georges looking at him with a quizzical expression. Mike asked, "What?"

Behind his bubble helmet, Georges shook his head. "You just looked...thoughtful, I suppose."

Mike smiled. "Nothing wrong with that, I hope." Georges shrugged and he and Mike followed Govanek as she led the way to the base of the cliff.

Dave Creek

*****

They made three jaunts to the cliffside over the next eight hours, taking only one brief rest break and a longer one for a meal. Mike and Georges took samples of the spherical fish. Govanek concentrated on the cliff-dwellers, since their relationship with their rocky environment particularly fascinated her as a geologist. They turned out to be six-legged creatures, mostly tan or brown, with thin, dart-like bodies and an odd bulge on their backsides.

They watched as the *Egg* extruded long slender arms from its port side that thrust deep within Jilan's surface, taking samples of dirt, rock, and the microscopic lifeforms within. They retrieved their own samples of Jilan's atmosphere.

Then it was time to leave. Mike paused a moment at the side of *Cosmic Egg* as he stowed away digging equipment in a hold in the shuttle's starboard side. He looked into the sky as if he could see the nano-bots that would be taking their own measurements and gathering more samples.

But there's something about a person being here, he thought. *It's not quite real, otherwise. In fact, it's frustrating even having to wear the lifesuit. If I could just take off this helmet and breathe Jilan's air in its purest form, take off these gloves and push my naked hands into its earth -- I feel I'd be able to understand this world in a way I'd never be able to from within this shell.*

It would also be the last thing I'd do. Jilan has a little more atmosphere than Mars, but not much. Lift off this bubble, and Jilan would start claiming all the moisture in my body for itself. I'd cry out, but you'd barely be able to hear me in the thin air.

At least I'd pass out within seconds. Then within minutes I'd enter a sleep both sweet and final, my brain starved of oxy.

Looks like I'm keeping the helmet on. What even brought about such a thought?

Maybe the answer's the same -- life. *Maybe your brain has to consider what death would be like to make life seem all the more precious.*

Maybe.

Govanek walked up to Mike. One of her eyes looked toward him as the other swiveled toward the sun, Moruteb. The primary descended through the deep blue skies slowly, still a couple of hours from setting. Within minutes, though, it would disappear behind the broad cliff. "It's good we're packing up," Govanek said.

"Why's that?" Mike asked.

"You'll see."

Within a few minutes Mike, Georges, and Govanek finished stowing their equipment and samples. Govanek changed from her spacesuit and Mike and Georges deactivated their lifesuits. They all sat in the *Egg*'s cockpit in their previous positions. Moments later, Moruteb disappeared behind the clifftop. To the north and south, Moruteb's light still illuminated the sides of distant mountains and jagged scarps, but immediately in front of the *Egg*, a dark translucent curtain appeared to lower over the landscape.

Mike twisted in the pilot's seat to look back at Govanek. "What now?"

"We wait," the Sobrenian said. "And I ask you to recall my question about whether your lifesuits become armor. Fortunately, we'll all safe inside here, and I have recorders running."

They didn't have to wait long. The first *pop*! from the cliffside came seconds after Govanek spoke. A small plume of dust rose from the ground several meters in front of the *Egg*.

"What the hell was that!" Mike exclaimed.

Another pop, and another plume. And another, and another.

Georges said, "It looks like the cliff is shooting at us."

"Not at us," Govanek said. "At the fish. It's the cliff-dwellers. Their bodies build up a small amount of methane gas that propels them out of their small, narrow homes on the cliffside."

"That was the bulge on their butts!" Mike said.

"Confirming what I suspected from the sensor scans I made while still in orbit. The cliff-dwellers shoot themselves down onto their prey -- the spherical fish. The fish, in turn, burrow deeper once they hear and feel the cliff-dwellers striking the surface. Individuals of each species live, or die. The ecology maintains its balance."

Georges asked, "Why didn't you tell us all this earlier?"

"Basic science. I didn't wish to prejudice your responses, in case we discovered something open for interpretation." She pointed a thick green finger at the cliffside. "As it turns out, this is all refreshingly straightforward."

Two of the cliff-dwellers spattered against *Cosmic Egg*'s forward viewport. "Damn," Mike said. "I hate seeing that. Anyone mind if we go ahead and lift?"

No one objected, and Mike made a quick preflight check and lifted the ship toward orbit.

As the shuttle cleared cloud cover, Georges told Mike, "There's that look again."

"Thoughtful?"

"Yeah. You know, it's just...*life*. We find it everywhere."

"A tiny fish in a shell? An almost-as-tiny little creature that launches itself out of a cliff by shooting methane out its ass? OK, not particularly dignified life, perhaps. But still marvelous in its own way."

"They don't have awareness. They can't know they won't live another month. Hell, some of them didn't live out the day."

"But all the same, it's something rare and precious. Left to itself, who knows what might rise up on this world one day? Become aware? Learn...to love one another."

Georges said, "I understand. Maybe I wouldn't have just a few weeks ago."

Mike understood. "Your mother."

Govanek spoke up. "You Humans! You think the galaxy revolves around you, and what you think important."

Mike stared at her in disappointment. This was the first glimpse he'd seen from Govanek of Sobrenian condescension toward him because he was Human. "And Sobrenians don't?"

"Sobrenians think it *should*," Govanek said. "But we know it does not."

Mike had nothing to say to that. He guided the *Egg* toward the *Meradeus*, where Govanek would rejoin her crew.

CHAPTER SEVEN

That night, Mike sat in his room, tempted to open up the detailed holos of Moruteb system again, to study Heuri as closely as possible from the safety of *Asaph Hall* before taking the *Cosmic Egg* down into the unknown depths of its atmosphere.

Who knows what kind of beings live there, he wondered. *The Drodusarel certainly brought some kind of lifeforms up with them.*

Could they be intelligent? Might they even be related to the Drodusarel? They've been so secretive about their interests all along on this journey.

Those thoughts flew away as Linna called on his datalink. "Mike? Am I disturbing you?"

Mike's face broke out in a broad smile, one he hoped his voice reflected. "Never."

Linna voice grew quieter, more thoughtful. "I talked to Teresa today. Just like this, just over the link. After that scare the other day, I had to check in to see how her child's doing."

"You have to be worried about it."

"Him. Lauren told me."

"Oh."

"And he's doing fine. You know, I want children one day."

"You've...never told me that."

Linna went on: "I already love my children."

"The ones you...don't have yet?"

"There's no hurry -- I'm only 43."

"Hmm."

"You've always told me how different you felt not having a family. You should create your own."

Is she hinting? Mike wondered. *But this is a woman who won't even let me tell her I love her. Time to fall back on an old standard.* "I'm an explorer."

"Not forever. What happens if...*when*...you get close to a hundred? Won't it be time to settle down?"

"I haven't thought about it that much."

Linna sounded amused. "I bet you *try* not to think about it. A home -- *one* planet to live on. How do you even pick, right?"

"Do we have to talk about this?"

"Don't have to. I'd like to."

"It's a challenge for you, isn't it?"

"Without the empathy, you mean?"

"Yeah."

"It's one I could do without. But it *is* intriguing."

"See?" Mike said. "We came here to learn about Moruteb. About the other Galactic species with us. Now we're learning more about each other."

"And ourselves."

"Yeah. And ourselves."

"Good night, Mike. Don't worry. We'll do this in person sometime soon, I hope."

"So do I. G'night." After a moment, Mike opened up the holo-files on Heuri. His thoughts, however, remained close to home.

*****

As previously arranged, Mike was taking the Cetronen explorer Natai to Heuri with him. He was glad the Cetronen paired symbiont was smaller than their species' norm; otherwise they'd have had a difficult time fitting into the *Cosmic Egg*. The red-furred Natai major, with the minor cradled in his arms, was a tough fit in the *Egg*'s co-pilot's seat as it was. The minor's deep-set eyes, though, looked out at Heuri with the same fascination Mike had seen in countless other explorers. His wide, pointed ears flicked at every sound, no doubt due to being on an unfamiliar craft.

The tough part was the major's tail, which was curled up in what looked like a very uncomfortable position behind and beside him. *If trading crewmembers among species becomes common,* Mike thought, *we're going to have to make better accommodations for one another.*

In the seat behind the co-pilot's position sat Rishona Kwan. As the *Hall*'s resident expert on the Cetronen, Mike had insisted she come along. But they weren't the only Galactic species on Mike's mind. "You have to wonder what originally brought the Drodusarel here."

Rishona said, "It's a mystery, all right. Did they know something we didn't?"

Mike understood Rishona's concern. What were the lifeforms the Drodusarel had scooped up from Heuri's atmosphere? Were they, indeed, intelligent? "If they did," he said, "they didn't share it with the rest of us. And you have to wonder why."

Natai said, "Look just beyond the planet -- that bright star, with two fainter ones accompanying it."

"I see them," Mike said. "Neska and her two planets?"

"Yes."

Rishona said, "They'll enter this system within a month."

Mike said, "Current projections say one of Neska's planets could strike Heuri head-on."

Natai said, "With so little time left, why'd the Drodusarel leave for Itherin?"

"The only way we can find out is to go there ourselves."

The ringed gas giant Jilan and its bands of clouds dominated the shuttle's forward screen now. Rishona said, "It resembles Saturn."

Natai's minor asked, "Is that a planet in the Human home system?"

Mike said, "Yes, a ringed world much like Heuri. And it brings up something about gas giants -- it's easy to look at them and imagine they're all alike. But they have just as much variation as any other type of world. It just means you have to look more closely."

"Please explain, Mike Christopher. I'm only a beginning explorer."

"Well, Heuri's only about half the size of Saturn. It's only a little larger than either Uranus or Neptune -- those are other, smaller, gas giants in Earth system. But the surface of Uranus looks like a solid blue globe -- very few surface features. At Neptune, you can see cloud features, and even storms along its surface. But it doesn't have the cloud bands that Heuri does."

Rishona said, "Don't forget the rings."

"That's right. Both Uranus and Neptune have ring systems, but nothing as extensive as Heuri. Another similarity it has with Saturn, though it's much smaller."

Natai's minor said, "Then Heuri combines qualities of worlds you are already familiar with."

"Exactly."

"And that experience helps you interpret your findings on new worlds."

"Or in this case," Mike said, "*into* new worlds. Look, we're coming up on the rings."

Again Mike saw the four main sections of rings. He looked in vain for structures similar to the braiding present in parts of Saturn's rings -- that phenomenon had always fascinated him. Heuri's rings, however, were much more "solid" looking. They weren't really solid, of course, being composed of chunks of ice ranging from the size of marbles to small moons.

Natai's minor leaned forward to initiate a sensor scan, then said, "I understand those rings may have intrigued the Drodusarel -- since life on their planet initially came from their own rings."

"As I told Rosa -- Captain Sandage -- earlier, it's a mystery, at least to Humans."

"And to Cetronen, as well. But if I am using your sensors properly, I detect no life within these rings."

Rishona said, "Our scans from the *Asaph Hall* didn't find any, either. Of course, there's no reason life should exist there. Although the idea could be what drew the Drodusarel to Heuri to begin with."

"And," Mike said, "it seems they found something."

Natai said, "Or someone."

"That's right." Mike guided the *Egg* past the plane of the rings and down toward Heuri itself. "Let's see what -- or who -- we can find."

Within half an hour *Cosmic Egg* was skirting Heuri's upper atmosphere. Skies above were still dark enough to reveal stars, although in some areas reddish wisps of hydrogen clouds obscured both the heavens and the lower cloud layers.

Look directly overhead, and Heuri's rings were a gigantic arch, lording over the sky so effectively that Mike felt an urge to duck, his instincts telling him that something so large yet so insubstantial *had* to be about to fall at any moment.

Natai's minor was performing another sensor scan. He was so intent on his duties that for Mike, the major on whose belly hump the minor was sitting had faded into the background. When the major grunted and shifted in his seat, Mike nearly jumped. He could feel his blood pumping in his neck.

Don't let him -- them -- spook you, he told himself. *Though sometimes I can't help it. I know better, but part of my mind keeps trying to figure out whether the major or the minor is the "real" Natai. Or worries that they'll get into a hopeless argument, with one storming away from the other.*

Never mind that simply seeing them apart would be even more disconcerting. He stole a glance back at Rishona. She was looking at the Cetronen with obvious fascination. He hoped she would learning something practical from this experience.

Mike took the *Egg* down into a lower level of clouds. With more atmosphere roiling overhead, the sky turned a dark blue and all but the brightest stars faded out. That meant so did most of Heuri's dozen moons, none of which was large enough to be visible from the planet as more than a swiftly moving point of light.

Both Natai and Rishona were working on sensor scans. "Anything?"

"No," the Cetronen minor said.

"Yes," Rishona said.

Mike asked, "Which way?"

She transferred several coordinates from her console to Mike's. "There."

Mike headed the shuttle in that direction, about two thousand K to starboard, and another few hundred deeper into Heuri's clouds.

Natai's minor said, "I see the readings now. They're lifeforms. And I can see why the Drodusarel would be interested in them."

"Methane breathers?"

"Doubtful. Not enough of that substance in this atmosphere. But living, as the Drodusarel do, in a planetary atmosphere, which is a rarity, would attract them. It's something we Cetronen can understand."

Mike felt his face redden. This was something Cetronen seldom spoke of. He was glad it was Rishona who asked the next question: "What is it that you understand?"

Natai's minor said, "Cetronen, too, are a rarity. We are the only sentient species not made up of singletons."

Rishona uttered a quiet, "Oh."

Natai's minor stood in the major's lap and faced Rishona. *Talk about disconcerting*, Mike thought. The minor said, "Do not be embarrassed. I do not share the prejudices some Cetronen do regarding singleton species."

Again from Rishona: "Oh." Then she said, "Well, I'm glad."

Natai's minor sat down on the major's hump again.

Rishona worked her controls, pointed out the front viewport, and said, "There!"

Excitement welled up within Mike. *This is why I'm so many hundreds of light-years from home*, he thought, *to make such discoveries. And again, life! Sometimes it seems there's hardly a place in the galaxy where it isn't present.* "Can you get us a visual?" he asked.

On the center viewscreen, Mike saw an image of a wall of dark clouds hanging before them. At first he had no sense of scale, and wondered whether he should throttle back to keep the shuttle from entering that roiling wall.

A quick sensor check, and the cloud wall's true scale revealed itself. Not to worry -- it was nearly seventy kilometers distant, though it stretched from one horizon to the other.

It seemed to move so quickly, though, that Mike realized the forces that wall must be wielding. *It looks like the eye wall of a hurricane*, he thought. *A hurricane that could swallow up Earth's Moon.*

And before that wall floated a series of...the only term Mike could come up with was ribbons. They were flat lifeforms of a dark purple that approached black, each of them about three meters long. Over a dozen strong, they undulated "sideways" across Heuri's skies at a leisurely pace.

"I've seen snakes trace paths just like that across a desert," Mike said. "Do you think these are the same lifeforms the Drodusarel were interested in? They're not very similar to them."

Natai's minor said, "Only in being atmosphere-dwellers. That may be enough."

Mike made a quick sensor check. "They're about four and a half meters long. I can't tell if they're gliding along with the prevailing winds or trying to tack against them."

"Look at their spines," Rishona said.

Mike focused the viewscreen more closely on one of the creatures. Sure enough, a thin ridge was visible down its back. They all appeared to have barely visible segments every few centimeters. Their bodies flared out at either end before forming a rounded tip that resembled an arrowhead. "These beings are just large enough to imply others are here, too. Either something they prey on, or something that preys on them."

Rishona said, "Look just ahead, at ten o'clock -- another pack, or herd, or whatever you'd like to call them."

"Well, I'd like to call this species 'ribbons,' Mike said. "So I'd say 'herd' is good enough. 'Pack' makes them sound like something that comes in a box." He glanced back and saw Rishona dour expression. "OK, so 'ribbons' isn't that clever. You got a better one?"

"Not just yet," Rishona said.

Natai's minor asked, "Can we go closer to them?"

"Perhaps a little bit," Mike said. "But I don't want to take the chance of harming them."

"Remember," Rishona said, "these appear to be some of the lifeforms the Drodusarel took along in the *Dirat*."

"Yeah. Maybe to dissect them."

"We could pull a maneuver I used to see on whale-watching cruises."

Mike said, "Excuse me -- whale *watching*?"

Natai's minor asked, "What is a whale?"

"Earthly ocean-dwelling being," Mike said. "Air breathers, and sentient, even though they're confined to water. Humans can communicate with them."

"How can a being who lives in the ocean breathe air?"

Rishona asked, "Don't you have such beings on your world?"

"Of course not. How would they breathe?"

"They spend a lot of time on the surface."

"That seems unlikely, not to mention inefficient."

Mike said, "Please -- just accept it for now." He turned to Rishona. "But why would anyone just watch whales? Why not talk to them?"

Rishona said, "Not all Humans have datalinks when they're children, you know. I saw this when I was about eleven. Humans weren't even talking to whales yet."

"So what's the maneuver?"

"We go ahead of the...*ribbons*...God, I hate that."

Mike raised his eyebrows at Rishona. "Something better?"

"*Not yet*. Anyway, we get ahead of them and sit right in their path."

"So we don't interfere with them, but we still get a good look. I like it. We'll try it."

Mike guided the *Egg* leisurely around the ribbon herd and eased the shuttle into position about half a kilometer from them, directly in their path.

And waited. The ribbons drew nearer, undulating effortlessly through Heuri's skies.

Rishona said, "It looks as if some of them form subgroups within the herd."

Mike said, "I'll have the comp ID each individual and track them. We'll see which ones stay together as they go around us."

Natai's minor said, "What if they don't go around?"

"Don't worry. I'm not going to let them get closer than a few meters. Then I'll back off."

The herd of ribbons approaching the *Egg* didn't change course right away. When it was about twenty meters away, however, the individuals within it angled around to form a straight line, as if they were an arrow pointing directly at the *Egg*. At about four meters, the individual ribbons separated again, each in a slightly different path as they slid past the shuttle.

When all the ribbons were past, Mike flipped the shuttle around to get a glimpse of them as they continued onward. "They seem none the worse for wear," he said. "I wonder what that maneuver around us was about."

Rishona said, "Maybe they have prey -- or a predator -- that gets confused when they do that."

Natai's minor rose on his major's hump once again and stretched his arms and rolled his neck in an oddly Human manner. As he sat down again, he said, "What seems clear is that these beings are not similar to the Drodusarel. If they are searching for beings like themselves, perhaps that's why they've gone ahead to Itherin."

"I don't know. These are just the first lifeforms we've found here. The Drodusarel only stayed a matter of days. You can't explore a planet in that short a time."

"We're attempting to explore an entire system in a matter of a month."

Mike couldn't help his bitter tone. "That's only because of delays in getting this mission together."

Rishona muttered, "Delays that weren't Humanity's fault."

"Nor were they the fault of Cetronen," Natai's minor said. "It was...others...to blame for that."

"The Drodusarel?" Mike asked.

"No. If anything, they were too eager to go. They wanted to take a small starcraft that was closer to our staging area rather than waiting to bring a more capable one. And you saw how they lost their patience -- boosted away to Moruteb ahead of us."

"Then...it must have been..."

"The Sobrenians," Natai's minor said, and his reluctance in saying that was apparent even across the datalink translation.

"Codari said Cetronen-Sobrenian alliances don't favor you right now."

"That's something we learned only during negotiations for this exploratory mission."

"And it meant enough to try to change that, so you delayed the mission."

The Natai minor said, "Perhaps I've said more than I should. I will focus on exploration now."

Well, that subject's closed, Mike thought. Once a Cetronen moved his focus from one topic to another, that was it. Then he looked down at his sensor readout and his eyes went wide. "Drodusarel shuttle, ten K behind us, approaching rapidly." He opened a comm channel. "Drodusarel ship, please identify yourself."

No response. Mike whipped the shuttle around again, this time to face the oncoming Drodusarel craft.

Rishona said, "Maybe we want to power up weapons."

Mike said, "Passive sensors don't show them powering up."

"I'd hate to be the one to shoot second."

"I don't want to shoot at all. These are supposed to be our colleagues."

Natai's minor said, "Colleagues would identify themselves when asked."

Mike opened the channel again. "Drodusarel ship, please respond."

Rishona put the image of the Drodusarel craft on the main screen. "It's silver, and it's an oval. Big surprise."

"And it's got the *Egg* outclassed when it comes to its drive, weapons, shroud -- you name it. They can do whatever they want to us."

The Drodusarel craft approached to within half a kilometer, then slowed in relation to the *Cosmic Egg*. Ribbons eased their way around it as they had the Human craft minutes earlier. "At least we get another good look at that trick," Mike said. "It's quite pretty, actually."

The Drodusarel craft held its position just long enough that Mike went back to studying the ribbons -- he was just starting to notice that the various herds appeared to be converging on a single point in the far distance when the Drodusarel ship rose through the upper layers of Heuri's atmosphere until it was out of sight.

"Hmph," Mike said. "Not even a goodbye."

Natai's minor said, "I wonder who they were more interested in -- the ribbons, or us."

"No way of knowing. But Drodusarel shuttles don't have stardrive. That means the *Dirat* has to come back from Itherin at some point to retrieve it."

Rishona said, "That gives them less time to explore there -- not to mention if they're interested in any other worlds."

"Most of the rest are all 'dirt worlds' -- they couldn't care less. But it makes me wonder what they're doing -- what they think is so interesting here that they leave that shuttle while *Dirat* heads for Itherin."

Natai's minor said, "It's a risk most Cetronen would be reluctant to make."

Mike looked up toward Heuri's thick clouds as if he could still spot the Drodusarel craft. "Humans, too. But something here must have been worth it."

CHAPTER EIGHT

By the time Mike dropped Natai off at the Cetronen starcraft *Cerenam* and arrived back on *Asaph Hall* with Rishona, he'd been piloting the *Egg* for nearly eighteen hours -- it was past midnight, ship's time. *I'd like nothing better than a hot cup of soup and about twelve hours sleep*, he thought.

Mike went to his quarters, shut the door quietly. Stood there a moment. Knew he couldn't sleep just yet.

I should be the one to call first sometimes, he decided, and touched behind his left ear. "Linna?"

It took a moment, and when Linna finally responded her voice sounded as if she was straining to keep it steady. "Mike...glad to hear from you." But what sounded like a suppressed cough and a sniffling sound punctuated her words.

"Are you all right?"

"Uh...fine."

"Don't bullshit me. You don't sound fine."

"Well...maybe I'm not."

Mike went to his bedroom and sat on the edge of his bed. "I suppose coming over to see you would just make things worse."

"I'm growing more sensitive every day. I'm going to have to move down farther into the ship, maybe close to engineering. There's a room there next to the new-space regulators...."

"What the hell are you talking about?"

"Mike, everyone on the ship is closing in on me."

"You need help. Maybe Lauren -- "

"I've *talked* to Lauren. There's nothing she can do. Empaths are too rare, no one knows enough about us."

"Maybe when we get back to Human space...."

"I may have to be sedated before then. We don't have a way to put me into cold sleep."

"Don't talk that way."

Linna's voice grew somber again. "I know. This is the tough part. Normally I'd come to you. We could talk. You could hold me. Maybe we'd make love. All that's closed to me now."

"Tell me what I can do. I'll help you if I can, Rosa will, we all will."

Silence.

"Linna?"

More silence for a long moment, then: "I have faith in you, Mike. And in Rosa. But I think it's going to take more than that to help me. I've got to go, Mike. Good night."

"Good ni -- " Mike began, but she was gone. He tumbled into bed and a restless sleep.

*****

Mike guided the *Cosmic Egg* across the icy surface of the Moruteb system's outermost planet, Risula, at about one kilometer's height. This time the Sobrenian Govanek was in the right-hand seat, with Alice Nicolson sitting behind him. Alice asked, in a low voice, "How's Linna doing?"

"She's been better," Mike said. He felt uncomfortable talking to Alice about Linna; he'd thought from the time he first joined *Asaph Hall* that she was attracted to him. He'd teased Linna about it once, hoping she would be able to confirm Alice's feelings. The possibility flattered him, though he was quite happy with Linna and would never do anything that might hurt her.

As usual, Linna refused to reveal anything she may have perceived about another crewmember, but her amused smile told him all he need to know. That, and her comment, "Of course, the two of you could do anything you wanted on shore leave and I wouldn't have anything to say about it, would I?"

Linna laughed out loud when Mike blushed; she enjoyed tweaking his "Earther" morals, and found it particularly funny that he hadn't realized until that moment that he was attracted to Alice, as well.

He'd made even greater pains to keep his and Alice's relationship strictly professional thereafter.

Mike turned his attention to Risula's surface. *Being named after a mythical being who renewed the world after winter was a damn poor pick,* he thought. Risula was a world frozen in time -- dark ice covered its entire surface.

Mike saw little evidence, even through detailed scans, of enough internal heat to crack that icy surface open anywhere on the planet. Its icescape featured shallow craters and occasional spires that barely reached fifty meters tall and were the remnants of hills eroded away over the centuries. Risula was only three A.U. distant from Itherin, the planet next-in to Moruteb, and was suspected to be a world which Itherin had captured and brought into the system.

Dark dust from meteor impacts pitted and pockmarked Risula's frozen surface. Lighter-colored ice stood in places where a particularly large meteor had struck the planet's surface, punching through the surface ice to reveal the newer, fresher ice beneath.

The scary part, Mike thought, *is looking into the sky. Neska is so close. The star and its two planetary companions still only appear to be bright stars. Knowing what they are, though, it's easy to imagine them rushing into view and filling the viewscreens at any moment.*

Risula would be the first of Moruteb's planets to feel the effects of Neska's approach. Even now, Neska's apparent size was about half that of Sol's from Earth. Its light cast a harsh illumination across Risula's surface at skewed angles to its primary Moruteb's light.

Govanek said, "I'd like to land."

Mike nearly did a double-take. "Land! We're lucky that Rosa and Codari -- not to mention Syradok! -- approved this fly-by. Do you realize how much more work the gravitics are doing, and the nav unit? And the comp! This is a planet that's liable to be inside that oncoming star within a week."

"I'm aware of that."

"*Thank* you."

"I want to land."

"*Why?*"

"I told you earlier I'm a follower of the Giver."

Alice spoke up. "The Sobrenian moral god."

"That's right. As opposed to the Shaper, who created all things."

Mike said, "So, if you don't mind me asking, what does that have to do with landing on Risula?"

"I want to spend a moment on this world that soon will no longer exist. I don't care about ice samples or how the planet formed or anything else. I just want to stand there for a few moments."

"Govanek, you're putting me in a hell of a position."

"If you're worried about the danger -- "

"I'm more worried about the ass-chewing my captain's going to give me!"

"Sorry? Failure to translate properly."

"Let's hope so. Did you talk to Captain Syradok about this?" Govanek started to speak, but Mike barreled on quickly: "Because if you did, I'd have to take your word on that, since you're his First."

Govanek's eyes stared down her snout at Mike. The Sobrenian said, "I can't lie when my purpose is to feel closer to my God of morality."

"That's a point, I guess."

Alice said, "I might be interested in how difficult nav is within all these conflicting gravity fields."

"We've taken the *Asaph Hall* to some strange star systems," Mike said. "It's knowledge that could save the ship someday."

"Govanek's right about the danger," Alice said. "In fact, the longer we wait, the more dangerous this becomes."

"I understand," Govanek said. "This becomes something we must do quickly, without recourse to our superiors."

"Dammit," Mike said, "let's quit talking about it and start doing something. How's that smooth plain to the west look?"

Alice made a quick sensor check. "It's nice and stable, just like most of the planet."

"Then here we go."

"Shouldn't we let *Asaph Hall* know what we're doing?"

"We will -- soon as we set down."

But they didn't even get a chance to wait that long. Even as Mike positioned the *Cosmic Egg* over that smooth plain, Rosa called: "*Asaph Hall* to *Cosmic Egg*. Are you declaring an emergency?"

Mike was settling the shuttle down onto Risula's icy surface. Alice responded, "Negative, *Asaph Hall*. We'll explain in a few moments." When she cut the connection, Alice told Mike, "By 'we,' I mean 'you.'"

"Fine," Mike muttered, and eased the *Cosmic Egg* down onto Risula's surface.

Govanek rose from the co-pilot's chair and, as she had on Jilan, took off her robes and put on her spacesuit. She stood there holding her helmet in her rough green hands. "Mike, I'd like you to come along."

"*Me*? Why?"

"You were kind enough to allow this. We're here to learn about one another as much as about this doomed system."

Rosa's voice came over Mike's datalink this time. "Mike, what's happening? Is everything all right?"

A quick glance at Alice and Govanek told him Rosa hadn't aimed her transmission at either of them. "We're all fine, Rosa. Just...a chance we shouldn't pass up."

A moment passed in silence, which worried Mike more than the fabled ass-chewing would have. Then Rosa said, "I'll expect to hear all about it when you get back."

Great, Mike thought. He told Alice, "We'll be right back. Keep the home fires burning."

"Don't worry. *I'm* not going anywhere."

"I love that mock-exasperated look you're giving me."

"It's not so 'mock.'"

Time to go, Mike thought, and pressed his left middle finger into his palm to activate his lifesuit. He followed Govanek into the airlock and they stepped out onto Risula's dark rough surface. Mike made his first steps onto the icescape tentative ones in the planet's .27 grav. "Not at all slippery," he said.

Govanek said, "This ice has been battered so many times, its surface has much rock mixed in with the ice. I'd love to know its composition, to -- "

"I thought you weren't going to concern yourself with such things."

"Apologies. Ever the geologist, I suppose."

"Just a minute. Alice?"

Over the datalink, Alice replied, "Yes, Mike?"

"While we're here -- "

"A few samples. I was listening. I'll get the *Egg*'s protocols started up."

Govanek said, "Thanks to you both."

Mike had made sure to land in an area where it was just past local dawn. Looking across the dark pitted icescape to the east, Moruteb was still rising. Risula's day was nearly thirty hours, so local noon would be some hours in arriving.

"Look just above and to the right of Moruteb," Govanek said. She was pointing to a large star, brighter than any others in the sky.

"That can't be Neska. It's on the other side of the planet."

"You're correct. It's Itherin."

"Ah. Where the Drodusarel are."

"I heard about your encounter with them at Heuri. It must have been interesting."

"On my world," Mike said, "the idea of something being 'interesting' is sometimes used as a curse."

"Then what is about to happen here on Risula will truly be interesting."

Mike knew what Govanek meant. The very idea of standing on a world that soon would not exist filled him with amazement at what the universe was capable of. *That's the unspoken motivation for coming here*, Mike thought, *at least for us Humans. Deep down, part of us craves spectacle.*

Just about a dozen meters away was a shallow crater with rounded rims. They were the norm here; the heat of an impact by an asteroid or meteorite would turn surface ice into water that splashed, then flowed across Risula's surface, leveling the nearby icescape before freezing within moments. Water would also at least partially fill the crater, making it shallow.

That was the case with the crater Mike was eyeing. He stepped gingerly over to its edge, still aware this *was* ice, however gritty, still aware of the .27 grav. The crater was nearly fifty meters wide, but he knew if he were so daring (so stupid!) as to jump into it, he'd still be able to poke his head out and wave to Govanek.

I've been thinking of the coming catastrophe as worlds colliding like billiard balls, Mike realized. *Risula really is one, the most-perfectly round world I've ever seen this side of Jupiter's moon Callisto.*

He thought of Govanek and turned to see what she was doing. The Sobrenian was where he'd left her, standing stock-still, both her hooded eyes staring at the stars.

No, Mike thought. *Not at them. Into them. As if she's losing herself in them.*

Now's when I need Linna here. What is Govanek experiencing? Some sort of religious ecstasy? Is that even an emotion distinct from other forms of euphoria? Or is this another example of the Sobrenian "calm" they can turn on at will?

Mike left the crater behind and went back to Govanek. He only approached to within about ten meters of her, not wanting to disturb her. *Although*, he thought, *we've got to leave sometime soon. Rosa's patience may be wearing thin. Not to mention Syradok's or Codari's.*

Finally, he said, "Govanek?"

The Sobrenian's gaze fell from the stars and both her eyes looked directly at Mike. "Yes?"

"I'm sorry, but we have to go soon."

Govanek looked around at her surroundings as if becoming aware of them again. "Do you know that thoughts of the Giver fill me with an unmatched awe?"

"I...don't know what to say."

"Humans have their gods, do they not?"

"Many of us do. I'm not one of them."

"How do you bear the sadness?"

"It doesn't cause me sadness."

Govanek said, "I wonder what Linna would say to that."

"One day I'll have to ask her."

"You are intimate sexually, are you not?"

"Well, uh...*yeah*."

"Then other intimacies should come naturally to you."

Mike asked, "Are you an expert in Human psychology, now?"

"Not at all. But you do fascinate me as a species. Your religions, your sexual roles, your families."

Mike muttered, "I don't know much about that last one myself."

"About Human families?"

"I was created by scientists, from scratch. Even called 'artificial' sometimes. No family. No ancestors. It all starts with me. You asked about gods earlier. I know a god didn't create me."

Govanek said, "I apologize if I've offended you."

"It's not anything I think about very often these days -- gods or families."

"You never even had a substitute family?"

"No one wanted an artificial Human. You wouldn't think it would matter. But it was a harsh time back on Earth then. The Great Human War started the year I was born. That distracted everyone, as you can imagine. And this was about the second or third generation, at least in the continent where I grew up, that was used to what they called the 'culture of plenty.'"

"You refer to replicators? My people went through a similar cultural transition about two hundred years ago."

"Yeah. No need to work unless you wanted to. So people didn't. No need to sacrifice. So they didn't."

"Seems contradictory, given that your species was fighting a war with itself."

Mike smiled. "Humans manage quite well embracing contradictions. Sure, there were people fighting the war, but they were the minority."

"And you grew up alone?"

"Mostly in a series of orphanages -- seldom even had a chance at becoming part of a foster family."

"I apologize," Govanek said. "I was overly curious."

"Not at all. I'm curious about some things, too."

"Such as?"

"Why the Sobrenians are suddenly so interested in this system. Why they didn't accompany the fleet from the beginning."

Govanek's eyes looked away again, the left one staring out toward the stars, the right one peering across the icescape. "My people do not appreciate such questions. I have not interrogated you about Human motivations."

Mike spread his hands wide. "Which are very clear. We want to learn about this system, and about other Galactic species."

"Including Sobrenians."

"Yes."

"That's one of two reasons we were reluctant to go on this mission."

"What was the other reason?"

"The Cetronen would not allow us to lead the mission."

Mike said, "You dislike having 'pre-sentients' in charge, don't you?"

Govanek's eyes spun toward Mike again. "I've never used that word to refer to you or any other Human. Not even in private among other Sobrenians."

"Then I apologize."

"You caught me at an inopportune time, Mike. My reaction to the stars...to standing on this world that soon will no longer be here...I hope I didn't ask too many personal questions."

"You didn't," Mike said. "We should get back to the shuttle."

Govanek led the way back inside, but Mike paused at the bottom of the ladder leading into the airlock. *Everything's transient*, he thought. *Nothing lasts. This world, so solid, so perfectly formed, will be random ice and dust within a week.*

A dead world, yet I find its destruction oddly affecting.

He scrambled up the ladder and into the *Cosmic Egg*. As he lifted the *Egg* off Risula's surface, Rosa called. "We need to talk. Right now."

Mike's face felt warm all of a sudden. "I understand, Rosa...uh, Captain. But can't this wait?"

Rosa's voice was conciliatory. "Oh, you thought I meant your, well, spontaneous jaunt. This is something else -- don't return to the *Hall* just yet."

Mike traded glances with Alice and Govanek. Alice shrugged, and Govanek stared blankly, both eyes facing forward. "So where *are* we going?"

"A little diplomatic visit to the *Cerenam*. Once you arrive, Captain Codari will be waiting for you. I've already sent two others ahead of you."

Mike frowned. "OK, I'll take the bait. Who are the two others?"

"Well, Linna for one. And Ambassador Song, for another. You met the Cetronen Natai before. He'll meet you at their hangar deck. Let Govanek know Captain Syradok has already approved her presence, as well. Oh, and I hope you're hungry."

CHAPTER NINE

My biggest fears are being realized, Mike thought. This was an event he looked forward to about as much as coming out of a stardrive jump into the center of a planet or waking up naked in a methane atmosphere. Natai, who had accompanied him and Rishona into the atmosphere of the gas giant Heuri, led Mike and Alice and Govanek into the *Cerenam*'s equivalent of *Asaph Hall*'s common room. It was much bigger, though, obviously intended for such diplomatic functions -- not to mention that the pairings of Cetronen majors and minors were somewhat larger than the average Human.

In the room's dim light, Mike could barely make out a long, high table that appeared to be of wood, set for a dozen beings. Several Cetronen scurried about, carrying platters of food and tall pitchers of drinks which they placed onto the table. The majors did all the carrying as the minors barked all the orders and, presumably, did all the worrying.

The rich smells of various types of Human food at the table were a good sign, but Mike also caught whiffs of sour-smelling Cetronen dishes and musty Sobrenian ones. *No doubt,* he thought, *the Cetronen and Sobrenians have their own opinions about other species' tastes and smells, none of them good.*

A glance at Govanek, though, and it seemed she was entranced by the spread. She lifted her snout and took a deep breath. When she noticed Mike looking at her, she said, "Apologies. It's been a long time since I've had a scent of food this delicious."

"I hope you enjoy it," Mike said, a sincere wish, knowing that his own fate was hopeless.

Natai's minor said, "The other guests will be here soon. Please make yourself comfortable. I must attend to Codari."

"Thanks," Mike said, noticing that the Cetronen did some pretty good scurrying of his own as he departed.

Alice asked, "Shall we sit down?"

"I'm not about to make a move toward that table just yet. Delay -- delay is the order of the day."

"Mike, you're rambling."

"Sorry."

The wall holos came on. He squinted, blinked a couple times, then was able to open his eyes enough to check out their displays.

To his right were the now-familiar Cetronen wonders he and Georges had seen in Captain Codari's quarters -- the Sorrowful Mountains, with more than one summit topping out at over 14,000 meters and all of them eternally shrouded in fog, and the broad and deadly Plain of Itherin, the desert where mythology said a god split the Cetronen in two, making them more than mere animals.

Mike recognized a third Cetronen wonder depicted in the holos -- Sullor, a sprawling metropolis of fifty billion that was two hundred kilometers across at its widest point.

On the opposite wall, Mike saw several holos devoted to scenes from the Sobrenian homeworld. He turned to Govanek, who still appeared to be taking in the smell of the food, and asked her, "Can you tell me what some of these holos represent?"

Govanek indicated the closest image, one that showed a valley filled with dense vegetation, red and green and yellow. "That's the Sharaith Valley. It's where many of our families perform their *koraht* rituals."

Mike nodded understanding, even at the word that didn't translate. He'd heard of the ritual in which Sobrenian youngsters had to make their way across a wilderness armed with only a sword and their own resourcefulness. They had to survive individually in an area with many poisonous plants and fruits as well as large roving predators called *adrono*.

"The next holo," Govanek said, "shows the Path of Victory. It's a narrow strip of land from which the ocean recedes only twice a year on average."

"How does that work?"

"It involves a conjunction of our world's two moons. The great astronomer and warrior Syrilla centuries ago calculated the exact moment when his troops would be able to rush across the strait in force and capture the island that held the fortress of his enemy, Turellen."

Alice asked, "Was Syrilla a good and kind ruler?"

"He ruled," Govanek said. "For our people back then, that was sufficient."

Mike looked around. "There don't seem to be any other Sobrenians here."

"No others are expected. That, at least, is what Captain Syradok has told me."

Uh oh, Mike thought. "Couldn't anyone else from the *Meradeus* make it here?"

"None was invited. This event was apparently organized very quickly. I am here only because I was already with you, and you would have missed this event had you returned me to my ship."

Uh oh again, Mike thought. *Now you've really stepped in it.*

Fortunately, Govanek was ready to move on, asking, "Are these next images from Earth?"

"They are," Mike said, and explained the significance of the 1700-meter-wide curtain of water that was Victoria Falls, the repository of geological history called the Grand Canyon, which Mike had already referred to back on Risula, and the Human-constructed wonders of the kilometers-long Unity Starcraft Assembly Habitat. The latter was a familiar sight to most people on the planet as it traversed Earth's skies every 90 minutes.

And, Mike thought, there's nothing at all from the Drodusarel homeworld. *What does that mean, if anything?*

Linna and Teresa entered the room. They would've arrived earlier aboard the *Asaph Hall*'s other shuttle, *Phobos 2*.

Mike went to Linna and embraced her briefly. He tried to keep his voice light as he told her, "Glad to see you're getting out more."

Linna's grin was the most glorious thing he'd seen in some time. "Glad to *be* out." Mike couldn't help but notice, however, that her grin quickly faded. The expression that remained was...resolute, perhaps even grim. *I can only imagine,* he thought, *what it must be like for her -- around so many individuals, and of four Galactic species!*

Teresa spoke up: "So, what was that you told me several weeks ago about about how a joint dinner wasn't a good idea?"

Mike saw Linna aim a withering look at Teresa of a sort he usually saw directed at *him*.

Mike only gritted his teeth. He wasn't about to get caught up in an open disagreement in front of the representatives of the four Galactic species who had sent starcraft on this mission.

And all four *were* represented here, Mike realized as, wonder of wonders, a Drodusarel delegation arrived.

There were two of the methane-breathers, an energy shield protecting each of them from the deadly oxygen in the atmosphere and allowing them to hover above the deck. The shields were a grayish-blue, and nearly opaque -- Mike could just barely make out their oval, tentacled, robin's-egg-blue bodies within.

The Drodusarel approached Mike. As they drew closer, he caught a whiff of the odor their shields generated -- as usual, Mike perceived it as something akin to ozone mixed with cat fur.

"Greet the Human ones!" the lead Drodusarel said. "I am Captain Dresk. Here is a crewmember, Kahtora. He explores."

Mike gave a slight bow. "Pleased to meet you." He introduced Linna, Teresa, Alice, and Govanek.

Dresk said, "I abhor such gatherings. Hive mind, however, reserves judgment, so I am here."

Mike had to bite his lip to keep his face as blank as he could, even though it was unlikely the Drodusarel could interpret Human facial expressions. "Very well, then," was all he managed to say.

The Drodusarel moved away. Once they were out of earshot, Alice said, "Charming."

Govanek said, "I've never encountered such beings personally before. Do you become used to them?"

"Never," Mike said.

Teresa said, "I'm going to see if I can talk to them some more."

"Don't go too far away," Linna said, and she grabbed Mike's elbow and took him aside from the others. "She's here at Captain Codari's insistence."

Mike said, "Didn't Rosa explain about her? *Ow*, don't squeeze so hard!"

"Listen, dammit, Codari doesn't care. He likes her."

"He saw her *once*, months ago, over a viewscreen. For all of about three seconds. And she was *late*."

"Mike, just shut the hell up and listen. I think that's the part he liked. She was...unassuming."

Mike cast a glance toward Teresa, who was still schmoozing with the Drodusarel. He leaned closer to Linna. "What she is, is totally inexperienced. She's liable to put us all in the middle of a diplomatic incident."

"Not much we can do about that now."

A discordant musical fanfare bleated from one end of the room, and Captain Codari entered, his two-and-a-half meter major an impressive presence. But it was the minor, as usual held in the major's arms, who acknowledged everyone's attention with outspread hands, a nod, or a brief word. Natai stayed close by his commander.

The room grew quiet as Codari sat at the head of the table, the major carefully inserting his thick tail through a hole at the back and easily settling into the broad-backed wooden chair. The minor, sitting on the major's belly hump, had to lean forward slightly to place his folded hands on the table.

Mike looked around for guidance on where he was expected to sit and found none. But it was clear that individuals were grouping themselves by species, with the other Cetronen nearest to Codari, everyone else farther down the line.

Linna said, "We should both stick close to Teresa. I'll sit next to her. Why don't you sit across from her?"

Yes, ma'am, Mike wanted to say as sarcastically as he could muster, but avoided the temptation. Instead he said, "I'm there," and worked his way around to the opposite side of the table, getting to the chair opposite Teresa just as she was sitting. To Mike's surprise, the Cetronen explorer Natai stood right behind her, his major even pulling out her chair and guiding her with a hand on one shoulder as she sat down. The smile Teresa gave Mike was suitably smarmy.

Natai took the seat to Mike's left, and it was a tight squeeze for the paired symbiont. Natai's minor said, "Even now, it is as if I have only begun analyzing everything we saw within Heuri. Learning more of the nature of the ribbons alone could take a lifetime."

Mike said, "It's unfortunate we won't have more time to study them directly." Then he sat, and it was apparent that the *Cerenam* wasn't equipped for Human visitors. The table rose to the middle of Mike's chest. He tried placing his hands in front of him and felt as if he were about to pull himself up the final centimeters of a steep mountain. Hands in lap, and he felt anyone looking across the table at him would perceive him as a disembodied head. And the tail hole was just big enough that if he leaned back the wrong way he feared he would fall backwards.

Linna sat immediately to Teresa's right. Being shorter, her head was even closer to the tabletop than his, looking nearly edge-on to the plate in front of her. He told her, "It's like sitting at the children's table."

Mike discretely tilted his head to indicate Govanek, who was several chairs down on Linna's side. Being even shorter than the average Human adult, her eyes barely saw over the tabletop. Linna chuckled softly. "Poor thing," she said.

Alice sat to Mike's right and reached for the closest platter. "Let's see what we're having," she said.

For his part, one look at Teresa's Cheshire-cat grin and Mike knew the menu. "Lemme guess," he said. "I bet it's sautéed fish."

"*Sole ala meunière*," Teresa said.

Alice had to lean forward to see over the lip of the platter. "Right the first time."

Linna asked Mike, "How'd you know that?"

"Never mind."

Teresa indicated a large bowl. "You'll also have to try the Vietnamese soup. The vegetables and herbs are delicious. It comes with either rice or vermicelli noodles."

Fortunately, although the Cetronen didn't use utensils, they had supplied them to the Humans. As they spooned out portions of fish and soup and began to eat, Mike had to admit it was a marvelous meal. Watching Teresa as she, in turn, watched the Cetronen consume *their* meal was especially entertaining.

It was exactly as Mike had described earlier -- Natai and the others ate unreplicated meat, from actual dead animals. Each of the dozen Cetronen crewmembers had a large slab of flesh on his or her plate. The major held on to the minor, who pulled off chunks and ate.

I wonder, Mike thought, *whether the lip-smacking and swallowing are as loud as Teresa imagined them when I described them.*

Govanek, the sole Sobrenian present, was comporting herself in a much more civilized way than the Cetronen, at least by Human standards. She employed utensils, and appeared nearly dainty as she carefully speared a chunk of meat or what looked like a blue vegetable.

As for the Drodusarel, the methane-breathers sat at the far end of the table, eating nothing, silent in their energy shields that still emitted the occasional ozone smell that wafted down the table.

Taking another look at the Cetronen as they fed, Mike also marveled at how much storage capacity the *Cerenam* must have to provide food that once was living beasts to the entire complement of a starcraft for nearly a year. When he sneaked a peak at Teresa's obvious discomfort, it was his turn to grin.

Natai's minor paused in his feast. As his major lifted the meat slab over the minor's head and took his turn eating, the minor asked, "So, Humans do not consume real meat?"

"Some do," Mike answered. "Most spacers, however, prefer replicated meat."

Natai's minor's pointed ears tilted from side to side, like those of a cat straining to hear an intriguing sound. "Because you don't want to kill to eat."

"Some Humans still kill to eat. But for most of us, that's correct -- we would rather not enslave or kill animals."

"Interesting. Also, to most Cetronen the idea of a liquid as a meal rather than refreshment is...unusual."

"Liquid? Oh, the soup. Well, uh...we enjoy it." Across from him, Linna stifled a giggle, which had Mike biting his lip to keep from busting out in laughter himself. *I'm just glad to see her laugh*, he thought, *even at my expense.*

The Cetronen servers appeared once again, this time with dessert. Inevitably, the Human treats were cream puffs filled with banana cream -- drizzled, of course, with chocolate sauce. Once again, Mike had to admit, they were delicious.

Once the meal was done, Captain Codari's major stood, effortlessly cradling the minor in his arms. His fur moved rhythmically as a draft wafted through the room. The nictating membranes in his nostrils opened and closed, opened and closed. The minor looked around at those assembled and said, "I wanted to speak of my dedication to exploration, and of the alliances that we Cetronen love to create -- and those who sometimes stand in the way of those alliances."

Oh, hell, Mike thought. *No good's coming of this. At best we're in for a snoozefest, at worst someone's gonna get their feelings hurt. Thousands of light years and five months out from even moderately civilized space is no place to start a grudge.* Mike glanced at Govanek. *Or*, he thought, *make an existing one deeper.*

Codari's minor extended a hand toward Mike, then swept it across to include the other Humans -- Linna, Teresa, Alice. "My Human friends. You were the first Galactic species we invited on this journey, and the first to accept our offer. That is only appropriate, perhaps, as we named this planetary system after the great Cetronen explorer Moruteb, best remembered for making first contact with both the Kanandra and Sobrenians. My crewmember Natai has told me of the fascinating journey within the gas giant Heuri that he made accompanying Mike Christopher and Rishona Kwan -- of discovering the atmospheric beings they call ribbons. They are beings our Drodusarel friends have also encountered, after their misguided decision to leave the rest of our little fleet behind."

Great, Mike thought. *As a diplomat, Codari's an excellent starcraft commander. He makes Teresa seem credible.*

Codari paused, as if giving the Drodusarel a chance to speak up. They didn't take advantage of it.

The Cetronen continued: "This brings us to our fourth Galactic species present. Codari's minor's gaze turned to Govanek. "I did not invite this representative of the Sobrenian species to this event, but I welcome her. Perhaps we can create a new understanding of what it means to forge a civilized alliance."

Govanek gathered her robes about her and stood on her chair, otherwise no one more than a couple of seats away would have been able to see her. "I must protest such ignorance and presumption. We Sobrenians are as civilized as anyone." She indicated the Drodusarel at the opposite end of the long table from Codari. "You gloss over the *Dirat* abandoning you, while the *Meradeus* remained."

Codari's minor pointed out, "The *Meradeus*, being uninvited, would not have been missed."

"These Drodusarel look down upon all non-methane breathers as inferior!"

Mike felt as if he were at a tennis match, as he looked back and forth from Codari to Govanek and back again as they spoke. *This is getting good*, Mike thought. *But it would be a shame if this mission ended right here before we got to see these planets collide.*

Codari's minor said, "Have I not repeatedly heard Sobrenians refer to individuals of other Galactic species as 'presentients?'"

Govanek gathered herself up and stood as tall as she could on her chair. "That's an unfortunate prejudice I do not share. And I've also heard more than one Cetronen express disdain for 'singleton' species."

Mike, without conscious thought, stood up, every instinct in his body screaming, demanding to know what the hell he was doing. "Captain Codari -- Govanek. Each of you has harsh words for the other. Aren't we here to try to learn more about each another? Shouldn't we explore one another's natures rather than criticize them?" He indicated Dresk and the other Drodusarel, what was his name -- Kahtora? "Perhaps we should take an example from our other friends here. They don't seem to harbor such resentments."

Dresk spoke up: "Have them. Not speaking."

"Well, so much for that," Mike muttered, and sat down.

Codari said, "I appreciate your sentiment, Mike Christopher. But I believed this *was* our exploration of one another. Am I wrong?"

Mike considered that. "Well...I'd just hoped we could do it without...such conflict, I guess."

"Mike Christopher -- when Neska and its worlds enter the Moruteb system, what do we expect to happen?"

"Well..they'll disrupt much of the Moruteb system, certainly. A couple of worlds may even collide."

"Conflict, correct?"

Mike leaned back in thought. "I suppose."

"And with these worlds under stress, perhaps to destruction, we will learn much about them, will we not? How much gravitational strain a particular world can take before it pulls itself apart. What the interior composition of these worlds might be, each an individual. And from these individual worlds, we learn more about worlds in general. Correct?"

"Uh...certainly."

"I hear your concern even before you speak of it. But don't worry. Because *that* is the reason for having several Galactic species on this mission. We create the strain, we endure the strain, but do not force matters to destruction." Codari's minor spread his arms wide, though that was barely wider than his own major. "The dinner is done. Go in peace, thinking only of what new wonders we will learn in the next few days."

Codari lowered his arms, Mike marveling once again at the Cetronen ability to focus, laser-like, on a single topic only to abandon it just as quickly.

That's when Teresa threw up, violently and loudly, all over the nice wooden table.

CHAPTER TEN

So it turned out no one left right away, either "in peace" or otherwise, because Codari and Natai and all the other Cetronen, along with Dresk and Kahtora and the other Drodusarel, and the lone Sobrenian, Govanek, had to get a close-up look at the ailing Human.

Meanwhile, Linna abandoned Teresa, leaving the table in a rush and covering her mouth with her napkin. When Mike tried to get near her, she waved him away and stood in a corner, as far away from Teresa as she could get. He knew the best thing he could do for Linna was to move away from her -- his presence was at least as upsetting to her as anyone else's. He went to Alice, who was standing over a crying Teresa Song, hands on the ambassador's shoulder, trying to comfort her. He asked Alice, "Can you get Govanek back to the Sobrenian ship and Linna back to the *Hall*? I'll take Teresa."

Alice said, "Gladly."

But Mike found himself with nothing to do for a few moments except dodge nosy questions from *Cerenam* crewmembers, Govanek, and the Drodusarel regarding the specifics of Human pregnancies and why nature would create a species that became ill during the reproductive process. That, and glance every few moments at Linna, who was still standing in that corner trying to remain inconspicuous and recover her composure. Within a few moments, she and Alice started making their way toward the hangar bay.

Teresa wiped her nose and sniffed. "I'm so sorry," she said. "I so wanted the banquet to go well."

Mike managed to pull Teresa away from the press of the other three Galactic species crowding around her, and got her on the way toward the hangar deck.

*****

Within half an hour, Mike got Teresa safely back to the *Asaph Hall* and handed her over to Lauren Takahashi. He pushed thoughts of Teresa away as he headed for his quarters -- he only wanted to think of Linna. She was his shipmate, his love, his strength.

She was the one who'd suggested becoming shipmates; it was a big step for both of them, as neither had entered such a relationship before. Both feared what might happen if they broke up -- would they be able to continue working together afterward, or would one of them leave *Asaph Hall*?

The question never arose. They stayed together, and after the first few years of their relationship seldom even had other lovers during shore leaves or other off-ship jaunts.

But soon we could be separated, Mike thought. *Perhaps never to see one another again.*

That's when Mike reached his quarters and found Linna waiting for him.

She was sitting on the couch and looked up as he came through the doorway. He started to speak, but she rose quickly from the couch, one finger to her lips, and embraced him.

Her body shook with fright and she held him tighter. Mike closed his eyes, ran his fingers through Linna's hair, took a deep breath of her. "This is where I belong," he said.

"Where I wish I could stay more often," Linna said.

Mike looked deeply into Linna's eyes. "This makes me think -- what's the big deal about being an explorer? Sure, I made that sort-of first contact with the Drodusarel, a decent second contact with the Jenregar, helped save two sentient species on Splendor, and just months ago survived being stranded on the Station of the Lost. It's not as if I haven't accomplished anything.

"But in all the universe, no matter how many worlds I travel to, I'm holding the only Linna Maurishka in my arms."

Linna chuckled. "I'm sorry. You're being very sweet, and not just your words -- I can feel all the love you're projecting just washing right over me. But I keep thinking of Teresa." She laughed until tears came to her eyes. "I'm sorry, it's not really funny."

Mike said, "I actually feel sorry for her -- urping like that in front of everyone. I'm sorry the banquet was so awful for you right at the end."

"At the end? God, the whole thing was *hideous*. The slurping, the cracking sounds, burping and farting noises, Codari's big speech and Govanek getting pissed -- Teresa throwing up was the only thing that redeemed it."

Mike ran his fingers across Linna's cheek. "We have better things to talk about."

Linna placed her hand over his and closed her eyes. "I can't stay long."

"I'm glad you showed up at all."

Linna opened her eyes, looked into Mike's. "You're the only one who knows what I'm feeling."

"I'm sure Rosa has an idea."

"Yeah. Probably." Linna kissed Mike, just a quick peck. "Gotta go." She took his hands in hers. "Sorry."

"Yeah."

"Once this is over...if I can just be by myself for the better part of a couple days...."

"That would be great."

"Then we'll get together -- and both walk bowlegged for a week."

"Looking forward to that."

Linna left. Mike stood there a long time afterwards, staring at the door.

*****

Rosa called Mike to her quarters when the rogue star, Neska, was only about a day and a half from its closest approach to Risula, the Moruteb system's outermost planet.

As Mike entered, Rosa was standing in the middle of her main room, but motioned Mike to the nearest chair. "Anything to drink?"

"No, I'm fine." *Odd*, Mike thought. *I've worked with Rosa for nine years and seldom been here.*

Little had changed from that last time -- the sensor and comm console she'd installed were of more advanced design. The inevitable small holos scattered around the room showed different views than before of her beloved Mars.

The "still" holos of her parents remained on a nearby table, though the one he'd noticed once of a German Shepherd, a long-dead pet, was gone. But the centerpiece of that table was still an actual book, her doctoral thesis turned bestseller *No Honor Given*, her classic history of the Great Human War.

Rosa was still standing silently, apparently deep in thought. Mike asked, "Everything OK?"

The *Asaph Hall* captain shifted her weight from one foot to the other. "What's that? Oh, yes, everything's fine. As much as it's going to be, I suppose."

"That doesn't sound encouraging."

Rosa shook her head, then sat down in a chair next to Mike's. "I'm sorry. There's just so much to cope with. And you're at the center of a lot of it."

Mike groaned. "That *really* doesn't sound encouraging."

"I wouldn't give you something I didn't think you could handle."

"That means it's especially bad."

"And here it is. Govanek -- and more importantly, Syradok -- wants you aboard the *Meradeus* when Moruteb approaches Risula."

"Oh," Mike said. "I'd imagined a much worse fate."

"Such as what?"

Mike shrugged. "It was indeterminate. But still pretty bad."

"Don't be complacent. That's not all."

"Uh oh."

"Yeah, uh oh. The next big encounter after Risula is at Itherin, and you can watch it here. But then you have yet another invitation, this one from Codari himself. He wants you aboard the *Cerenam* for what will probably be the destruction of Heuri." That was the world where the Drodusarel had gathered up lifeforms and taken them into the *Dirat*, where he and Rishona and the Cetronen Natai had discovered the ribbons.

Mike said, "I'm going to be a busy boy."

"Busier than you might think. Codari also wants Linna along."

"I hope she can handle it."

"She has to. Teresa's going, too."

"Ah, *finally* -- the worse fate. Why in hell does he want her along?"

Rosa threw up her hands in frustration. "Cross-reference under that wonderful banquet you attended, I suppose."

Mike looked at Rosa with narrowed eyes. "I should've brought a to-go box for you. With plenty of Cetronen recently-live meat."

"*Not* hungry, thank you. And apparently Teresa's learned her nose is a little too sensitive for such events."

"Good for her. You should've been there, though. You know, sometimes I can't even remember the last time you were off the ship."

Rosa smiled gently. "Sometimes I can't either. But my place is here."

"Codari told me the same thing, back when Georges and I visited him on the *Cerenam*."

"Cetronen or Human -- we're both captains. We know these things."

"He told me then he wanted me to keep an eye out for anything important -- and let him know about it."

"I'd have asked the same thing in his place."

Mike squirmed in his seat. "Ask a crewmember of another ship -- of another *species* to spy on everyone else?"

"Not spy. Keep an eye out." Rosa paused for an instant, then went on. "Have you told him anything?"

"Not a thing. And I've told you *everything*."

"As it should be."

"I'm confused," Mike said. "I thought you said you'd have done the same thing in Codari's place."

"I would have. To find out if I could trust that person. Anyone who would report back to me before his own captain could never be trusted."

Mike said, "So maybe I passed a test with Codari."

"Which could be why he wants you along on that trip to witness the end of Heuri. Codari's the leader of this mission, and he's done an excellent job. But I only trust him so far. When it comes down to it, he'll look after his own ship and his own people first."

Mike grinned. "He gave me similar warnings about the Sobrenians and the Drodusarel."

"Fine advice. But guess what?"

"It applies to us, too?"

"Got it the first time," Rosa said.

*****

Things happened quickly once Mike guided the *Cosmic Egg*, with Linna and Teresa aboard, to dock with the water-drop-shaped Sobrenian ship *Meradeus* for the first of his invitations aboard another Galactic species' starcraft.

As they exited the *Egg*, Mike couldn't help but notice that Teresa didn't wrinkle her nose at the ship's musty, organic smell as she had on her first visit. *Given her recent history, I can't imagine she's used to it*, he thought. *But at least she knows better than to show her distaste.* Our ambassador!

Mike had expected Govanek to meet them at the hangar deck, but it was a different Sobrenian who welcomed them. He was wearing the familiar blue robes, featuring several lines of yellow and red running through them. "I am Sejagar, Captain Syradok's head of security," he said, and extended a rough-skinned hand to each of the Humans in turn. "It's an unusual custom, to touch someone immediately upon meeting them. But I see that it could be comforting."

I'll take whatever comfort I can get right now, Mike thought. "We're glad to be here," he said, not altogether lying.

Sejagar said, "Captain Syradok would like you to come to our bridge immediately."

Teresa spoke up. "We'll be honored to join him."

Sejagar led the way out of the hangar deck. They had to walk single-file down the *Meradeus*'s narrow, shadowed, dark-green corridors. A couple of times Mike and the other Humans had to duck beneath equipment hanging from the ceiling or where a corridor narrowed to accommodate blast doors.

Mike expected to see more of the same when they reached the bridge. He was wrong. Sejagar stepped aside to allow him and Linna and Teresa to precede him, and with his first step onto the bridge he found himself squinting and raising his hand against blinding light in all directions.

I knew Sobrenians could withstand brighter light than most Humans, Mike thought, *but I've never seen an interior of one of their ships illuminated so intensely.*

Then he heard Syradok speak: "Mike Christopher and Linna Maurishka and Teresa Song! What a pleasure to see each of you again."

As Mike's eyes adjusted to the light, he could make out Syradok, who stood with his back to an oval table in the center of the bridge. A quick glance around, and Mike saw viewscreens and holos in ever direction, each centered on one of the ships of the fleet or one of the worlds of the Moruteb system. As many as a dozen crewmembers bustled around the various sections of the bridge. *There* was Govanek, busy working a sensor cluster to one side.

Syradok's blue robes rustled as he waved the Humans closer to the table. Mike stared down at it, Linna and Teresa taking positions immediately to his right, and he realized he was seeing a display of the dark, pitted surface of Risula. "Look closely," Syradok said as he stood on the opposite side of the display from the Humans. "This is the last glimpse any Galactic intelligences will have of Risula."

The light was harsh and bright on this display, as well, but that was from the proximity of the rogue star Neska to the planet. Though the display didn't show the star itself, its light thrust sharp shadows across Risula's surface. The lighter portions of the icy world, indicative of meteor strikes, stood out even more now.

The display switched to another view, this one focused on the side of Risula toward Neska. Already ice vaporized from the planet's surface, revealing dark earth and rock beneath. Giant cracks the size and length of rivers spread across what remained of Risula's icy surface. Mike imagined the destruction of the landscape he and Alice and Govanek had visited on their brief trip to that world -- the shallow craters splitting apart, the fifty-meter-tall ice spires crumbling. Alice had told him earlier that she'd actually gained some insights into the interactions of bodies large and small coexisting within conflicting gravity fields -- her cover story/excuse for Govanek wanting to stand on the surface had turned out to be real.

Mike felt a presence to his left and realized Govanek was standing at his side. He wondered how much she'd told Captain Syradok about their brief jaunt to this doomed world. Probably not a lot, he mused.

Govanek kept one eye on the display while aiming the other toward Mike. She gave him the slightest nod, then turned the other eyeball toward the display, as well. *I don't think nods are a Sobrenian expression*, Mike thought. *I imagine that ranks up there with the handshakes all around when we arrived. That was her way of thanking me for that trip.*

Which makes me all more grateful that we took the chance.

As Neska drew Risula closer, Mike and the others sat and watched as the star stripped the planet of the rest of its ice cover, and as the planet's surface soil and rock tore away, revealing its center. Risula's interior contained only a small iron core, much less than a planet such as Earth -- it had never grown hot enough during its formation to separate the iron from the rock.

Then some balance of Neska's heat and gravitational forces versus the integrity of Risula's rocky structure tilted in favor of the star, and Risula crumbled and broke apart. *It's as if I had a dirt clod in my hand*, Mike thought, *and gave it a big squeeze.*

The fractured, continent-sized pieces of the planet also began to break apart, and over the course of a very few minutes Risula crumbled away.

It had been a lifeless world, but Mike still felt a profound loss, as if something vital had been snuffed out before him. Risula was named after the Cetronen mythological being who sacrificed herself to set the seasons in place. *I'd like to know*, he thought, *what this Risula has sacrificed itself for.*

Mike stared at the display showing the continued advance of Neska across the Moruteb system, its composition unchanged, its path undisturbed even after overwhelming a planet.

Mike turned to his left, meaning to speak some words of comfort to Govanek, but she was gone. He wondered what the Giver might be telling her about this event.

A glance to his right, and Linna looked to be holding up well, but Teresa was turning her back to the display and wiping away tears.

She should wait until something happens to Heuri or Jilan, Mike thought. *How will she take it when she watches as a planet with at least primitive lifeforms on it dies?*

Syradok spoke in much quieter tones than Mike had heard from him before. "Now, my friends," the Sobrenian captain said, "After witnessing such an event together, after sharing this marvelous yet troubling experience, we must speak. Let us go to my quarters."

Mike let Syradok lead the way into the corridor as he and Linna and Teresa followed. *I wonder if I wouldn't rather be having a beer*, Mike thought. *Even if I had to go the Accretion Disk to order it.*

CHAPTER ELEVEN

To Mike, Syradok's quarters stood in sharp contrast to the bridge of the *Meradeus* -- shadowed rather than brightly illuminated, simply furnished rather than filled with viewscreens, compact rather than spacious. Mike was also more aware of the higher humidity and musty organic smell.

Syradok said, "I must apologize that there are no seats suitable for Humans. I will keep my remarks short, Mike Christopher and Linna Maurishka and Teresa Song."

Teresa smiled. "You know, Captain Syradok, with Humans you're familiar with -- and I believe we qualify -- you can just call us by our first names."

Syradok tilted his head. "Ah! That is good to know. And a marvelous timesaver. Why, out of all the Galactic species, is it only Humans who seem to require two or more names to identify themselves?"

Mike shared a glance with Linna, who passed it on to Teresa, who looked back at Mike, who said, "Not really sure."

"Another time, perhaps," Syradok said. "What I am about to tell you, I was originally going to pass on through Govanek, unofficially. But I realized it would be best for me to explain matters myself, especially in the presence of Linna Maur...of Linna, the empath."

Teresa spoke up again. "We're honored, Captain Syradok."

Playing ambassador, Mike thought.

Syradok continued: "I would still like you to consider this an unofficial meeting, given what I have to say. We Sobrenians were interested in the Neska system because we believed our Galactic precursors first sent the system on its journey as a rogue star."

Mike said, "Your...precursors?"

"Many of our scientists believed we were the progeny of a more advanced species which seeded our homeworld with life. We had hoped to find evidence of that species here. We'd even dared to think such beings were the inspiration for the Giver and the Shaper. But, even using our nanoprobes throughout the system, we could not find them."

Mike asked, "Would these beings be similar to what we Humans call the Determinants?"

"No. The Determinants are said to mediate between sentient species, though we've never encountered them."

Linna said, "Neither has Humanity. At least, not in a way anyone's been able to confirm."

"Our precursors would never mediate -- only conquer. We'd hoped to find some sort of overwhelming weapon here. Again, we did not."

Ah, yes, Mike thought. *The Sobrenian emphasis on weaponry and conquest. Never mind that when the shit strikes the recycler, they're as likely to bluster as shoot.*

Teresa said, "Captain Syradok, you can at least take some comfort in that -- after all, it means current Sobrenians are your species' greatest achievement. *Your* science is the most advanced. *You* are among the most civilized of Sobrenians."

No, Mike thought. *You don't tell someone that their gods, or near-gods, are all but obsolete.*

But Syradok didn't seem to take offense. "You're kind, Teresa. But we find no comfort in such thoughts."

Mike asked, "Why are you telling us this?"

"I believe Govanek told you the story of our great warrior Syrilla?"

"She did." To Linna and Teresa, he explained: "Syrilla was also an astronomer. That let him predict the exact time he should take his troops across a strait where the ocean only receded twice a year."

"Exactly," Syradok said. "He struck at the most opportune time. I intend to do the same thing."

Mike swallowed a sudden lump in his throat.

Syradok spread his arms wide. "My friends -- I understand how these words may concern you. But don't let them. I pride myself on seeing farther than most of my species. Knowing that these so-called precursors do not exist is a blow, but one we can recover from."

Mike said, "Something tells me you're looking toward what happens after more Sobrenians find this out."

"I believe we must all accept our place in the universe. And I do not subscribe to the militarism that many of my species do. Also, you will notice I have no ancillary -- no Garotethan aboard."

"I did notice that."

"I believe retaining such a being is close to slavery. I refuse to employ them."

Teresa said, "Captain Syradok, you impress us with your higher morality."

Don't lay it on too thick, Mike thought.

"Again, my thanks, Teresa," Syradok said.

Mike let out the breath he'd been holding.

The Sobrenian captain continued: "I believe it's time for Sobrenians to accept the Cetronen offer of an alliance."

Teresa said, "The one you didn't want any part of before," and Mike gritted his teeth. *Let* him *say that*, he thought.

This time Syradok didn't complement Teresa on her insight. "A harsh truth. But a truth all the same. Many of us believe we rose up from a primitive state, aided by our precursors, only to fall and rise again, many times over. We believed it was fated. Finding no evidence of those precursors makes that uncertain."

Linna said, "*Everything's* uncertain," which made Mike turn and look at his shipmate as if seeing her in a new way. *I've never heard her say something that cynical before*, he thought. *Has coping with her increased empathy had something to do with that?*

"In this case," Syradok said, "I cannot disagree with you. That would include the reception my people will have for me when we return with word that we found no evidence of the precursors. If I can bring back a Sobrenian-Cetronen alliance, perhaps all will be well. That is how I intend to strike first.

What I would ask of you, Linna, is that you confirm my sincerity in everything I've told you."

Linna said, "I do so gladly."

"Mike, Linna, Teresa -- please pass on what I have said -- again, unofficially, to Captain Sandage and Captain Codari."

"Of course," Mike and Teresa said, simultaneously. Teresa smiled at Mike as he frowned at her.

Mike told Syradok, "We'll talk to Rosa at once. And Codari very soon." After a few more pleasantries, Mike led the way to the hangar deck and lifted the *Cosmic Egg* toward the *Asaph Hall*.

*****

Immediately upon their arrival back at the *Hall*, Mike asked Rosa to meet him, Linna, and Teresa in the viewing sphere. It had its own grav controls, and as many as a dozen people could float comfortably within it and call up flat or holo images on its walls. Many *Asaph Hall* crewmembers, however, also used it as a private place to turn the lights down low and make love in zero-G. Mike and Linna often used it for that very purpose.

When Mike, Linna, and Teresa arrived, they found Rosa already there, perched in zero-G on the opposite side of the sphere, watching a replay of the breakup of Risula. *I hope*, Mike thought, *this isn't designed to match her mood.* He cast off from the doorway and drifted over to join her, Linna and Teresa close behind.

Rosa asked for a summary of what Syradok had told them. Mike did most of the talking, with Linna and Teresa adding their own comments occasionally. Afterward, Rosa asked Linna, "Do you really trust Syradok?"

Linna said, "He's sincere in what he says. Whether his superiors have deceived him is a different matter."

Mike said, "He strikes me as being particularly bright -- and perceptive. I think anyone who tried to get him to pass on lies or even half-truths would discover that he'd figured it all out."

Rosa rubbed her hands down her face. "What would you call that, Mike -- secondhand empathy?"

Mike felt his face go red. Rosa grinned, put an arm around his shoulders, and squeezed tight. She told him, "I happen to agree with you, based on what you've all told me about our good Sobrenian captain. But it's thin stuff to take back to the Unity."

Teresa stared down each of her companions in turn. "Is this how diplomacy really works? It's like you're...."

Linna said, "We're reading tea leaves. Looking to see who's standing on the reviewing stand next to the dictator. It's an inexact art."

Rosa wrung her hands, seemed to notice she was doing it, and stopped. "We'll get this information to Codari as soon as we can. But it has to be in person. Teresa, I think it would be best if you stayed here. No telling what kind of diplomatic emergency we may be in for next." Mike realized the true subtext was to keep Teresa close to prevent such an emergency. Rosa continued: "Mike, don't wait for the encounter at Heuri. Go now -- the Itherin encounter's coming up, you can watch that one with him, too. Linna, you feel like going along?"

Linna said, "For now, I think I can take it."

Rosa told Mike, "Set up that trip to *Cerenam*."

"Sounds great -- I shared the destruction of Risula with Syradok. Codari and I can take in whatever happens at Itherin together."

*****

As Mike guided the *Cosmic Egg* toward the mushroom-shaped Cetronen starcraft *Cerenam*, he asked Linna, "You're sure about this?"

Linna glared at him. "For the thousandth time, I'm *fine*. Stop asking."

That reply doesn't make you sound fine, Mike thought. Through years of experience in being intimate with an empath, though, he didn't say a word.

The unusual thing, Mike realized, was that Linna didn't reply to his unexpressed emotion, didn't remind him that he couldn't hide his real feelings from her, or make a joke about how he should stop radiating his emotions at her.

It's the silence that's frightening, Mike thought. *She's shutting down, trying not to let anything bother her. Which may be the worst thing she could do.*

Or is her alternative to let the emotionalism all around her overwhelm her?

Then it was time to bring the *Egg* in for a landing at *Cerenam.*

Natai escorted Mike and Linna onto the bridge. It was quite a relief after the bridge of Syradok's ship -- muted lighting, few viewscreens, and only a handful of crewmembers.

And one more thing. "Uh, Natai, a question."

Natai's minor said, "Yes, what can I answer for you?"

"Where do we sit?"

Natai's minor's ears waggled and he stared blankly for a moment. Then his body shook with laughter. "Well, I suppose that's something that doesn't occur to us. You see, we minors are almost always sitting."

Linna said, "The majors sat at the banquet."

"Meals and sleeping periods are the only times majors are not standing. Here -- it is always work, always on their feet."

Mike said, "Well, then, we'll stand. When in Rome...."

"Sorry," Natai's minor said. "Failure to translate."

Linna said, "Never mind. Earth idiom."

"We'll go to our main viewscreen. Neska should be coming up on its closest approach to Itherin in just awhile."

That main viewscreen turned out to be a wall-sized display that made Mike feel as if he were standing on the edge of space, ready to fall off.

Itherin dominated that view. It was a small gas giant, its surface a dark blue-green with only faint banding visible across its hydrogen, helium, and methane atmosphere. Less than an A.U. distant, Neska was only .86 Solar masses, yet seemed nearly half again the size of Sol, a bright, deadly presence in the firmament.

Captain Codari entered the bridge. His major carried the minor toward the viewscreen to stand next to Mike, Linna, and

Natai. "It is so good to see you again, my Human friends. I understand you have much to relate to me."

Mike glanced around the bridge. "Should we discuss this here -- and as a world is about to be ripped to shreds?"

"I trust Natai and all my bridge crew. And if what is rumored is true, then this is news my entire species will need to know."

"Very well, then," Mike said, and summarized Syradok's offer of an alliance between his people and the Cetronen. When he finished, the minor repositioned himself in the major's arms before saying anything: "This is marvelous to hear. A Galactic species known for its aggressive actions toward so many others -- including your own, Mike Christopher -- and we may be able to forge an alliance with them."

"We can only hope," Mike said.

Linna spoke up. "Look at Itherin."

The blue-green world was losing its atmosphere. Hydrogen, helium, methane, it was all streaming off into space, mostly from the side of Itherin closer to Neska, forming a "tail" similar to a comet's.

Codari said, "How quickly even an entire world can be ravaged, soon to be destroyed."

Mike agreed -- it *was* disturbing, watching Itherin in the process of being stripped bare.

"Soon," Natai's minor said, "Neska will begin to pull Itherin from its orbit. Moruteb will barely notice, but the cost to Itherin will be high -- it will probably lose most of its outer layers of gas and be reduced down to its core."

Mike said, "I understand the Drodusarel haven't left the planet yet?"

"They have not. Display: show the path of the *Dirat*." An image of the Drodusarel starcraft appeared in a corner of the display. It was well away from any danger, but Mike still couldn't believe what he was seeing. "So they *are* still here? What about their shuttle I encountered at Heuri?"

"It remains there. And I share your surprise. It's an impressive technology that they're able to leave such a relatively small craft alone on a long-term basis."

Linna said, "Heuri's similar to the Drodusarel homeworld in many ways. Maybe they can live off the land, so to speak -- take in atmosphere and process it, use its elements to renew their equipment."

Mike said, "Sounds reasonable."

Linna's voice grew strained. "Or maybe...maybe they *can't*. Maybe they're all going to *die* over at Heuri." Tears flowed down Linna's face. Mike took her arm, but she pulled away from him. "Leave me *alone*."

Codari's minor asked, "Linna Maurishka, are you ill? How may I help you?"

"I'm not ill...I'm...."

Mike took a step toward Linna and she took two steps away from him. He told Codari, "It's her empathy. It's become too strong. I have to get her back to the *Asaph Hall*."

Linna held up her hands as if to ward Mike away. "No," she said. "Not *you*."

Mike understood immediately, and asked Codari, "Could Natai take Linna back to the *Hall*?"

"Of course, but -- "

"Being near me makes her empathic overload that much worse."

As Linna buried her head in her hands and sobbed uncontrollably, Natai spoke up. "Perhaps it's best if Linna Maurishka and I are on our way."

"Thank you," Mike said. "Linna -- "

She wiped away tears with one hand, caught her breath. "Yes. I heard. Let's go." She led the way through the wide doorway off the bridge, Natai's major carrying the minor close behind.

Mike stared at that doorway for some time. Then he touched behind his ear. "Mike to *Asaph Hall*."

Rosa answered over the datalink. "*Asaph Hall*."

"Linna's on her way back. With Natai. Prepare to receive a Cetronen shuttle. Be ready to show Natai every courtesy."

"I understand. I'll get you an update soon as I can."

"Thanks, Rosa. Mike out."

"*Asaph Hall* out."

Codari's minor said, "She will recover, will she not?"

Mike returned his attention to the Cetronen captain. "I don't know."

"Such beings...empaths...are unknown among my people."

"They're rare among mine. We're lucky to have her."

"I can see how an empath would be an asset in a first contact situation."

Mike couldn't help but grin. "Sometimes among our own people. She helped save Teresa from some Humans in a bar just as this trip was beginning."

"Ah -- an unfortunate thing, to have to fight your own people. If you don't mind me saying, several Galactic species have grown beyond that."

Mike *did* mind. *But after all*, he thought, *I suppose it's what Codari would expect from a "singleton" species. I'm not about to tell him that, though.* Instead, he said, "All the better if we can also avoid fighting each other. Which makes an alliance between Cetronen and Sobrenians an excellent idea."

"I would agree," said the Codari minor. "But such alliances often begin well, yet end up -- " The minor indicated the viewscreen, where Itherin displayed a perceptibly smaller globe. " -- as ephemeral as that."

Just as Linna told me awhile back, Mike thought. *Everything changes.* He told Codari, "If you don't mind, Captain, I'll be heading out in a few minutes, as soon as I know Linna's safely away."

Codari's minor rubbed his tiny hands together, as if in worry. Mike didn't know if the gesture was the same for a Cetronen as for a Human. "I understand, my friend. Your first loyalty should be to your mate."

Before Mike left, he viewed more of the spectacle of Neska's effects on Itherin. The rogue star continued ripping the planet's atmosphere to shreds -- soon, he knew, some of its rocky, metallic core may even be visible, a repeat of what happened to Risula, on a larger scale. And despite himself, he delayed his departure for *Asaph Hall* and watched, fascinated and appalled, as Neska's gravitational pull tossed Itherin's two icy moons out of orbit like rocks thrown from a sling, never to return.

CHAPTER TWELVE

As he piloted the *Cosmic Egg*, alone, back toward the *Asaph Hall*, Mike contacted Rosa. "Is Linna all right?"

The answer came back: "I don't really know. I'm not with her -- it's best to have as few people around her as possible. Lauren says she's started disassociating. She's not sure what's real and what's her own perception."

"I want to see you the moment I get back."

"In my quarters. Natai's already here."

A quick landing in the *Hall*'s hangar bay next to Natai's shuttle -- even it looked like a mushroom turned on its side -- and Mike made it to Rosa's quarters within moments. She and Natai were both there, the Cetronen major sitting on the edge of a chair, the minor positioned as usual on the major's hump.

Rosa embraced him and gave him a peck on the cheek. "I'm frightened for her, too," she whispered into his ear.

"Have you heard anything else?"

Rosa's eyes were hooded, her features firm. "I just talked to Lauren again. She's sedated Linna. It's the only thing that can give her some relief."

"Relief -- from me and you and everyone else on the ship."

"Lauren says Linna should be all right in the morning -- but eventually this is all going to get worse. She thinks Linna needs at least a week alone. She'll die otherwise -- or be driven mad."

"She can't stay asleep all the way back."

"I know that."

Natai asked, "Do you have stasis technology that can preserve her until she can be treated?"

"No," Mike said. "It's never been standard equipment on Human ships, except for short-term use -- days, maybe a couple of weeks at most."

Rosa explained, "It's a technology that Humans sometimes abused decades ago -- keeping unwanted children in stasis for years at a time, for instance. I know someone that happened to, and I'm not sure she ever forgave her parents."

Natai's minor's pointed ears pivoted like a cat's and the nictating membranes in his nostrils opened and closed. "That seems -- "

Mike filled the silence Natai left. "Barbaric? You're right. That's why it's much more regulated now."

Natai said, "My people use it sometimes, purely for medical purposes. But I don't believe our tech could be adapted quickly or easily for a Human. Please, may I stand as you too are doing?"

"Of course," Rosa said.

Natai's major stood. "Thank you," the minor said. "I understand your people's custom, to ask people to sit. This is ours, to stand."

Mike said, "I remember from the banquet. We're learning about one another all the time on this trip, aren't we? Natai, I can't thank you enough for bringing Linna back here."

"I believe I may have had a calming influence upon her. Perhaps she wished to appear more in control around someone of a different species. And you are correct, Mike, we are learning about one another. I am learning much about the depths of Human emotion. Your and Captain Sandage's caring for Linna -- it's quite touching."

For mere singletons? Mike wondered, then dismissed the thought as unkind.

Rosa's features took on a pained expression that made Mike's own sorrow even harder to bear. She said, "We have to figure out what the hell's going to happen once Linna wakes up."

"She has to leave," Mike said."

Rosa said, "It won't do any good for her to go to the *Cerenam* or *Meradeus*. She reads other Galactic species nearly as well as Humans. Even the Drodusarel."

"I know. We have to separate her from everyone."

"How? I've thought about it. The radius she receives from is expanding all the time, and this ship isn't that big. There's nowhere on board she can crawl into and be totally alone."

"Which means we have to set her up to live for a week or so aboard one of the shuttles, far enough away that she can't pick up any emotional radiation."

Rosa folded her arms and looked away from Mike. "How can we do that? I mean, we push protocols sometimes -- you came back here aboard the *Egg* all alone just now. By rights, I should've sent someone over to the *Cerenam* to accompany you back here."

"Except it would've meant sending *three* people over there in *Phobos 2*. Four crewmembers and both shuttles tied up instead of me coming back alone under minimal risk."

"*This* risk wouldn't be minimal -- letting someone stay out there in a shuttle all alone for a week?"

"Linna is dying! The hell with protocol. Sure, it means giving up one of our shuttles for awhile, but we don't need the shuttle as much as we need her -- *alive*."

Rosa's features grew tight with determination. "I'll talk to Lauren about getting Linna in good enough shape to transfer her over to a shuttle. We'll use *Phobos 2*. You and Georges get it ready to go."

"Right away."

Rosa turned to Natai. "We're in your debt. If there's ever anything this crew can do for you, let us know."

Natai's major bowed for them both. "Merely that offer is honor enough. I'm returning to *Cerenam* now, and I'll tell Captain Codari of your appreciation."

Mike said, "I hope one day to show him just how far that appreciation extends." He left to start work on *Phobos 2*.

*****

Mike and Georges didn't delay. *Phobos 2* was a tough little ship, more functional and utilitarian than the silvery *Cosmic Egg*. That Linna could survive aboard it went without saying; its life-support systems and food replicators were more than up to the task. And the shuttle would seldom be more than a few minutes away from docking with the *Asaph Hall* in an emergency.

But I don't want Linna just to survive here, Mike thought. *I want her to be able to* live, *to become aware of herself once again.*

That meant upgrading the *Phobos 2*'s replicators to deliver a wider food variety than just snacks and drinks, and transferring over plenty of music and both fiction and non-fiction cube files. And installing an actual bed taken from ship's stores. *This at least has to resemble a home*, Mike thought. *Or at a minimum, a hotel room -- something that's a lot less makeshift than this really is.*

Several times while they were working, Mike called up a holo to check on Itherin's progress. The resemblance to a comet was even more marked now, only no Human eyes had ever seen a comet the size of a small Jovian. The world was noticeably smaller now, its atmosphere burning off quickly.

Another quick check, and Mike saw that the Drodusarel craft *Dirat* was still observing Itherin. Did they intend to follow Itherin's continued demise until the bitter end? What about their shuttle back at Heuri?

As Mike worked on installing that bed in the shuttle's small cargo bay, Georges told him, "I think I understand your frustration. If you don't mind me saying."

Mike was still considering the pieces of the bed before him. He wondered if it wouldn't have been easier to research a replicator program and have construction nanites make the thing from scratch. "What's that?"

"Your frustration involving a loved one. You can't even go near Linna right now."

This is the last thing I want to talk about, Mike thought. *I want to help Linna. I don't want to talk about helping her.*

But he knew Georges meant well, though this mission had become something drastically different from the Hero's Journey he'd hoped for. "Well...you're right. It *is* frustrating."

"I know I was incredibly frustrated not being able to go home when my mother died. I didn't want to admit for awhile that it wasn't possible. But I knew I couldn't expect the ship to abort this mission for me. It turns out, though, that I understand my brother better now than I ever have."

"How's that?"

"I turned away from their -- our -- life in Avignon. It drove a wedge between me and Renaud ever since. But now I want nothing more than to be with him, and the rest of our family. No matter how many months it may be before I can return to Earth, I intend to stand with Renaud in our dining room, lift a fine glass of Clairette de Bellegarde and toast our mother and the unchanging values she lived for."

Mike looked up at Georges. "Thanks for sharing that with me."

They worked well into the early morning. Their refit of the shuttle completed, Mike thanked Georges for his help, grabbed a sandwich in the commons, and took it to his quarters. He dropped onto his couch, called up a holo of Itherin, and began to munch his sandwich.

And stopped in mid-chew. The planet was noticeably smaller than it had been a couple of hours earlier. *As far as any Human knows*, he thought, *nothing lived there. Certainly nothing does now. But to watch even a dead world essentially being dismantled before your eyes -- there's something sad about it, almost undignified.*

Even as he began chewing his sandwich again, a voice over his datalink made him stop: Rosa. "Mike?"

"Here, Captain."

"Relax. Just wanted to thank you for the great job on the *Phobos*. And let you know I spoke awhile to Linna. Over the comm, that is."

"Yeah? Did she -- "

" -- She told me to tell you she wanted to talk. No matter the time."

"Oh. Then, should I -- "

"You *should*. Quit talking to me. Talk to her." Rosa broke the connection.

Mike touched behind his ear, and said, quietly, "Linna?"

A sleepy voice in response: "Mike?"

"Yeah."

"Great to hear from you."

"You, too. More than you can know."

"Hope I didn't embarrass you in front of Codari."

"He understands. He agreed right away to send Natai to bring you back."

"I'm grateful to them both." He heard her sob. "And I'm sorry I've been such a bitch."

"Linna...you're my darling. Always have been. Wish you always could be. Once you get better, when I see you again...it may just be a few hours at a time. A walk together or a drink or a meal or we make love...."

"I know. Mike, I spoke to you about children before."

"Yeah."

"Something occurred to me -- if my empathy is such that I can't be around other people regularly, how can I even have a child? Its consciousness would grow inside me, it would feel things even before birth, and how could I even stand to be around my own child?"

"You wouldn't have to carry it."

"But how could I care for it? What kind of life is that -- an artificial womb, then nannies or a foster home until he or she's grown?"

"The same kind of life I had."

"I'm sorry, I -- "

" -- No, no, I'm agreeing with you. It's not the best kind of life."

"Mike?"

"Yeah."

"I'm leaving this afternoon."

"I know."

"I just realized the other day -- back on Earth, it's about to be the New Year."

"Oh, boy -- happy 2149."

"I know such things don't mean much when we're hundreds of light years away. But it's home for me. And I'd like to think of it as a chance for a new beginning. Thank Georges...and thank you...for getting *Phobos* ready."

"Everything should work out fine."

"For awhile. Until I have to come back to *Asaph Hall*."

"We'll get you back. For good."

"I don't know how, Mike."

"I have faith."

"Hmph.   You always say you're not a religionist. Especially since you know a God didn't create you."

"My faith's in Rosa. In Lauren. In you and me."

"Mine, too."

"Well," Mike said, "let's hope we haven't misplaced it."

They signed off and Mike crawled into bed, then settled into a restless sleep in which planets eased toward one another only to merge like soap bubbles, while Linna was consumed by the fires of two suns.

*****

Mike wasn't about to go down to the hangar deck the next morning as Linna went to prep the *Phobos 2*. Making his presence known would've been the worst thing he could have done, given her condition. But nothing could've kept him from calling up the cube feed as he sat in his quarters.

He watched as Linna entered *Phobos 2*, and as it lifted off the deck and glided through the energy screen at *Asaph Hall*'s stern. Linna would maintain *Phobos* on a parallel track to *Asaph Hall*, its nav comp locked to that of the larger ship. Its station-keeping position would be about a half K to port, and slightly behind.

Not that far away, Mike thought. *I can call up a holo or go to a viewscreen or even a port and look out at her -- or at least the shuttle -- anytime. I can't give myself over to worry. She'll be back. She'll be fine.*

So why, when I think back on last night's conversation, does it seem so final?

*****

When the distress call from the Drodusarel ship came, not three hours after Linna's departure, Mike was manning a sensor console on the *Asaph Hall*'s bridge, trying his luck at interpreting the data pouring in from Itherin. So far, the only insight he'd gained was that the planet's atmosphere was ripping away faster than computer models had predicted -- its remnants were just over Earth-size now, its liquid hydrogen and helium only the barest layer of material covering its rocky, metallic core.

There's enough here for "real" scientists to study for years, he thought. P*lanetary composition, gravitation, orbital mechanics. For now, I'm satisfied that it takes my mind off Linna, at least for a few moments.*

Then Alice spoke up from the comm position: "Rosa, we're getting an emergency signal from the *Dresk*."

Rosa said, "Let me hear it."

The call was audio only: "Greeting the Human ones! Captain Dresk speaks! Hive mind in unanimity -- starcraft *Dirat* is damaged and needs assistance."

As Rosa responded, trying to get more information despite the usual roundabout translation of Drodusarel speech, Mike turned his sensor sweep into a search for the *Dirat*. Within moments, he sighted the smooth, silvery craft. "I found it. Close in to Itherin, or what's left of it."

Rosa ordered that sensor output onto the main screen. She said, "Too damn close! What the hell are they doing down there?"

"I don't know, but they took a pretty good hit. I think they strayed too close to that stream of atmosphere coming off Itherin. A lot of their nav capability is down, and it looks like several thrusters were disabled."

"Life support?"

"Hard to tell -- their needs are so much different from ours." Another sensor sweep -- *Dirat* was making a pass at the doomed world that took it dangerously close to a jet of hydrogen and helium being expelled from the planet. "Uh oh."

"I need better than that, Mike."

He checked distances. "That jet's ten thousand K wide -- and the Drodusarel are just over a thousand K away from it."

"They're going to hit it?"

"The atmosphere's streaming off the planet like a hurricane the size of the Earth. Even if the *Dirat* doesn't get any closer, that jet could reach out and destroy it any moment now. That's not even taking into account any number of smaller jets that keep forming."

Alice spoke up. "We're the closest to *Dresk*. *Cerenam*'s at the edge of the system. *Meradeus* is still at Risula."

Rosa studied the display. "How close in can we take *Asaph Hall*?"

Mike double-checked the distances. "Not at all. Not if we want to live. But a shuttle could make it."

Rosa touched behind her ear. "Captain Dresk -- we're sending our shuttles to try to rescue as many of your crew as we can. Linna, have you been listening in?"

"I have," Linna responded. "I'm already on an intercept course."

"Very good. You'll take aboard *Dirat* crewmembers who are in lifesuits. I'll have Luther work on reproducing a proper environment here on the ship for when they get here."

Alice said, "And Captain, she'll have to deal with some odd orbital mechanics with both Neska and Moruteb fighting over Itherin. I learned a few things at Risula that I can pass on to her comp."

"Do it," Rosa said. She turned to Mike. "Prep *Cosmic Egg* quick as you can. Take Georges -- he'll have to prepare the cargo hold for any *Dirat* crew without lifesuits."

"I'm on it," Mike said, and within ten minutes he was piloting the *Egg* off the *Asaph Hall*'s hangar deck as Georges worked to program the cargo hold's environmental controls to supply the proper methane atmosphere and bring the cargo hold down to a temperature the Drodusarel would find comfortable -- something like -150 C.

Mike contacted Captain Dresk and asked, "How many of your crewmembers are still aboard?"

The audio feed came back: "Nineteen. And...other beings accompany us."

Mike asked, "What other beings?" Then it came to him: "Are these the beings your shuttles removed from Heuri?"

"They are. We have approximately two hundred on board. You encountered them during your own trip into Heuri."

The ribbons, Mike thought. He magnified the view of the *Dirat* on the *Egg*'s main screen. The silvery craft edged ever closer to the gigantic jet of hydrogen and helium. "Captain Dresk, we're going to be lucky to save most of your crew, given the differences in environment between our species. To try to save so many others -- "

"You must try, Human. They are sacred to us."

What is it about this system? Mike thought. *The Sobrenians think their precursors sent Neska on its wild journey across the galaxy, and now the Drodusarel believe they've discovered something sacred.* "We'll do what we can," Mike said and signed off, knowing what he or Georges or Linna could do for those beings was limited at best. *Dresk will realize that by the time we arrive*, he thought. *He'd better.*

From behind him, Georges asked, "How long until we get there?"

Mike checked. "About fifteen minutes."

"I'll be ready."

Mike opened a private channel to Linna, aboard *Phobos 2*. "How're you doing?"

Her voice came back over his datalink: "Right on track. I should beat you and Georges there by a few minutes."

"That's not what I mean."

"Oh...well, *better*. I can already tell a difference."

"I'm sorry this happened. Having to call on you yet again."

"Hey, I'm happy to be the one to save everyone's asses all the time." Mike heard both confidence and concern in her voice. "We'll get in, grab the Drodusarel, get out. Couldn't be easier."

"Yes, it *could*."

"See you there, Mike."

"I'll be looking for you." Mike turned to Georges. "How's the cargo hold coming?"

"I've got it pretty cold, and the atmosphere's coming along. I've been speaking to Kahtora -- remember from the banquet?"

"Yeah. Explorer."

"We can land in their docking bay, open up the cargo hold, equalize pressure. Let as many of *Dirat*'s crew in as we can."

Mike said, "I hope this business with the ribbons isn't going to be a problem. Though I suppose we'll find out one way or the other pretty quick now." *If we make it past these smaller jets of atmosphere coming off the planet*, Mike thought. *What the* hell *were they doing there?*

CHAPTER THIRTEEN

A glance at Itherin, and Mike saw that the planet's core was becoming visible in places -- soon the heat from Neska would begin burning off the carbon dioxide and water locked up in that core.

None of that helps us, he thought as he guided the shuttle around a new plume of hydrogen and helium as it formed. *There's still enough atmosphere rushing off the planet to destroy a hundred* Dirats. *And probably about a thousand* Cosmic Eggs. *Comforting thought.*

Soon the silvery Drodusarel craft loomed large in the *Egg*'s viewscreen. Mike saw a broad gash in its side, and Mike realized the opening was *flowing* open, rather than having a door that slid across or opened outward. *Nice tech*, he thought, jealous to learn its secret sometime.

But not now. He guided the *Egg* through that mysterious opening and though the energy field that retained atmosphere within the bay. He set the shuttle onto the dark, shadowed floor of the *Dirat*'s hangar deck. As he peered out the forward viewscreen, his initial impression was of a series of arches forming a low dome. Obtaining more than that impression was difficult given that he was looking through the ship's sluggish methane atmosphere, but he could see the area was cramped by Human standards.

A closer look just ahead, and Mike realized Linna had been right about beating him. *Phobos 2* was already there, and a line of Drodusarel with their energy shields activated was entering it. Mike touched behind his ear and asked Linna, "How's everything proceeding?"

"Fine for now, Mike. Talk to you later."

She sounds frazzled, Mike thought. *But damn if I'm not, myself.*

From all around now, the oval, tentacled forms of Drodusarel crewmembers without energy shields were converging on the *Cosmic Egg.* Georges said, "I'm still equalizing pressure -- letting *Dirat*'s atmosphere in. Mine was pretty close."

Mike contacted Captain Dresk. "It's going to be just a few more moments for your crew without energy shields."

Dresk responded, "Thanking the Human one! Hive mind is approving!"

The *Dirat* shook violently as unseen forces pounded its exterior. It was a frightening idea, given that the Drodusarel ship had inertials the same as any Human starcraft. Forces that could overcome them enough to make the ship shake like that must be on a scale that could easily destroy it.

Linna's voice came over Mike's datalink: "I've got seven on board, including Kahtora, and I'm ready to haul mass!"

"Good luck, Linna. See you back at the *Hall.*" Mike watched as *Phobos 2* lifted, glided carefully past the *Egg*, and headed out of the hangar bay. That magical door flowed open again.

Behind Mike, Georges said, "Ready to accept passengers."

On a small viewscreen to one side, Mike saw the rest of the *Dirat*'s crew making their way into the cargo hold. There was just room enough, Mike hoped, for the twelve remaining crewmembers to squeeze inside. "Captain Dresk, are you among those in the hold?"

"Entering as we speak, Human friend! Looking for room for a container of ribbons."

"With all respect, Captain, we don't have time for this." As if to punctuate Mike's thought, the *Dirat* shuddered again.

"Looking! Not finding! Centerpiece of mission! Hive mind displeased."

Mike thought, *I'd like to tell the hive mind they're suffering from a cranial-rectal inversion if they think I'm waiting a moment more than I have to.* "Captain Dresk, we have to *go.*"

"No!" Dresk exclaimed, and left the cargo hold.

Georges peered through a porthole looking into the hold. "Where's he going? No, wait -- now more of them are headed after him."

"To pull him back into the hold, I hope."

"Not yet."

Mike's hands gripped the *Egg*'s controls so fiercely they ached. He told Georges, "Get ready to lift."

"You don't mean -- "

"I *do* mean! We've got half of Dresk's crew counting on us. Not to mention I don't intend to die here, and neither do you."

"Wait! It's Dresk -- he's coming back."

"And the others?"

"They're with him. They're carrying something -- some kind of container. It's long -- about three meters."

"*Dammit.* It's a ribbon, maybe several of them, it has to be."

Georges said, "They're fitting it in. Length isn't a problem, but several of them are having to hold it above their heads."

Mike could feel and hear the *Dirat* take yet another hit, a more prolonged one this time, as if a gigantic bell were ringing beneath his feet. "No more time! Close the hold!"

"Closing!"

"Lifting!"

Once away from *Dirat*, Mike had to resort to fancy flying to dodge the many jets of methane, ammonia, and hydrogen shooting out from Itherin. Although the planet was nearly reduced to its core, enough atmosphere remained to destroy the *Egg* many times over.

They hadn't left *Dirat* a moment too soon -- Mike checked a holo-image looking back toward the Drodusarel craft just in time to see several atmospheric jets engulf it and reduce it to random debris.

Mike's next thought: *What about Linna?*

He spoke to her over his datalink: "Linna -- how are you doing? Are you going to make it?"

Her response was curt: "Flying, not talking."

The corner of Mike's mouth turned up in a reflexive smile. *Very Drodusarel sounding*, he thought. *Hope their speech patterns aren't rubbing off on her.*

But he certainly understood her abruptness -- for the next several minutes, avoiding those jets, not conversation, had to be the priority.

They were about ten minutes from the *Asaph Hall* at maximum boost. *I can only hope*, Mike thought, *that we'll be out of danger from these jets within the next two or three minutes.*

Then proximity warnings chimed and Mike was desperately dodging new jets as they formed to either side of *Cosmic Egg*. The small craft shuddered as something struck in its rear. He yelled back at Georges, "What's going on back there?"

"We're fine. Minimal damage, and it doesn't look as if any of the Drodusarel are hurt."

Linna's voice came over Mike's datalink. "We're nearly out of the worst of it."

"I know," Mike replied, catching a glimpse of *Phobos 2* as it dodged one of the smaller jets. For an instant, Mike was more transfixed watching Linna's piloting than paying attention to his own. *Can't let myself do that*, he thought an instant later, and aimed his attentions back to his own craft.

And the instant after *that* was when a jet of atmosphere struck *Phobos 2*.

"No!" Mike exclaimed as he saw Linna's shuttle falter, then veer off on a new trajectory taking it off on a tangent from its intended course toward *Asaph Hall*. Debris and gases trailed the shuttle's path. "Linna, come in! Are you all right?"

Rosa spoke up from *Asaph Hall*: "Mike, this is an order. Do *not* go after *Phobos*. You've got more survivors aboard than it does, not to mention that one of them's *Dirat*'s captain."

"But Linna -- "

To Mike's relief, it was Linna's voice that broke in next: "She's right, Mike. *Keep going.*"

"How are -- "

"I'm hurt, but I can still fly. I'm trying to return to the right heading."

Rosa said, "Linna -- just a few more minutes, and we can get an enticement beam on you."

Linna didn't respond, and Mike said, "Linna -- are you still with us?"

Phobos 2 was still headed on its wayward path, and Linna didn't respond. *I'm about to do something I've never done before*, Mike thought. *Violate a direct order from Rosa.*

But then the *Asaph Hall* captain came back on the line: "OK, Mike, try to catch up to *Phobos*. But I'm bringing the *Hall* down, too."

Mike wanted to protest that it was too big a risk. *But*, he thought, *it's the very same risk I'm taking*. He altered course to intercept the *Phobos 2*. To Georges, he said, "Everything holding up back there?"

"So far," the answer came.

Rosa broke in, over Mike's datalink: "Have you taken a sensor reading on *Phobos*?"

"No time. Rosa, what is it?"

"It's Linna. She...."

"*What?*"

"It's bad."

"I'm getting there fast as I can."

"Make it faster."

Georges came up to sit in the co-pilot's seat. "The problem is, what the hell are we going to do once we get close to *Phobos*? I mean, *look* at it."

Mike understood Georges' concern. "I see what you mean. It's off on a wobbly course, spinning like crazy."

"Absolutely right. Try to match speeds *and* spin."

"By the time we managed it, *Asaph Hall* would be here."

"What's that mean for Linna? She can't be in good shape to..."

Mike told Georges, "It's all right. I'm thinking the same thing."

Then a weak voice came over Mike's datalink. "Mike..."

"Linna?"

"Yes..."

Mike told Georges, "I'll be in the back. Take the controls."

"Got 'em," Georges said, as he gave Mike a sideways look that said he understood Mike's interest wasn't in the cargo hold.

Rosa cut in: "Mike, latest scan shows...Linna doesn't have much time."

Dammit, Mike thought. *If I could just get over there.*

The channel to *Phobos* was still open. "Linna...what's happening over there?"

"Never mind that. *Asaph Hall* -- on the way? Did I hear that right?"

"You did. And I'm close -- not fifty meters behind."

"Don't try anything stupid, Mike. *Phobos* is tumbling. You can't make it over here." Linna groaned, a sound all the more heart-wrenching since she was obviously trying to suppress it.

"I'd take my chances."

"With the Drodusarel, too? You'd risk a dozen of them for one of me?"

Two deep breaths, then he told Linna, "You'd be just as tempted." He stepped to a sensor station next to the hold and called up two readouts -- a flatscreen image of *Phobos 2* and Linna's lifesigns. *Rosa was right*, he thought.

"Mike, just listen." Another pause, another low groan. "I have to tell you something."

In the instant before she said the words, Mike realized what her words would be, and what her saying them meant. "Linna, *no!*"

"I love you."

Mike pressed his lips together and closed his eyes against tears. He leaned with one hand on the side of the cargo hold, barely able to catch his breath. He said, "And I..."

Asaph Hall snatched *Phobos 2* away, even as Linna's lifesigns flatlined.

"...love you," Mike said, and collapsed against the hull.

CHAPTER FOURTEEN

Mike paused in the corridor outside the *Asaph Hall*'s hangar bay. Beyond that doorway, Linna's casket stood, awaiting her memorial ceremony. He was waiting until the last possible minute to enter. *I don't want to be the center of attention on this day*, he thought. *I can't handle it emotionally, and besides, any notice I draw will be that much less for Linna.*

The hangar bay's doors eased open as he approached them. As he expected, nearly everyone looked toward him as he entered, the low murmur of conversation dying down for a moment, then rising again.

He stood at the rear of the group who sat in neat rows before Linna's casket. Fourteen of *Asaph Hall*'s crew were gathered here, with only ship's pilot Darwin Haidar minding the store on the bridge. Beyond the edge of the hangar bay, beyond the force screen holding in atmosphere and heat, Neska was grasping the hard core of Itherin and dragging that world's remnants along as it completed its pass through the Moruteb system.

Captain Codari had come over from the Cetronen starcraft *Cerenam*, along with the explorer, Natai. The Sobrenian captain, Syradok, was also present, as was his geological specialist Govanek. Captain Dresk of the late Drodusarel craft *Dirat* was, at least temporarily, a guest aboard *Asaph Hall*, as were fourteen other *Dirat* crewmembers, but they all remained in a section of the ship set aside for them. Another four Drodusarel out of seven aboard *Phobos 2* had died along with Linna.

Rosa stood next to Linna's casket. "Good afternoon, everyone," she said, and even though her voice was low all attending quieted down again. "We're here to remember Linna

Michelle Maurishka. If anyone would like to come up here and share their memories of her, please feel free."

Alice was the first to come forward, and praised Linna as her friend and as family. Luther Kindred was next, and marveled at her calm while helping rescue Teresa from the rockhoppers at the Accretion Disk.

Then came more praise from the rest of the *Asaph Hall* crew. Her friends.

After that, the Cetronen Codari came forward. The shared symbiont simply stood there for a moment, the major carrying the minor effortlessly as usual. Then *both* beings cleared their throats and began to sing.

The major's voice was deep and full-throated, bringing power and resonance to their harmonies. The minor's contribution was a soaring tone that rose above the major's voice and gave it life.

Mike's datalink apparently couldn't cope with translating lyrics, but none of that mattered. *I can't imagine any words that would add to the sheer beauty*, he thought. *And this from a starcraft captain! I can't imagine what it would've been like to have heard Jilan, the singer the planet's named for.*

The end of Codari's song was followed by a thoughtful silence. Then, as Mike had feared, Rosa caught his eye, urging him to come forward. He moved toward Linna's casket.

In the instant before he turned to face everyone in the hangar bay, Mike looked upon Linna for the last time. Her round features were at peace. *I wish I could see her eyes*, he thought. *I always loved those brown eyes, so pretty and bright.*

He faced those gathered to remember her. "I didn't want to come here today. I didn't want to see Linna lying there. I've never gotten comfort from seeing someone in their casket or visiting their grave.

"But I'm glad I came after all. I can't help but think back to meeting Linna right here aboard *Asaph Hall*. We didn't hit it off quite so well at first. Our whole relationship might've soured from the very beginning. But as most of you know...it got better."

The scattered laughter arose from both relief and nervousness, Mike knew. He continued: "I remember the dangers we faced together against the Jenregar at Korolev Station, and on countless other worlds, right down to this very mission here in Moruteb system.

"I can barely think of that now. It's probably too much to pour out in front of you, as well as I know all of you, as much as I love you. Maybe some quiet or drunken night on the way back, but not now. I'm sorry. Those are the only words I have. They aren't enough. They never can be.

"Except for one word. Love. In her most difficult, her most hurtful times, love is what she counted on -- and what she gave in return. And the most heartening thing is, you can be sure -- more sure than you could be about anyone -- that she knew it."

Mike stepped away from Linna's casket, wishing he could just fade into the crowd. As Rosa and Alice closed Linna's casket, Mike closed his eyes and stood without thought, keeping himself as unaware of his surroundings as he could. When he couldn't sustain that trick any longer, he opened his eyes and Linna's casket was at the edge of the hangar bay, placed now on top of a small booster.

Rosa and Alice stood back. Rosa said, "As stardust we begin, and as stardust we return." Then she gave a quiet voice command, and Linna's casket moved smoothly out of the hangar bay, though the energy shield. Once clear of *Asaph Hall*, it would boost toward Itherin and crash upon it, even as that planet's remnants continued its new journey with its new primary, Neska.

Then there was only silence. After a few moments, everyone began to drift away, back to duty or a meal or to gather together and console one another. Mike went to Rosa and said, "There's one thing I meant to ask. Why Itherin? Traditionally, spacers are shot into a star."

Rosa gave Mike a gentle smile. "Don't worry about that just yet. We're picking up the crew of *Dirat*'s shuttle over at Heuri next. But we'll be back here at Itherin sometime soon. I'll tell you more then."

Well, Mike thought, *that was cryptic enough.*

*****

Three weeks later, Mike watched from *Asaph Hall*'s bridge as the effects of Neska's presence on the planet Jilan became apparent. *No visits for me for awhile*, he thought. *Go to* Cerenam *or* Meradeus, *and I'd have to listen to another round of sympathy, of inquiries about how I'm coping, of endless regrets that Linna isn't here to share these final moments of life for the countless cliff-dwellers and spherical fish about to die on Jilan.*

Oddly enough, I do grieve for them. Self-aware or not, Linna's absence makes me realize just how precious life is, how rare, in any form.

Mike watched the multiple readouts on the main viewscreen. Most of the effects on Jilan weren't visible from orbit, but one was about to be quite apparent -- the Mars-like world was about to lose a couple of its small moons.

Neska wasn't approaching Jilan as closely as it had Itherin, so its grav wasn't exerting nearly as much of a pull. Already, though, the rogue star was pulling Jilan into a more elliptical orbit. Calculations showed that Moruteb would be able to hold on to Jilan, but at great cost to the planet itself.

Alice, from a sensor station behind them, reported to Rosa, "I'm detecting massive stresses deep within the planet. Pretty soon its crust will start cracking. That means it'll remain pretty active geologically even after Neska leaves."

"Look," Rosa said. "One of the moons is heading in."

"It's called Reulo," Alice said.

Mike's eyes widened as he watched. The rate of speed at which Reulo was approaching its primary was astounding, mostly because Jilan's new trajectory just happened to coincide with Reulo's orbital path.

The moon was only a few kilometers wide, but Mike knew the effects of its collision with its primary would be as catastrophic as that of the asteroid that ended Earth's Cretaceous Period (and the dinosaurs' reign) and ushered in the Tertiary Period.

The two worlds drew together in a slow-motion dance that ended when Reulo took only five seconds to burst through Jilan's thin atmosphere and impact the larger world. Reulo disappeared within a bright yellow fireball that spread across dozens of kilometers within seconds.

Over the course of the next half-minute, the fireball faded and debris from the impact crater splashed into space. *It's like watching a stone strike the surface of a lake*, Mike thought. *Only that's an impact that will change this world forever. The cliff-dwellers, the spherical fish, they're all dying in this instant.*

Alice said, "That's absolutely amazing."

"There's another impact coming," Mike said. "Nilanu should crash into Jilan during its next orbit. It'll probably get to keep Tyaila, though."

"And Jilan itself should stay with Moruteb. It's orbit will be screwed up, though."

"Sometimes," Mike said, "I guess you just have to be satisfied with what you have left."

*****

Three weeks after that, Mike watched the most catastrophic event of Neska's encounter with Moruteb, once again while standing on *Asaph Hall*'s bridge. Rosa, Georges, and, Teresa, and Alice were also there.

It was Heuri's time to die. The home of the ribbons was soon to meet one of Neska's planets, Lasira. Neither gas giant would survive the encounter.

Rosa asked Alice, "How are the Drodusarel these days?"

"As good as we could expect. We've adapted one full level of crew quarters to a methane atmosphere for now, and another area for the ribbons."

Mike asked, "Did we ever figure out why they kept the *Dirat* so close to Itherin?"

"As much as I can figure out," Rosa said, "they had some sort of vague history involving life from beyond their homeworld seeding its rings. Those lifeforms then traveled down to the planet itself."

"And then they found the ribbons within Heuri's rings."

"That's right," Rosa said. "They thought Itherin was their true homeworld, so to speak -- the place that seeded the homeworld they know."

Alice said, "It all sounds so unlikely that they would believe that."

Rosa said, "Don't underestimate the power of creation myths. Imagine if we suspected the genetic material that became Humanity didn't arise on Earth. The Drodusarel were trying to find out every nugget of information they could, even as the planet was dying underneath them."

Mike said, "Getting away from the Drodusarel for a moment -- did the Sobrenians ever decide whether to pursue that alliance with the Cetronen?"

Rosa pursed her lips. "That's not going to happen."

"Why? I thought Linna -- "

"I wish I didn't have to tell you this. It's *because* of Linna that they're not pursuing it."

"But she's the one who was vouching for Syradok's sincerity."

"And the one who lost control right in front of Codari. They're uncertain whether to trust her perceptions. I'm sorry."

"Damn," Mike muttered.

"Look at Heuri and Lasira," Rosa said, indicating the main viewscreen. "It's happening."

The two worlds were drawing together slowly but inexorably. Though they were both gas giants, they contrasted greatly; Heuri had its tan, brown, and red cloud bands and its rings, while Lasira, a world about three-fifths Heuri's size, was a nearly featureless aquamarine ball with no rings.

As Mike watched, the two gas giants' atmospheres began to flow toward one another, briefly creating a barbell shape. That flow disrupted Heuri's rings, and they began to fly apart, most of the debris remaining in Heuri's equatorial plane.

The barbell shape soon dissipated as the planets continued to draw closer. Then the two worlds began to crash into one another.

It's a catastrophe taking place in even slower motion than Reulo's impact upon Jilan, Mike thought. As he watched, Heuri's tan sphere bowed inward as Lasira struck, as if it intended to take the blow for an instant only to deflect the intruder away.

Which was impossible. Instead, the inevitable happened -- debris thrust outward from Heuri's surface, as Lasira, the less-massive world, began to split apart.

I'm grieving yet again, Mike thought, *this time for the ribbons, even though I've no way of knowing if they're sentient.*

Then came the paradox: slow as the gas giants' self-destruction played out, when it was nearly complete it seemed to have passed within moments. Mike checked the time; it had been barely an hour since the two worlds began to collide. Now they were mere debris, merged clouds of deep blue and purple with ever-extending fingers of tan, brown, red, and aquamarine.

And the ribbons were dead, except for the small sample of a couple dozen the Drodusarel had saved, first by snatching them from Heuri, then by retrieving them from the starcraft *Dresk* before it was destroyed at Itherin. After that evacuation of *Dresk*, the Drodusarel had lost four of their own aboard *Phobos 2*, just as Mike had lost Linna.

If I can grieve for ribbons, for cliff-dwellers, and for spherical fish, I can certainly grieve for those Drodusarel. They were sentient beings, they have an advanced culture, presumably they love and care for one another and are curious about the universe. And surely they grieve.

But as Mike continued to watch the two worlds devour one another, it was Linna who remained uppermost in his mind. No matter his determination to identify with any forms of life, sentient or otherwise, it was Linna he'd lived with all these years, Linna he'd loved, and who'd loved him in return -- no matter that she'd never allowed the word to be spoken until the very end.

Afterward, watching the debris of two star systems go their separate ways, Mike didn't think of the stupendous forces he'd witnessed as much as he thought of the dead. *Even planetary collisions*, he thought, *don't affect the soul as profoundly as watching a loved one die.*

I wonder at our own preconceptions, our self-centered presumption, he thought. *We see an event literally astronomical, and believe our most private concerns are as large as those events we're chasing. That our actions and reactions have galactic import.*

After nearly two hours, Mike decided he'd seen enough. As the years passed, Heuri and Lasira's remnants would form a ring around Moruteb. He wondered if Humans would be around someday to witness that.

As he was about to make his way off the bridge, however, he felt a hand on his shoulder. Alice. She said, softly enough that no one else should hear, "You're not alone. And you're not the only one who misses her."

Mike took her hands in his. "I know," he said, and realized her eyes were looking at him as if making a silent appeal for help. *Time to consider someone other than myself*, he thought. "Do you want to talk?"

Alice managed a brave smile. "I was counting on it. How about the sphere?"

*****

When Mike stepped into the sphere, he took a misstep in the zero-G and went tumbling across the dark room. That was bad enough, but Alice's laughter at his expense caused him to start laughing, as well.

Mike struck the far wall and Alice grabbed onto him as he bounced off. They looked at one another. They embraced, held on tight.

Mike kissed Alice's cheek, a gesture born of affection rather than sexuality. But then Alice kissed back, on the lips, and they were pressing against one another. When Alice began pulling at Mike's clothing, he grasped her hands to make her stop.

"Damn Earther," Alice said. "What would she think of you now?" And she waited for him to continue. He did, and then they were naked and Alice wrapped her legs around his hips and he slipped into her.

And after some initial thrashing around, he was spent even as Alice was still becoming aroused. "I'm sorry," he told her, and tried to pull away, grateful she couldn't see his face flushing.

But she held on that much tighter. "Don't be sorry, *don't*. Being with an empath all those years...."

Mike could barely get out the words: "It was too easy. I'm *sorry*."

"Not the point, Mike. I'm holding onto you, you're holding me, *that's* the point."

Mike's shoulders shook as the tears began to flow.

*****

Mike was asleep three days later when Rosa awoke him with a call over his datalink. "Come to the bridge," was all she said, and didn't respond when he asked for more details.

He dressed quickly, worried that some emergency had broken out in the middle of ship's night and that Rosa was too busy dealing with it to talk. Down the corridor, up the grav tube to the command level, then onto the bridge.

Which was empty except for Rosa, who was facing the main viewscreen.

"I don't understand," Mike said. The *Asaph Hall* was orbiting a planetary remnant, but it wasn't Heuri and Lasira. "Where are we?" Then he realized. "Itherin?"

"Yes," Rosa said.

"We've...returned to Linna. Why?"

Rosa indicated the main screen. "Look at what's left of the planet."

Mike saw that Neska had stripped Itherin to its rocky, metallic core, which was just smaller than the Earth. Rosa turned to a console and punched up a closer view. It showed wide rifts in Itherin's surface the width and length of the Grand Canyon, and smaller cracks as wide as the Mississippi River. Already Mike could tell some gases were venting from those rifts and cracks. Mike shook his head. "I'm sorry, Rosa, I still don't -- "

"Itherin's giving off carbon dioxide and water from its core. What happens next?"

"Rosa, if this were anyone but you trying to give me a lesson in planetary science -- "

"Just *think*, Mike."

He forced himself to suppress his growing anger and consider why in space Rosa felt it important to call him up here in the middle of the night.

Then it dawned on him. "Carbon dioxide. Water. Sunlight."

Rosa said, "Water vapor. Clouds. Rain. *Oceans*."

"And eventually -- life?"

Rosa nodded slowly.

"*That*'s why you wanted to bury Linna *here* -- not within Neska."

Tears flowed freely down Rosa's cheeks. I couldn't help thinking of a very old quote...from the poet John Dryden...that to die is landing on some distant shore."

Mike went to Rosa and held her. "And you found Linna's for her." After a time they stood and watched Itherin and Neska.

Eventually Mike asked, "How long?"

Rosa said, "Probably millions of years. Who knows if Humanity will even be around by then? Other species may have replaced us and the Cetronen, the Sobrenians, the Drodusarel, all the rest." Rosa paused, then said, "We're heading back tomorrow."

Mike didn't say anything. After a moment, Rosa said, "I'm going to bed. You staying?"

"Yeah. I'm fine."

"Luther should be here in an hour or so to start his shift."

Mike managed a wan smile. "Thanks. I appreciate you bringing me here for this."

Rosa took Mike's hand for a moment. Then she left.

Mike faced the viewscreen and Neska's light shone full in his face. Itherin's core was a dark crescent, giving few clues as to whether life would, one day, evolve there.

How odd, he thought. *I've always believed I didn't hold anything to be sacred. But perhaps I do, after all. Perhaps life itself is sacred for me -- certainly it's the most glorious and mysterious of Nature's manifestations.*

Images shot through Mike's consciousness -- the first time he and Linna made love, the first time he noticed the reddish highlights in her hair, the last time they'd spoken together before that fatal mission and he'd called her his darling and wished they could just take a walk or share a meal.

I couldn't comfort her in her final moments, he thought, *not by taking her hand or even with a look or finally being able to tell her I loved her. As I still love her, will love her until my own final day.*

I also have to envy her. She's embarking on her greatest and longest jaunt. She'll be exploring the galaxy long after I'm gone, as long as Neska burns. And she'll be there on Itherin as that cold dark world comes alive.

He stood there watching Itherin, which he came to think of as Linna's own, until Luther Kindred arrived to begin his bridge shift. Luther nodded toward Mike, then went without words to a console and made a point of appearing busy.

Mike stood another moment, then left the bridge and Itherin's glories, seen and unseen, behind.

CHAPTER FIFTEEN

Five weeks out from the ruins of the Moruteb system, Mike set the shuttle *Cosmic Egg*'s controls to plunge at what he knew was a dangerous rate into a gas giant's atmosphere. "Hive mind insists you lack understanding," the Drodusarel commander said from behind him and Luther.

It took every bit of restraint Mike could summon not to tell Dresk to shut the hell up. *After all*, he thought, *it was the Drodusarel's carelessness that led to Linna's death.*

Dresk hovered behind them within the gray-blue energy shield that protected him from the *Egg*'s Human-friendly atmosphere and temperature. As usual, it was impossible for Mike to perceive the Drodusarel's mood by looking at him, anymore than he could tell if a jellyfish were having a good day.

Mike guided the shuttle through a turbulent area of the planet's hydrogen-helium atmosphere, thankful for the inertials that kept their ride smooth even as titanic forces from without buffeted the craft. "Captain Dresk," he said, "I'm all too aware the ribbons were dying aboard the *Hall*." The two dozen beings were in the cargo bay behind them. He said, "We can only hope this planet will be a place they can survive."

Dresk had insisted upon accompanying Mike and Luther on this mission. The fleet had paused at the nearest star system that had a gas giant with a similar atmosphere to Heuri.

They were diving toward the north pole of this unnamed world in this unnamed system. Mike caught a glimpse of an aurora, waves of emerald and azure stretching hundreds of kilometers across the planet's sky. Then the *Egg* dove through a massive cloud bank and left the aurora far behind.

Luther was checking sensors. "This is our best bet," he reported. *And*, Mike thought, *it feels right here. The skies are the same dark blue as when we first saw the ribbons on Heuri, and all but the brightest stars are obscured.*

Mike brought the *Egg* to a near-standstill and told Luther, "Do it." Luther punched the control that opened the *Egg*'s cargo bay to the planet's atmosphere. The flat, three-meter-long beings had been lying helplessly on the shuttle's floor; now, with the grav turned off and the shuttle's own atmosphere rushing outward, they lifted from that floor and began their usual undulating motions that propelled them forward.

Even over the datalink translation, Mike could hear the awe in Dresk's voice. "Hive mind approves. If only this can be their new home."

Mike tried to consider what it must be like for the Drodusarel commander, to have the chance to save beings he held sacred. *Although*, he thought, *the ribbons aren't out of the woods yet. We don't know if they can survive here. But they had to leave* Asaph Hall. *Our best efforts weren't enough for them.*

A quick glance at Luther. Those broad shoulders shrugged and he raised his eyebrows in a gesture that said, "Who knows?"

Mike turned around to face the Drodusarel. "Captain Dresk, I can only hope -- "

Dresk said, "Thanking you, Mike Christopher. I trust you personally. Even as hive mind reserves judgment."

The hive mind, Mike thought, *is a pain in the ass.* To Luther, he said, "I'm going to spin around to see how they're doing. Keep a sensor lock on them."

As *Cosmic Egg* turned, the ribbons became visible in the forward viewscreen. *Something's wrong*, was Mike's first thought.

The ribbons' snakelike movements weren't smooth as they'd been in Heuri's atmosphere, and weren't coordinated with one another -- several collided. The arrowhead-shaped tips at either end of their bodies seemed to be trying to guide them in different directions, as if they wished to pull themselves apart.

"Questioning the Human ones!" Dresk said. "Unacceptable! Ribbons must live!"

Luther said, "Their lifesigns are fading fast."

Dresk demanded, "Returning the ribbons. Hive mind cannot bear this tragedy."

Mike punched controls. "I'll try to get an enticement beam on them."

"Too late," Luther muttered.

The ribbons' bodies were shriveling, and they'd ceased their usual undulating movements; the harsh winds high in the gas giant's hydrogen-helium atmosphere were scattering them.

Luther said, "It's over."

"*Dammit,*" Mike said. *So now I've killed the Drodusarel's deities*, he thought. *How's that going to help interspecies relations?* He paused with one hand over the enticement beam controls. He asked Dresk, "Shall I gather their bodies?"

After a moment's silence, the Drodusarel commander said, "Refusing the Human ones. Returning to *Asaph Hall* -- immediately!"

Mike set a course out of this unnamed world's atmosphere and back toward *Asaph Hall*. He was at a loss for anything to say. *How*, he wondered, *do you comfort methane-breathers whose emotional lives are largely a closed book to you? And who are generally disdainful of you, anyway?*

Something tells me we haven't heard the last of this.

*****

The fleet returned to stardrive. Captain Codari demanded a full report as soon as possible, which was why Mike, Luther, and Rosa soon gathered in *Asaph Hall*'s commons to compare notes. Luther was wolfing down a roast beef sandwich. Mike sat and stared at his orange juice.

Rosa leaned against a counter, arms folded. "So the very thing we feared would happen -- "

" -- happened," Mike said. "We took them to a world we knew nothing about -- and threw them out like garbage."

"None of which was your fault."

"You didn't see the ribbons curling up as if a fire was consuming them. They didn't last half a minute."

"Mike, you knew the whole thing was a crap shoot from the beginning. What were the chances we'd find a gas giant that just happened to be able to sustain the ribbons? It'd be like the Drodusarel dumping us on Mars or Venus -- similar planets to Earth in many ways, unless you want to keep breathing."

But Mike wasn't listening to his captain. "I was there for every discussion. I could've given us more alternatives. Georges and I might've fine-tuned the ribbons' environment here on the ship, or...*something*."

Rosa sat across from Mike. "I know why this hurts so much."

"Cheap psychology," he said, getting up. "Excuse me." He left the commons for his quarters, the whole time telling himself he hadn't been thinking of Linna, he *hadn't*, that he'd placed memories of her gentle hands, the freshly showered smell of her skin, the sight of her body shooting off toward a ravaged world, into a safe, secure compartment.

*****

Then Mike reached his quarters and all the lies he'd been telling himself came rushing back into his consciousness. The door to his quarters slid shut behind him and he began sobbing convulsively, until just drawing a breath became a struggle. Tears ran down his cheeks and dripped off his chin.

A small part of him watched his body give itself over to this physical display and felt betrayed. Linna had the audacity to die when she knew how much he'd needed her, *still* needed her.

The ribbons had died, just as Linna had, and the death of anyone or anything brought the moment of her passing back to him to relive in vivid detail -- how the remnants of the doomed planet Itherin seemed determined that she shouldn't escape, how she said she loved him and before he could even say it back she was gone.

They were the words they'd never said to one another; in that instant, Mike knew when she spoke them that meant she'd accepted the fact of her death, something he refused to accept then and wouldn't now.

Mike wiped his face with his hand, and the damp hand on the front of his shirt. He threw clothing off and headed for the sonno. When the dry shower was done, he took his time dressing again, then sat, quiet and still on the edge of his bed.

*****

Several hours after Rosa passed along her findings on the incident with the ribbons to Codari, Captain Dresk demanded a meeting, and he insisted it be on the deck that had been turned over to him and the other fourteen Drodusarel. Within minutes Mike and Rosa stood at an airlock that opened onto that deck.

Before cycling the lock, Mike asked, "How'd the report to Codari go?"

"Could've been better," Rosa said. "But he basically understands we did the best we could."

It was a moment before Mike said, "I'm sorry for how I acted earlier."

"Don't worry about it."

"I can't let my grief for Linna affect how I act toward other people. I need all of you too much."

Rosa indicated the lock mechanism. "Let's get to work."

Mike activated his lifesuit, checked that Rosa's was on as well, and cycled through the lock. Captain Dresk and another Drodusarel were awaiting them on the other side.

It was one of the few times Mike had ever seen a Drodusarel in his natural environment, or at least as close to it as the *Hall*'s systems permitted. The grav was minimal, and the methane atmosphere was palpably thick and gave everything a greenish tint.

"Greeting the Human ones," Dresk said. "And here is Kahtora again." Mike remembered him from the fiasco of a banquet aboard *Cerenam*. Both Drodusarel waved their tentacles gently to keep themselves suspended before the Humans.

Rosa said, "Pleased to see you both again."

"Hive mind not pleased. I am not pleased."

Mike said, "I've worked with the crew to make everything as comfortable for you as we can. What else can we do?"

Now it was Kahtora who spoke. "Life-support insufficient. Deadly oxygen leaks into Drodusarel habitat."

And Dresk again: "Desire to leave *Asaph Hall*."

Mike's first thought was, *Good riddance*, but Rosa said, "I hope it doesn't come to that. It would be a shame to have to move your people again."

Captain Dresk said, "Hive mind fears death for individuals, possibly its own demise. Same fate as ribbons."

Mike said, "What happened to the ribbons was unfortunate. But you were there. We did everything we could."

"Still, ribbons die."

"Do you believe they were the beings who seeded your homeworld with life?"

"Hive mind disappointed. No evidence. Mission...a waste."

"I'm sorry about that. I assume you want to transfer to the Cetronen ship, *Cerenam*."

"Hive mind does not assume. Humans should not."

Mike started to speak again, but Rosa gestured for him to be quiet. "Let me talk to Codari. As fleet commander, he'll have to approve this -- especially since it would mean dropping out of stardrive again to make the transfer."

"Thanking the Human ones," Dresk said, and he and Kahtora whipped around and floated down the corridor. Mike waited until he and Rosa had cycled back through the lock and deactivated their lifesuits before saying, "You couldn't have just agreed to let them go? We've spent weeks trying to accommodate them and they are never satisfied. And they take the ribbons from their natural habitat and expect *us* to instantly find a proper world for them when they start to die off. And Linna...."

Rosa gave Mike a hard look. She said, "Do you realize how little contact with Drodusarel Humanity has had? I want to maintain this relationship -- rocky as it is -- if at all possible."

"The Cetronen haven't always been on the best terms with them, either. What if Codari wants them for himself, to improve the Cetronen relationship with them?"

Rosa started up the ladder. "Let's find out."

*****

Within minutes, Mike and Rosa arrived on the *Hall*'s bridge. Darwin Haidar was piloting and Katarina Diop was working the comm. Katarina told them, "Message coming in from the Sobrenian ship. It's Captain Syradok."

Rosa said, "Let's see what he has to say."

As Syradok's image appeared on the main screen, Mike thought, *Things are about to get even more complicated.*

The Sobrenian commander was dressed in his usual blue robes with lines of green, red, and gold running through them. He raised a rough-skinned, greenish hand and said, "It's so good to speak with you again -- or should I say, 'Greeting the Human ones?'"

Uh oh, Mike thought. *A* lot *more complicated.* He was impressed, however, at the poker face Rosa presented to Syradok as she said, "It's good to speak with you again, as well."

The Sobrenian said, "Captain Sandage, I will speak plainly to you, because I respect you. I know of the Drodusarel's concerns."

It took all of Mike's control to keep from showing the anger that flared within him. *How the hell can he know that*? he wondered. *The Drodusarel just spoke with us about three or four minutes ago.* He said, "You're already working with the Drodusarel on this, aren't you?"

The Sobrenian bowed slightly. "Just one of the many reasons I admire you, Mike. And so wonderful to address you by only a single name."

Rosa tilted her head wonderingly at Mike.

"I'll explain later," Mike told her. "Captain Syradok, why are you so eager to bring the Drodusarel aboard your starcraft?"

Syradok spread his arms wide. "I've told you I do not subscribe to my species' usual militarism. I simply wish better relations with the methane breathers -- as does Humanity."

Rosa said, "I can't deny our own interest, Captain."

"I believe I can trust you to represent all our views fairly to Captain Codari. Please let me know if he would care to speak to me directly." Syradok's image faded.

Rosa told Mike, "I hate it when someone trusts us to do the right thing."

Mike wasn't much for returning quips these days. He told Rosa, "Syradok's still holding a grudge toward Codari for making him pledge allegiance to him before allowing *Meradeus* to join the fleet. Not to mention that he wasn't invited to that awful banquet. I knew he could be sneaky, but I'm still disappointed in him. I was starting to like him."

Rosa pulled at one ear, apparently lost in thought. Then: "If Syradok's motivated by politics and revenge, I have to wonder if he would take good care of the Drodusarel."

Mike stepped close to Rosa and lowered his voice. "I don't care what he does. Of the three other Galactic intelligences on this mission, we share the least with the Drodusarel and the Sobrenians. They deserve each other. Trying to save Drodusarel got Linna killed."

Rosa squeezed Mike's arm. "And what would she say now, hearing you? You've devoted yourself to discovering life, to understanding it. I heard about how you reacted to that little spherical fish on Jilan, knowing it was about to die. That's the Mike Christopher I know."

Mike tried to pull away, but Rosa just held on tighter. "*Don't* pull away from me. I love you every bit as much as I did Linna, and I need you every bit as much as I needed her. You have to take up the slack for her."

"Damn, that's harsh," Mike said.

"If you'd quit filtering your memories, you'd realize Linna could be pretty harsh, too."

Mike hissed, "That's unfair."

"What's unfair is you don't realize how much you leaned on Linna for insights to yourself. You've got to do that on your own now."

Mike looked away from Rosa, was suddenly aware that Katarina and Darwin were paying conspicuous attention to their instrument consoles. He said, "Let's get Codari on the horn. If he refuses to allow the move, then it's settled."

"And if not?"

"If not, then I guess you and I will find ourselves on the hangar deck waiting for the Sobrenians to come pick up their new friends."

*****

Mike, Rosa, and Teresa stood on the *Asaph Hall*'s hangar deck, where the Drodusarel had gathered to transfer over to the Sobrenian starcraft *Meradeus*. *I believed I'd be happier to see them go,* he thought. *But I guess Rosa infected me. Their departure means we're losing face among the Drodusarel and, maybe, the Sobrenians, as well.*

Captain Dresk and the fourteen other Drodusarel who were the only survivors of the *Dirat*'s destruction back in the Moruteb system hovered within their energy shields, pointedly paying no attention to the Humans. The giant doors at the far end of the hangar deck began to slide open. Beyond the silvery shimmering of the energy shield that retained the air within the deck, they could see the large Sobrenian shuttle, yet another teardrop shape, approaching.

Cosmic Egg and the heavily damaged *Phobos 2* were well off to one side of the deck, allowing the Sobrenian craft plenty of room to touch down. It settled onto the deck, its emerald hull and slender struts giving it an insectile appearance. The outer lock opened and Syradok appeared in the doorway. He raised his blue-robed arms in greeting. The lines of green, red, and gold fabric laced through them shimmered.

It's as if everyone has gathered here to honor him, Mike thought. *I'd believed better of him than to lord this over us.*

Rosa leaned close and said, "Welcome to hell. Oh, yeah -- and we seemed to have forgotten to celebrate -- Happy New Year."

Mike only groaned.

Syradok stepped down from the shuttle. Mike was glad to see Govanek exit right behind him. *Thank goodness,* he thought. *A fellow explorer, someone without a political agenda.*

I hope.

Syradok approached Rosa and reached out his rough-skinned, thick-fingered hands to envelop hers. "So good finally to meet you!" he said.

Rosa said, "I've been looking forward to this, as well." Mike suppressed a grin as he thought of the accusatory expression Linna would've aimed at their captain for uttering such a lie.

Syradok went to Teresa next and said, "And also so good to see our friend Teresa here."

"Our honor, Captain," Teresa said.

Syradok stepped toward Mike and took his hands now. "I invite you to come to *Meradeus* soon and inspect our facilities for the Drodusarel. I'm eager to hear your opinions on them."

Mike said, as sweetly as he could, "I doubt I'd have much in the way of advice, Captain. You seem to have some very clear ideas on what you want."

Syradok's eyes looked intently over his snout. Mike wondered how much of Human voice intonation and body language the Sobrenian captain could read. "The invitation remains open," Syradok said, and moved toward the Drodusarel.

Govanek approached Mike. She wore her usual blue robes with red lines of fabric running through them. "I hope we have another opportunity to explore together as we return to familiar space."

Mike forced himself to smile. "So do I, though I wonder, given our circumstances, whether we'll have the opportunity."

"Let's hope for the best in all things," Govanek said, and moved to catch up with Captain Syradok.

Within moments Captain Dresk herded the rest of the Drodusarel into the Sobrenian shuttle. As it lifted off the *Hall*'s hangar deck, Mike told Rosa, "Captain Dresk didn't even say goodbye."

Rosa said, "I'm not exactly surprised. Certainly not disappointed. But what Govanek said was interesting."

"About exploring together again?"

"I wondered what you thought about the idea."

"Of exploring something with Govanek?"

"Of exploring at all."

"Hard to say," Mike said.

"I know."

"I just want to get home, Rosa."

"An odd thing to say. I know you don't mean going back to Earth. Isn't the *Asaph Hall* home?"

"I...I just want things the way they used to be."

The Sobrenian shuttle eased through the hangar bay's energy shield and the massive doors began to close. "Linna's not coming back," Rosa said. "The Drodusarel aren't going to become un-pissed. The Sobrenians aren't going to become trustworthy."

"You're not being very comforting."

"I just think nostalgia isn't what being an explorer is all about."

"So we *will* be explorers again one day soon?"

"One day," Rosa said. "I don't know about soon." She left, leaving Mike staring beyond the hangar bay doors for a long time.

CHAPTER SIXTEEN

It turned out Linna was alive, but she was falling into the incandescent fury of a star. She was wearing an old-fashioned spacesuit of metal, plastic, and fabric, and had only seconds left before it would be impossible for Mike to save her.

Mike also hurtled toward that star, barely five meters behind Linna, but still much too far away, no matter how desperately he stretched out his arms, hoping desperately to grab her and pull her to safety.

Gigantic solar flares reached out toward Linna, as if with conscious effort. The star's flames ablated the surface of her spacesuit. Her body twisted and tumbled, and even though he couldn't make out her expression, he saw her agonized features as the star began to cook her within her spacesuit.

If I could only touch her, Mike thought -- *just one finger --*

But the flames enveloped Linna, and swept away the material of her suit, leaving her naked body exposed to space, to the star's searing fires.

But I can't feel those flames, he thought. *Linna's burning up, and I'm about to shiver from the cold. I don't under --*

Mike sat up in bed, gasping as if he were drowning. His face was moist with sweat and a vein pounded in his neck.

Even as his breathing slowed, part of Mike's consciousness remained in the dream, and *wanted* to remain there, because Linna was still alive there, even if it was just for another moment, and as long as she was alive Mike had hope.

Mike tossed and turned for over an hour before he could give himself up to a restless sleep, as remnants of the previous dream shot through his awareness. One moment his consciousness was ready to accept the dream's reality again, and the next it protested that enough was enough and it was ready to face reality.

When his datalink woke him, it was almost a relief.

It was Lauren: "Mike, we've got a medical emergency on our hands."

Now she had his full attention. "Who is it?"

"Teresa. Her pregnancy's starting to destabilize. I need you to come here to the infirmary as quickly as you can."

Mike got up, started looking for clothes to pull on. "I have to ask what the hell use I can be?"

"She's asking for you."

Mike finished dressing, then headed for the infirmary. Lauren was waiting for him at the doorway when he arrived. He could just make out Teresa's pregnant form lying in the operating room beyond. She was holding onto her swollen belly and groaning softly. Lauren's assistant Althea Canady was attending to her.

"What's this all about?" Mike asked.

Lauren shrugged. "She asked for you," she said, as Althea sent an imploring look his way. Once Mike saw Teresa's pained and concerned expression, and how desperately she clutched her belly, as if holding her child in place, he kept his voice quieter and calmer than he'd originally intended. "Why did you ask for me?"

"Lauren's going to have to take the baby -- place him into an artificial womb."

"So why am I here?"

"I thought you should be here to see him. I think Linna would want you to."

"What the hell does Linna -- "

"My pregnancy helped her realize how much she wanted a child -- your child." Teresa grimaced. "Please, the pain -- "

Lauren handed her patient a pill. "Nanotech tablet. Backs up what I've already injected." Teresa took it, chewed, swallowed. Althea activated the controls on Teresa's bed that activated the sterile field that extended about six meters in all directions. Energy fields extended across the doorways in either direction. The lighting grew brighter.

Lauren gathered her surgical equipment. Gloves controlled the automated instruments that cut tissue, retracted and clamped skin, then closed the wound and sealed it. Those same gloves allowed her to control the nanotech dust she'd already injected into Teresa's body that would do everything from occluding blood flow to alerting Lauren and Althea if Teresa's or the baby's vitals deviated from safe levels. They would also instantly provide the proper levels of medication.

Lauren told Mike, "You've got to stay out of our way."

Mike said, "Don't talk to me like I'm the proud parent or something."

Lauren bent over her equipment again. "Fine. Then leave." But Teresa looked up at him with such a plaintive look that he didn't move right away.

Lauren looked back at Mike and he thought she'd snap at him again. Instead, her expression turned kindly. "It's also all right if you stick around. Just stay out of the way."

"I'll stay," Mike said. "Though I don't know why."

Teresa said, "Thanks, Mike. I know..."

"Shh," Lauren said. "No time for any of that now." She checked a sensor at the side of the bed. "Good night." She pressed together her thumb and forefinger just above Teresa's head and the nanotech activated her sleep center. Her eyes closed and her breathing slowed.

Lauren and Althea began what Mike knew should be a quick and relatively bloodless procedure. Still, his eyes widened and he stood stock-still as Althea rolled the artificial womb next to Teresa's bed. It was a tall vertical cylinder about a meter and a half tall, with artificial uterine fluid filling its upper portion. Its clear top opened on its own, waiting to receive this child whose development had been halted at four months.

Mike told Lauren, "I'm amazed you have this equipment on hand."

"I had to replicate a few things -- remind myself of a few procedures. But I try to stay prepared for just about anything. Replicating Teresa's uterine fluid was the tough part -- making sure to get the sodium and potassium levels right, all the other factors. Ready, Althea?"

Lauren's assistant indicated she was. Lauren leaned over Teresa and with swift movements of her fingers and the assistance of the nanotech within Teresa's body quickly had her patient's belly laid open. Next, slower and more precise movements opened up the uterus.

Then everything happened so quickly that Mike nearly missed it. He had a brief glimpse of Lauren grasping a tiny pink-skinned being, umbilical cord still attached to the placenta, and lowering it gently within the artificial womb.

An instant later, though, Mike got a good look at the child as Althea rolled the artificial womb away to an adjoining room. The child's eyelids were closed. Not only were his hands and feet fully formed, but Mike felt a sense of wonder as he saw him make a fist.

Linna, poor dear Linna, he thought. *She wanted to have a child. I didn't, but if I did, I'd certainly want Linna to be my child's mother.*

Then Althea closed the door and by the time Mike thought to see how Teresa was doing, Lauren had already closed her up, with hardly a drop of blood spilled in the entire process. She put away her equipment, made one last check of the sensors showing Teresa's condition, then turned to Mike and said, "Just that simple."

Mike said, "You and Althea were amazing."

"I'm talking to a man who's always known he was different because he didn't have a family. I mean, the Cetronen call Humans 'singletons.' You're the ultimate singleton -- no family tree at all. But haven't you ever considered starting such a history?"

Mike glared at Lauren. "I haven't. Maybe you think that's some sort of tragedy. I just look at it as my own choice, as reasonable a choice as any."

Rosa's voice came over his datalink. "Mike, get up here to the bridge right away, please."

Mike told Lauren, "Gotta go. Rosa's calling." He left the infirmary and headed for the bridge.

*****

When Mike arrived on the bridge, he saw Rosa in apparent contemplation of the swirling colors of stardrive displayed on the main screen. Before her, Darwin was piloting and Katarina was at nav.

Rosa told Mike, "I know what happened down there. With Teresa, I mean, and..."

"Yeah. The child."

"How are they doing?"

"They're fine."

Rosa said, "The Drodusarel hive mind has been complaining to Codari about how the fleet is being run. Codari, of course, was more than happy to point out that the Drodusarel are dependent upon the kindness of the Sobrenians. Without their own ship, they're not in much of a position to demand anything."

"Let me guess," Mike said. "You want me to go over to *Meradeus* and placate the Drodusarel."

"*Codari* wants you to go. And while you're placating people, put in some good words with Syradok, as well."

"I'm going to be at a disadvantage, here. Syradok always seemed enamored of Teresa, and she's not going anywhere for awhile. And I'd always get a reading on his emotional state from Linna."

Rosa stared at Mike as if he were a stranger. "This has been tough on all of us -- perhaps you most of all. But you've got to get past that. I made you chief contact officer when you came aboard precisely because I knew you'd be great at it even if Linna weren't here. You've got to prove that to me now."

Mike cleared his throat and fought to control the tension in his voice. "You're right."

"Three ships -- four species," Rosa said. "It's never simple, is it?" Rosa turned to Darwin and Katarina. "Get ready to leave stardrive. There's a system up ahead. *Cerenam* will transmit the exit coordinates." She shook Mike's hand. "I've already asked Alice to go with you. Good luck."

"I guess a little luck never hurts." He headed for the hangar bay.

*****

Mike and Alice said little to one another as they performed the pre-flight on *Cosmic Egg*. By the time they finished, *Asaph Hall*, *Meradeus*, and *Cerenam* had exited stardrive. It was only after Mike guided the *Egg* through the hangar bay's energy shield that Alice said, "We haven't talked much. You know...the past few weeks."

Mike's throat clenched. It was all he could do to say, "We've both been busy."

Alice looked out the forward viewscreen. They would be at *Meradeus* within minutes. "I see. Busy."

Mike's hands gripped the shuttle's controls. "I'm sorry. You deserve better than that."

Alice's expression softened. "It's too soon. I know."

"Just because we went to the sphere together that time...listen, I wish I had better words to say this. That was about our grief. It was about Linna."

Alice said, "I know. I guess now *I'm* being an Earther."

"We'll...be OK."

They didn't speak anymore as Mike guided the *Egg* into the *Meradeus*'s hangar bay. For some reason, he was very aware of the many projections scattered across the teardrop-shaped craft that he knew were the Sobrenians' beloved weapons.

*****

Mike wasn't surprised that it was Govanek who met him and Alice at the hangar bay. As usual, she wore her blue robes with the lines of fabric that single color, red. *I wonder if she'll ever have a chance to win more colors*, Mike wondered. *In her culture, explorers aren't widely respected or admired.*

Sobrenians had few facial muscles, making it difficult to sense Govanek's mood. But she sounded pleasant enough -- if not completely happy -- as she said, "Once again we meet under less than ideal circumstances."

More thoughts of Linna. *Set them aside*, Mike thought. "But these are circumstances we can do something about," he said. "At least, that's our hope."

"May it be so," Govanek said, and led them down the corridor toward Syradok's quarters. When they arrived, both Syradok and Dresk were there.

Mike had anticipated the shadowed surroundings of Syradok's quarters, having been there with Linna and Teresa after they'd viewed the breakup of Risula. This time, though, many of those shadows were eliminated by the soft glow of Captain Dresk's energy shield. Mike could just make out the familiar jellyfish-like form of the Drodusarel within the gray-blue shield, which allowed him to float above the floor.

As usual, Mike perceived a faint whiff of ozone mixed with cat fur emanating from the shield. That, combined with the regular musty smell and higher humidity of the Sobrenian ship made Mike's stomach want to clench. He forced that feeling down -- didn't want to emulate Teresa -- and told Captain Dresk, "I'm so pleased to see you again."

"I suppose," Dresk said, "I am greeting the Human one. But it gives no pleasure."

Mike tried to show as little response he could as he told Captain Syradok, "And it's a pleasure to see you again, as well."

Syradok spread his robed hands wide. "I suppose I'm greeting you as well, admittedly with more enthusiasm than my Drodusarel friend. But then, I always try to get along with others."

Or at least want to seem like it, Mike thought. He said, "I'm sure you both remember Alice from the banquet aboard the *Cerenam*."

"Remembering," Dresk said.

Syradok said, "Once again, I must apologize that there is no place for Humans to sit. Captain Dresk has complaints. We should hear them."

Dresk said, "Hive mind disagrees with how fleet is run."

"What's the nature of that disagreement?"

"Drodusarel starcraft is destroyed. We should be provided with new craft."

"And how," Mike asked, "would that be possible?"

The Drodusarel's energy shield seemed to become brighter. "We would accept the use of *Cerenam*."

Oh, shit, Mike thought. *Is Dresk serious? And if so, does he intend to back up his talk with action? Possibly violent action? Is this why he picked the Meradeus to go to rather than remain aboard* Asaph Hall?

"Captain Dresk, with all respect, do you really believe Captain Codari would consider abandoning the *Cerenam* and turning it over to you?"

Dresk said, "Not Drodusarel problem. Cetronen problem."

Mike glanced at Syradok and wished he were better at interpreting Sobrenian expressions. The *Meradeus* captain's left eye was staring at the Drodusarel while his right peered at Mike. *And he's just standing back and taking this all in*, he thought. *The bastard. Syradok loves being the kingpin. Now he has everyone's attention, all four species on these three ships, focused on his ship. It's what he wanted all along, why he wanted on this mission.*

And if Syradok decides to back up Dresk with his ship's Sobrenian weaponry -- I don't want to consider what might happen. Mike told Dresk, "This goes far beyond anything I may address personally. I've got to speak to Codari."

"Speak, then." Dresk said. "Briefly. Then return."

As Govanek led Mike and Alice back toward the hangar bay, Mike thought, *I wish I could look through Dresk's energy shield, and that I understood Drodusarel body language well enough to get a reading on him. If Linna were here, she could've told me whether he's sincere, or whether this whole thing's a big bluff.*

Then there's Syradok. Suddenly his intentions have turned opaque. What's he getting out of this odd alliance with the Drodusarel?

As they arrived at the hangar bay, Govanek said to Mike, "I hope you can bring back good news from Codari. I wish we could become explorers again."

Mike paused at the steps leading to the *Egg*'s airlock. He told Alice, "Why don't you go ahead and start the pre-flight?"

Alice looked at Mike sympathetically and went up the short ramp into the shuttle. Mike told Govanek, "I wish I could be optimistic. But what in space can Codari possibly decide that could placate the Drodusarel?"

Before Govanek could reply, though, a low rumble resounded throughout the hangar bay, and the deck shook with a force that made Mike unsteady on his feet for a moment. "What the hell was that?"

Govanek's eyeballs went back and forth independently in their sockets and she stood with her bare feet spread wide, braced to repel any attack. "I don't know what's happening, Mike. But you should leave now."

From a vent overhead came a hissing sound. Mike couldn't see or smell anything, but in that instant his lifesuit snapped on. He touched his wrist sensor and aimed it upward.

Methane!

CHAPTER SEVENTEEN

Mike heard Alice's voice over his datalink -- she was standing in the doorway of the *Egg*'s airlock, also in her lifesuit, saying, "Co'mon, Mike, we gotta get out of here!"

But Mike took only a single step before he heard Govanek's coughing, and turned to see her bent over trying desperately to breathe.

Then she collapsed.

Mike didn't hesitate. Govanek didn't have lifesuit tech, and he had no idea where he might locate a Sobrenian spacesuit. He scooped her up and carried her aboard the *Egg*. He dumped her into the seat behind Alice, who punched controls sealing the lock and said, "Lifting." She brought the shuttle off the deck and into free space.

Rosa's voice came over the shuttle's comm. "Mike, what the hell is happening over there? We're getting all kinds of crazy readings from *Meradeus*."

Mike opened a supply bin next to Govanek's chair and took out a medical sensorpac. "It looks as if the Drodusarel are taking over. Tell Lauren we've got another patient for her -- Govanek."

"Understood," Rosa said. "And I'll alert Codari." She signed off.

Mike made a quick scan of Govanek's vitals, then accessed the scanner's databank for Sobrenian physiology. Alice asked, "How's she doing?"

Mike returned the scanner to the sensorpac. "Near as I can tell, she'll be OK. It looks like Sobrenian and Human reactions to methane exposure are similar. It's not in itself toxic, but she was right under that vent. I suspect the methane displaced the oxygen in the air."

"And the rest of the crew of the *Meradeus*?"

"Anyone who didn't get a spacesuit on is about to asphyxiate."

"It might take just a few Sobrenians to defend their ship against the Drodusarel."

Govanek started coughing, then bent double in her chair. Mike sat next to her and asked, "Are you all right?"

She took in her surroundings, eyeballs turning in different directions. "How did I get onto the *Egg*? We were on the hangar deck, and..."

Mike said, "The Drodusarel are trying to take over your ship."

Govanek tried to rise. "I've got to get back!"

Mike placed his hands on her shoulders and eased her back into the chair. "What you've got to do is stay still until we get you examined back on *Asaph Hall*."

"I'm no coward! I've got to help my people."

"No one's calling you a coward. If it helps, consider yourself kidnapped. This shuttle's *not* going back to *Meradeus*."

"I have to know what's going on back there."

Mike squeezed past Govanek and sat next to Alice. He ran a quick sensor scan on the Sobrenian ship. "*Meradeus* is quickly gaining a methane atmosphere."

"Sobrenian lifesigns?" Govanek asked.

Mike asked, "How many are aboard your ship?"

"Twenty-two, including me."

Another scan. *Damn*. "I'm sorry. Now there's seven."

Govanek leaned forward and placed one hand on the back of Mike's chair. "You *must* allow me to return there."

"Even if we turned around right now it would be too late."

Alice said, "Look there -- two lifepods leaving *Meradeus*."

"*Now* we can do something," Mike said.

Alice's fingers hovered over the nav console. "Intercept course?"

"You got it. And I'll get ready to receive the pods." He went to the rear of the cabin and waited by the doorway leading to the cargo bay. He watched through a window set into the door as he punched controls opening the rear hatch.

It only took about half a minute for Alice to bring *Cosmic Egg* alongside one of the lifepods. They were each about nine meters across and three wide, their dark green metallic finish reflecting starlight. "I think they'll just about fit," Mike said as he activated the *Egg*'s enticement beam.

Govanek joined him, though she had to go tippy-toe to look through the window into the bay. "I'm bringing them in one at a time," Mike told her. To Alice, he said, "Get ready to boost once they're in. I don't like the idea of hanging around out here too close to the Drodusarel."

Alice said, "Especially when they suddenly have Sobrenian firepower at their disposal."

Mike could hear the regret even in the datalink translation of Govanek's voice: "Our weapons, it seems, have done us little good."

Mike finished using the beam to guide the first lifepod to the cargo bay's deck. "Getting the second one," he said as he redirected the beam.

"Holy shit!" Alice exclaimed. "Mike, finish up quick, *Meradeus* just fired on the Cetronen ship."

"I've got a hard lock with the beam, go!" Mike replied.

Cosmic Egg boosted toward *Asaph Hall*, the enticement beam towing the second pod even as Rosa's voice came over the comm: "Codari's ship is taking severe hits. I'm sending Lauren and Althea to the hangar deck. Once they retrieve those pods, I want you two to stand by in case you need to get over to *Cerenam* to help out."

"Understood," Mike said.

Alice said, "We should be there in about two minutes."

Mike told Govanek, "Let's see who made it out." He hit a control, the doors to the cargo bay slid aside, and Mike approached the nearest lifepod. He asked Govanek, "How do you open it up?"

Govanek pressed a finger into a small opening in the side of the pod that Mike hadn't seen. A small handle, built for

Sobrenian hands, extended from the pod. Govanek turned it and the hatch pushed itself outward a few centimeters, then slid aside.

Mike covered his nose and mouth with one hand. *I've smelled burned flesh before*, he thought, *but you don't get used to it.*

The interior of the lifepod was filled with smoke and splashed with dark red, almost black blood. The still figures of three Sobrenians lay inside. Mike touched his wrist sensor. "Close it," he told Govanek. "They're all dead."

Govanek grasped the handle and closed the pod. She rushed toward the other one. This time Mike made sure to aim his wrist sensor at it before they opened it. "Two alive. One just barely."

Alice said, "Docking."

Govanek opened the second pod. She stared inside and said, "The Giver is generous!"

Mike peered over her shoulder. *Syradok.* The right side of his snout was covered in blood, as was his right shoulder. The Sobrenian captain looked up at Mike, but didn't seem able to form words.

That's when Mike recognized the other Sobrenian -- Sejagar, Syradok's head of security, who'd escorted him, Linna, and Teresa to the *Meradeus*'s bridge to witness the death of Risula. *He's in bad shape*, Mike thought. Much of Sejagar's chest was a bloody mess, his right arm was hopelessly mangled, and his robes were in tatters. Mike to Govanek, "He must've given the Drodusarel a hell of a fight."

The cargo bay's rear door opened, its ramp extruded, and Lauren and Althea entered, two spider-legged smart-gurneys right behind them. "This one's the worst," Mike said, indicating Sejagar. "The other one's Captain Syradok."

"Stand back while the gurneys get them out," Lauren said. One gurney extended its deft mechanical arms to gently lift Sejagar and place him on top of itself. Lauren went to work on him. Syradok went onto the other gurney, and Althea started on him.

Mike took Govanek gently by the arm. "It's best if you stand back and let them work."

Over his datalink, Mike heard Rosa's voice: "I need you up here, ASAP."

Mike caught Alice's eye as she left the *Egg*'s cabin and stepped down into the *Asaph Hall*'s cargo bay. "Can you stay here with Govanek? Rosa wants me on the bridge."

"Sure."

Mike took another glance at the two injured Sobrenians. He couldn't see much of what was happening, heard only the click of instruments and the hum of healing energies as he left.

*****

When Mike arrived on the *Asaph Hall*'s bridge, the first thing he realized was that Darwin, who was piloting, was backing the starcraft away from the dueling Cetronen and Sobrenian craft. Katarina, on sensors and nav, was laying in potential escape trajectories. The blue and black, mushroom-shaped *Cerenam* and green, water-drop-shaped *Meradeus* were visible on the viewscreen only through high mag. In a rarely-seen type of space battle, they were slugging it out like old-time oceangoing vessels, using thrusters to circle one another and try to gain advantage.

Looks like Meradeus *is more mobile and has superior firepower*, Mike thought. *But* Cerenam's *taking the pounding in stride while getting some pretty precise shots in.*

Rosa saw Mike's questioning glance and explained, "It was Codari who insisted we move back. He realizes we're outclassed in this fight."

Mike knew his captain was correct -- *Asaph Hall* had a paltry three banks of disruptors, meant to sting a potential enemy just long enough to power up the stardrive and make a quick escape. "All the same, maybe we could make the difference."

"And maybe we don't shoot at all," Rosa pointed out, "and if *Cerenam*'s destroyed we hope the Drodusarel aren't pissed enough to turn their weapons on us -- not that we'd stay around that long."

"Still, I hope we don't end up having to make the rest of this trip back all by ourselves."

Rosa asked, "How's our Sobrenians from those lifepods?"

"Everyone dead in one of them. Two alive in the other. Syradok's one of them. Sejagar's the other."

"Well, that's a little something, I suppose. I'm glad you got Govanek, as well."

On the viewscreen, *Cerenam* and *Meradeus* continued to trade energy bolts. In the vacuum of space, the beams themselves couldn't be seen, only the flaring of shields as they struck home and the damage they inflicting when one of those shields failed. Mike said, "Makes me wonder whether the Sobrenians' weapons are as great as they believe."

"Probably not a fair test," Rosa said. "With Drodusarel aiming them, and all."

"If *Cerenam*'s crippled, we could end up with Cetronen aboard, as well."

"But no Drodusarel, no matter what." Off Mike's surprised look, Rosa said, "I'm not being a species bigot. It's these particular Drodusarel I don't trust."

Mike folded his arms. "No reason we should."

The viewscreen emitted a brilliant flare of light, and when it faded, Mike took one look at *Cerenam* and said, "Oh, shit." The Cetronen craft had taken a severe blow at the "top" of its "mushroom." An expanding cloud of debris partially obscured the starcraft.

"Dammit," Mike said. "Now the Drodusarel are likely to go in for the kill."

Katarina spoke up: "*Cerenam*'s shields won't hold up very long now."

Then the Sobrenian-turned-Drodusarel craft *Meradeus*, which had been bearing down on *Cerenam*, halted, and began to back away. The teardrop-shaped craft executed a smart 180-degree turn and boosted away from *Cerenam*.

Katarina split the screen, half continuing to monitor *Cerenam* while the other half kept focus on the departing *Meradeus*.

Rosa told Darwin, "Contact Codari -- offer him any assistance."

Another flare from the screen, this one from *Meradeus* as its stardrive field began to annihilate old-space before it and create new-space behind.

"Well, that was polite," Mike said. "At least they put a reasonable distance between us before they jumped."

Darwin said, "Codari, Captain."

Rosa said, "Put him on."

The Cetronen's transmission was audio only: "I'm so glad *Asaph Hall* wasn't harmed during that exchange."

"I'm sorry we couldn't be more help," Rosa said.

"I must admit, Captain Sandage, my main concern was that at least one ship from our little fleet should survive intact."

Rosa said, "So what's next?"

"Match your stardrive signature to ours. We're going after the Drodusarel."

Mike spoke up. "With all respect, Captain Codari, are you sure that's our best course of action?"

Codari's voice held an unaccustomed mirth. "It may not be, but I believe it is the necessary one. These Drodusarel are dangerous."

Rosa asked, "Do you need to delay for repairs?"

"Perhaps I should. But I will not. We proceed within five minutes." He signed off.

Rosa stood with one hand over her mouth, her eyes focused far away. *I know what she's considering*, Mike thought. She's weighing whether we're better off following Codari or continuing on our own. It's a tough call. We're still nearly two months out from Human space.

Rosa asked Mike, "What do you think?"

He said, "I don't like the idea of following after the Drodusarel. I'd be pretty content to let them go on their way. On the other hand...."

Rosa said, "On the other hand, they're out there whether we're following them or not. We'll be a lot safer with Codari than all alone."

"I don't know. We might just become a bigger target."

"Chance we'll have to take," Rosa said, and turned to Darwin. "Do just as Codari said. Match signatures. Prepare for jump."

Mike watched without enthusiasm as Darwin and Katarina made their preparations. On the viewscreen, the kaleidoscopic swirl of the stardrive field appeared as *Asaph Hall* made its jump. *I just wanted to be an explorer*, Mike thought.

*****

During the next couple of hours, Mike paced the *Hall*'s bridge. He knew it could be hours or days before anything happened, but he was still unwilling to leave. Alice replaced Katarina at nav, but otherwise all remained quiet.

Eventually Mike made himself sit next to Rosa. Then came a moment when he could tell Rosa was listening to a private datalink transmission. After about half a minute, she said, "Message from Codari. He's giving up on chasing the Drodusarel."

Alice checked her sensors. "*Cerenam*'s in bad shape and getting worse. Parts of it are still falling off. It's venting a lot of volatiles and air."

Mike said, "He's going to have to find a place to stop."

Rosa said, "He has. We're heading toward that system we noticed on the way out -- where we thought we saw the comets. It's just a few minutes ahead."

It took Mike a moment to think back, and he snapped his fingers when the memory arrived. "That's right, it was an Earth-like world, wasn't it? All of which could make things even more complicated. Add a first contact situation into everything else we have going on here...."

A tone from Alice's console drew all their attention. Alice said, "It's Codari's ship. The *Cerenam*'s stardrive field is losing integrity."

Mike looked over Alice's shoulder at the sensor readings and said, "He's going to have to drop back into normal space pretty quickly."

Rosa said, "That would be right now. Katarina, stay with him. Alice, keep that sensor lock on him."

Mike realized how tense he'd been. He relaxed his shoulders and took a deep breath. He told Rosa, "I think he's doing the right thing. Giving up the chase."

Rosa said, "That's the great thing about being a spacer. We'll find out soon enough if it was the right decision or not. Why don't you take advantage of this breather and go down and check on our Sobrenian guests?"

CHAPTER EIGHTEEN

Lauren met Mike at the entrance to the infirmary. "Syradok's OK for now," was the first thing she told him. But she nodded toward one of the smart-gurneys, where a body lay covered with a sheet. She asked, "The other Sobrenian?"

"His name was Sejagar."

"You said he must've put up a hell of a fight. He certainly did as I was working on him. He just lost too much blood."

"What about Govanek?"

"I had her assigned quarters and told her to get some sleep."

Mike rubbed an earlobe, shuffled from one foot to the other. "You say Syradok's OK for now? What's that mean longer-term?"

"He's got a good chance. Althea's looking to him in the next room."

"I'd like to get this over with." Mike followed Lauren into the next room, where Althea was standing next to the Sobrenian's bed, taking readings with a hand-held medical sensor. Lauren caught Althea's eye, and both doctors left Mike and Syradok alone.

Syradok sat up. "It's so good to see you, Mike," he said. "Though I have presented you with a more dynamic presence during our other meetings."

The right side of Syradok's snout and his right shoulder sported bandages. His chest was bare. Mike had forgotten how heavily muscled Sobrenians were -- Syradok's torso was three times as thick as a Human's. His arms looked as if they could lift Mike over his head easily, even in his weakened state.

Mike glimpsed the Sobrenian's blue robes, in tatters, on a chair next to his bed.

Syradok followed Mike's gaze and said, "They were lovely, and look at them now. But what they represent is more important -- my achievements as a fighter and a starcraft captain. Those remain." Syradok folded his hands on his lap. "Doctor Takahashi told you about Sejagar?"

"She did."

"He fought bravely. He rushed to my quarters when he realized the Drodusarel were trying to take over the ship. He ignored me when I demanded he try to save as many of the crew as possible. He took a mighty breath of air before the methane could overcome him and rushed me to the lifepod."

"There was another pod I took aboard our shuttle."

"But they were all dead?"

"Yes," Mike said.

"Unfortunate. By then the Drodusarel had cut off the gravity, and were floating around in those damnable energy shields of theirs. They were much more agile, more used to a zero-G environment."

"They shot up the other lifepod?"

"Yes. Sejagar made his decision. He could not defend both pods. He fought to save me, not the other crewmembers."

"A tough choice."

"Not the one I would have made," Syradok said. "I wish the rest of my crew had lived. But Sejagar traded his life for mine. I remain grateful to him."

"Captain Syradok -- forgive me for prying, but how did the Drodusarel manage to take over your ship? I'd have thought *Asaph Hall* would've been a better target while they were still here."

"Ah, Mike, now I must beg your forgiveness. *Asaph Hall* would've been, as you say, the easier target. But *Meradeus* was the bigger prize. They overcame us before we could self-destruct. Sad though I was to see my grand starcraft taken by the methane-breathers, I was proud to see its weapons take on the Cetronen so efficiently."

Without thinking, Mike said, "Captain, I can't believe what I'm hearing! The Cetronen are our allies -- or at least

Humanity's allies. *Cerenam* is crippled, and is limping toward the next star system."

Syradok said, "Yes, again, you must forgive me. My own culture betrays me. Such feelings run so deep. Of course, my interest was purely intellectual. My people and the Cetronen do not always get along. But I did not enjoy the deaths and injuries of innocent Cetronen."

Though I have to wonder, Mike thought, *if it was because he wasn't the one shooting. Culture running deep, indeed.*

Syradok asked, "What is happening to our two remaining ships now?"

Mike explained about *Cerenam*'s damage and that they were halting for repairs in the system where Codari had mistakenly thought he'd detected unknown spacecraft months earlier.

Syradok said, "Mike, I must give you advice. And I hope a Sobrenian's wisdom can transfer to a Human."

Mike looked at Syradok. Both the Sobrenian's eyes stared directly at him and held their gaze, which was a rare enough sight. But Mike saw in those eyes a sad and wistful expression he'd never glimpsed on a Sobrenian's face before. *His injuries are more than physical*, Mike thought. *This has affected him on a deeper level than I'd have imagined.*

Syradok said, "I've failed my people in so many ways. My ship captured by Drodusarel -- you cannot know how shameful that is. My crew dead, and Sejagar sacrificing himself for me -- more shame. But those are nothing compared to the shame I'd already brought down upon my people."

Mike understood. "The precursors."

"Yes -- what I told Teresa was a 'harsh truth.' I wished to find the evidence of what so many of my people take on faith. We pride ourselves on our rationality, you see, and even the most devout believers in the Giver and the Shaper will require proof of those who helped us rise again and again from our primitive periods."

"Because your people are afraid they're about to enter one of those primitive periods now," Mike said.

"You are correct."

"Excuse me if I assume too much, Captain Syradok. But I'd say your species' doubts are reflected in how you've had to cope with your own dilemmas on this mission -- to nearly have to beg to be a part of it, to have to consider an alliance with the Cetronen because that business with the precursors didn't work out -- it had to be humiliating."

"I would argue that your analysis is overly simplistic," Syradok said.

"But essentially right?"

"Yes. I fear it is essentially right."

Mike said, "Captain, I have to get back to the bridge. We'll drop out of stardrive any moment now. Who knows what's waiting for us in this new system."

"I hope," the Sobrenian captain said, "it will be something better than I've found."

Mike turned away from the Sobrenian and headed back toward the bridge.

*****

We're about to come out of stardrive, Mike thought as he rushed down the corridor that led to *Asaph Hall*'s bridge. After living nearly a decade on this starcraft, he could interpret that distant rumble as the phase transition module working to insert the ship and its crew back into normal space.

And -- now, he thought, sensing without conscious effort those faint creaks transmitted through the hull as new-space dissipated behind the ship, and that slight change in air pressure as the *Hall*'s life-support systems adapted to the influx of extra power available as energies dedicated to the stardrive redistributed themselves throughout the ship.

He couldn't help indulging in a wry grin as he entered the bridge and saw on the main viewscreen that the *Hall* had, indeed, returned to normal space. There was *Cerenam*, a large chuck of the topmost part of its mushroom shape missing. *At least it's not venting any more debris into space*, Mike thought.

Rosa stood between Darwin, who was still piloting, and Alice, on nav. The captain said, "I was just going to call you. Captain Codari wants to talk to us both. Yes, Captain, go ahead."

With both ships out of stardrive, the transmission was a holo now, with the image of the Cetronen captain appearing in front of Rosa. The minor's deep-set eyes seemed haunted, and his wide, pointed ears moved listlessly. *He's exhausted*, Mike thought. *Not surprising, given what he's been coping with the past day or so.*

The Codari minor said, "Captain Sandage, I thank your crew for remaining with us."

"Don't thank us yet," Rosa said. "We know very little about this system or any possible inhabitants."

"That is the task I would like to set for your crew. My own is busy keeping *Cerenam* together, and many of our sensors are off-line. I'd like you to find out as much as possible about this system, and a world we're headed toward that looks hospitable. I'd like an overview of the system, then a focus on that planet, and especially those possible starcraft that may have been here."

Rosa said, "I thought those turned out to be comets?"

"I apologize. We've known of this world for some time -- we have named it Vuraso, after a great peacemaker from Cetronen history. I staged the exit from stardrive so we could do a quick long-distance scan of the planet."

Mike looked up from a sensor scan he was just beginning. "So all that business of dropping out of stardrive, and being mistaken about the comets -- that was just playacting?"

"I'm not sure of your reference," Codari said. "But our primary interest lies here at Vuraso. The journey to Moruteb had to be made first because Neska would not wait on us. But that part of our journey was, for us, only a precursor to this stop."

Rosa said, "This is not good, Captain Codari. I expected more trust, more openness, from a colleague."

"I apologize. Yet here we are, all the same."

Rosa wrung her hands a couple times, stopped. She smiled at Codari's image. *She's playing for time*, Mike thought. *Deciding.* Finally she said, "I'd feel a lot better if you weren't also repairing your ship in the middle of all this."

There's a surprise, Mike thought. *She just pulled a Cetronen change-the-subject on him.*

Codari said, "Even with *Cerenam* fully repaired, I do not intend to leave until we have explored Vuraso sufficiently to answer certain questions."

"Which means," Rosa said, "we'll be better off getting that over with while you repair your ship."

"Wise as usual," Codari's minor said.

To Mike, Rosa said, "Start the scan."

Mike leaned over the sensor console. A quick reading showed basic information on the system's star. Mass of 1.23 Sol for the primary -- it had probably been been on the main sequence for about three billion years, with another one and a half or two billion left to go. *A good, healthy star*, Mike thought. He sent a quick data blip toward the *Cerenam*.

As Mike worked, the Codari minor continued: "I hope to obtain help for my ship from any beings on or orbiting Vuraso. At a minimum, perhaps I and some of my crew can remain in this system while you take the rest toward Human or Cetronen space -- at least close enough to send a transmission requesting assistance."

"I hope it doesn't come to that," Rosa said. "I have to wonder if the Drodusarel are still out there waiting for us."

Mike worked on the overview of the system's planets. The *Hall*'s sensors had been carrying out standard scanning protocols and he accessed those readings. Ten planets altogether, five rocky ones close in, then Vuraso. Three Jovian-class gas giants were next, then a smaller gas giant. Another blip to *Cerenam*.

The Codari minor was saying, "Despite the Drodusarel's obvious success in taking over the *Meradeus*, they cannot be eager to continue operating a Sobrenian starcraft any longer than they must to get home."

Rosa said, "I'm sure you're right. I'd still rather make the rest of this trip in your company."

Mike focused now on Vuraso itself. He said, "Excuse me, Rosa, Captain Codari. But I've found a few things that may be promising."

The holo image of the Codari minor said, "I've noted the information you've already transmitted. "What else do you have?"

"The planet looks promising," Mike said. "It's nicely in the middle of the ecosphere. Oxygen-nitrogen atmosphere. 1.83 Earth masses, 1.24 Earth grav. Most of the land area is either dense jungle or barren desert, and the planet is hotter than Earth on the average -- about like your homeworld, Captain Codari."

Rosa asked, "Any signs of intelligent life? Orbital starports, maybe, or large cities on the planet itself?"

"Narrowing the focus. Hmm."

The Codari minor said, "Failure to translate."

"Sorry -- just getting a better reading. For now, I don't detect any large cities at all, and the ones I see are all pre-industrial, just villages. No ground vehicles or paved roads. No nuclear or nanotech facilities. I detect thousands of different species, and several of them could be intelligent. But they range in size from a large dog to something close to an elephant."

"From your experiences on Splendor, you certainly know more than one species per planet could be intelligent."

Rosa said, "That may be overly optimistic. All the same, let's go ahead and send standard greeting protocols -- you know the drill." Such protocols involved transmissions on everything from radio to subspace comm channels. They also included still images and cubes of planets the *Hall* had visited over the years, as well as of the Human form. Those images were accompanied by the sounds of natural radio sources, such as a pulsar, and mathematical formulas expressed in binary code. Such messages had a history that went back as far as the first Voyager probes just over one hundred seventy years earlier.

"Right away," Mike said, and bent over the console to get to work.

*****

Moments later, with every message sent across every medium the *Asaph Hall* could muster, there was still no response from the planet.

Mike balled his hands into fists. He wanted to smash them against the console. *Childish*, he thought. *God, how I need Linna here. That's what's making me so frustrated, not the lack of contact.*

Images flashed through Mike's consciousness in an instant:

-- Linna telling him she'd end her latest self-imposed quarantine from him the next night: "Supper in my room? Wine?"

-- A night within the viewing sphere making love, musky Human-smell filling the room, legs intertwined, only drifting apart in the zero-G because finding each other again was all the fun.

-- Eleven years earlier, their first meeting, as he stood next to Rosa in a corridor on *Asaph Hall* just outside an embarkation tube. Linna took one look at him, her mouth curled up, then became a full smile as she said, "He'll do." As the blood rushed to his face, Mike nearly went right back down that embarkation tube.

I'm glad I didn't, he thought. *Despite everything, I'm so glad. And right now, she'd have sensed my frustration and been right beside me with just the right words, or a hand on my shoulder. Funny how you begin to expect that, living so close to an empath all those years.*

Mike felt a presence behind him and turned. Rosa.

"Frustrated?" she asked.

"It's that obvious?"

"When you're bent over those controls and look like you're in some sort of trance, and don't have a single expression on your face, yes, it's that obvious."

"I wanted to come through for Codari. I don't know how long he can keep *Cerenam* together."

"I feel the same way." Rosa touched behind one ear. "Captain Sandage to Captain Codari."

The Cetronen's holographic image appeared before Mike's sensor console. "Yes, Captain -- Mike. Have you made contact with any beings on the planet?"

Mike said, "No, Captain. I don't even see anything we'd call cities. But that could just mean we need to look more closely..."

Codari's minor shifted position in the grip of the major. "Contact protocols are based upon past experience. These beings may represent something utterly new. They may be advanced, yet not gather together in large communities. Is that not why we become explorers?"

Mike said, "You're very generous, Captain."

"I'd like to speak to you for a moment to provide encouragement."

"Ah -- a pep talk."

"Failure to translate. But I perceive you understand my meaning."

"It's sort of my job," Mike said.

"Then listen -- I am desperate. It's a desperation that leads me to being an explorer in the purest sense -- to travel alone with no expectations about what I might find or how dangerous the territory ahead of me might be. If something happens to *Cerenam*, you're the only ones who may be able to help us. Finding someone on the planet technically advanced enough to help us seems unlikely, but we will make the attempt."

Mike said, "Your ship runs partially on biological systems. Could there be something down there that might help with repairs?"

"Perhaps. If nothing else, we may find a place of concealment. Also, I leave this decision to you, Captain Sandage -- perhaps you will need to abandon us and save *Asaph Hall*."

Rosa said, "I'd rather not have to face that decision just yet."

Mike said, "It's a risk -- approaching this planet without making some sort of preliminary contact first."

"The risk would be in allowing *Cerenam* to deteriorate any further. We'll enter into orbit around Vuraso soon."

Mike had to clear his throat before he managed to say, "Good luck, Captain Codari."

The Cetronen captain's image faded away. Rosa muttered, "I think they'll need that luck."

Within twenty minutes the damaged *Cerenam* eased into orbit around Vuraso. Its teardrop shape was illuminated on one side by the primary, and across its surface by running lights.

Captain Codari's voice came over the comm. "This is to reassure you that everything is going smoothly here so far. We are about to enter our parking orbit. We're concerned, of course, that we've not made contact with any beings on this planet."

Rosa said, "We intend to keep trying, Captain. Can we lend you any assistance?"

"Thank you, but no. Much of Cetronen tech is very specific to our physiology, and require four hands guided by a single brain to be operated properly. And Captain -- "

"Yes?"

"Our comm is about to go offline, and it will look as if we've had massive systems failures. But that's just a precursor to our repair effort. Please don't worry about us. We still have enough power to launch a shuttle to you. Natai will be aboard, and he should travel with you down to Vuraso."

"Do you think that's wise?" Rosa asked. "Isn't he needed on board to help you with repairs?"

"I can spare him. And although I anticipate that your crew will be its usual efficient self, I insist that a Cetronen be a part of the landing party."

"Of course," Rosa said.

"I can hear and understand your hesitation even through the translation, Captain Sandage...Rosa. But remember I am still the commander of this mission. One last thing -- you should ask Ambassador Song for more information about this planet."

A statement which brought utter silence to the *Asaph Hall*'s bridge. *What the hell does that mean?* Mike wondered.

Rosa broke the silence: "Captain Codari, please explain."

"Speak to your ambassa...SKKWWRRK."

Mike took an involuntary step toward the viewscreen, as if he could walk toward *Cerenam* and give assistance. Then he could only watch helplessly as, one by one, all of *Cerenam*'s running lights went out.

CHAPTER NINETEEN

Mike rushed to the sensor console as Rosa was saying, "This is Captain Sandage to *Cerenam*. Captain Codari, do you read?"

Mike took readings on *Cerenam* as quickly as he could. "Near as I can tell, everything's shutting down over there. Propulsion, weapons -- "

"Life support?" Rosa asked.

"Hanging in so far. But it looks like it's just barely there."

"Get us closer," Rosa told Alice, at nav. To Rishona, she said, "Prep the *Egg*."

Rishona asked, "We're headed over to *Cerenam*?"

"No. You heard Codari. You're going down to Vuraso."

"But you see their ship," Mike said. "How can we -- "

"How can we do exactly what Codari asks? He's right -- he is in command. He made it very clear what was about to happen to *Cerenam*, and what he expected of us. Rosa touched behind her left ear. "Lauren, get our ambassador up here right now. I think she's up to it." She asked Rishona, "Why are you still here?"

Rishona gave Mike a pleading look that let him know she'd want to hear the whole story of what was about to be said. Mike nodded (he hoped imperceptibly except to her), and she left.

Moments later, Teresa came onto the bridge. Mike was struck by how confidently Teresa strode through the doorway, shoulders back, looking at everyone as if she were suddenly in charge. Everything went still for a moment, as everyone's attention turned toward her.

A harsh look from Rosa toward Darwin and Alice, and they returned their attention to their instruments, at least outwardly. She gathered Mike and Teresa to her at the rear of the bridge. Rosa stepped close to Teresa, stared her down. "Why," she asked, "do I get the idea I'm not going to like this?"

"Captain Codari told me many of us -- Humans, that is -- have excellent instincts for grasping at the truth."

Mike said, "Which tells me the truth has been in scarce supply."

Teresa's eyes flashed anger. "Captain Codari has never lied to you, and never will. But certain truths were...set aside."

"You sound as if you've been speaking to him regularly -- beyond that awful banquet...and Linna's funeral."

"I have."

Rosa said, "Why would Codari approach you?"

Teresa pointed at Mike. "Blame *him*. Captain Codari wanted to learn of anything important he discovered as he met with the other species in this fleet. But he never received a single report."

"So much for passing that test," Mike said. He asked Teresa, "How the hell did you know about that?"

"I've been in touch with him the entire time. A private datalink, subspace tightbeam. Transmissions Human tech can't pick up. Now, though, I can't raise him."

Rosa asked, "When could you have had that installed?"

"During the banquet."

Mike said, "Dammit, I know when they did it, too. Natai's major touched you on the shoulder as you were sitting down."

"Exactly." Teresa touched her left hand to her right shoulder. "Right about here."

Rosa told Mike, "When we're done here, take her to Lauren, find that link -- and take it out of her."

"I protest!" Teresa said. "I was within my rights -- "

"Not when it jeopardizes my ship, you weren't."

Mike said, "Rosa, our ambassador here has been through plenty of medical procedures and testing here before her son's birth. If nothing detected it before, Lauren might not be able to set her nanotech extractors on it to lift it out."

Rosa said, "I don't care if she uses a dull knife. I want it out!" Bringing her attention back to Teresa, she asked, "So what the hell is so important here at Vuraso?"

Teresa looked around at them all, and Mike could tell Rosa was about to explode again when the ambassador finally spoke. "The Cetronen always intended to explore this system. In fact, for the Cetronen, Vuraso and not the Moruteb system was always their primary goal."

"Codari made that clear. But why? What's here?"

Teresa looked around as if she were going to say something filthy. Mike couldn't help leaning closer, and noticed Rosa was, too. "They believe another intelligent symbiont species may exist here."

Now Mike understood. *The Cetronen Holy Grail, perhaps waiting for them on Vuraso! No wonder they intended to come here.* "How do you know that?" he asked.

"The Cetronen sent a long-range automated probe here to Vuraso last year. It detected life that the Cetronen believes to be paired."

"*Believes* to be?" Rosa asked.

"The probe started to fail just before touching down. It destroyed itself as a precaution. But it detected enough lifesigns to know paired beings exist here. They may have just been animals, but that only made not knowing that much more unbearable."

"It adds up," Rosa said. "Our goals on this mission have been as much political as scientific. We wanted better relations with other Galactic species. All those other species had their motives, too."

Mike said, "All this is damn coincidental, don't you think? Three of the four Galactic species on this trip thinking they're going to find some great revelation about themselves?"

"A coincidence not borne out by the results," Rosa said. "The Drodusarel were wrong about the ribbons. The Sobrenians were wrong about their precursors. Myths and superstition drive even advanced Galactic species if they're strong enough within their cultures."

"I get it. When you're headed into uncharted territory, you fill it ahead of time with whatever you're most eager to find." *And what was I looking for here? Mike wondered, and have I found even the slightest bit of it? Oh, Linna....*

Rosa asked Teresa, "So why hide all this from us in the first place?"

Teresa said, "Most Cetronen won't speak of it to outworlders."

Rosa's tone was bitter: "Singleton outworlders, you mean."

Teresa looked defiantly at Rosa. "Codari admitted as much to me. Humans travel to the stars, and we see beings much like ourselves. The Sobrenians. Garotethans. The Arols. Two arms and legs, a single head. Complete unto ourselves. It wasn't like that for the Cetronen. The Drodusarel were their first contact. The methane-breathers were different enough from them in so many ways that they thought nothing of them being singletons. But their next contact was with the Sobrenians. Then they saw the pattern."

Mike said, "This really means so much to them?"

"They see it as a trick the universe is paying on them -- no other intelligent symbiont species. And there's a point to it -- they've heard the humor at their expense."

Mike felt his face grow warm as he remembered his words months ago to Georges, who had been concerned that since the *Asaph Hall* was running late for its rendezvous, that the Cetronen must be "beside themselves" waiting. And Mike had replied that as paired symbionts, they were always "beside themselves."

Teresa said, "Codari would never have told you of the hurt those comments cause, but he told me."

How would Linna advise me right now? Mike wondered. Would she pull me aside and tell me how sincere Teresa was, and how we needed to treat her emotionalism seriously and not just dismiss it because it sounded silly?

Or would she say Teresa's fencing with us, it's all bullshit to get us to go along with whatever she wants?

But goddam it, Linna isn't here anymore. I've got to trust my own instincts.

Mike said, "Either way, Codari's not going anywhere until we find out whether this world has intelligent pairs."

Teresa said, "A search I want to help with."

"*No*," Mike said, firmly enough that he even surprised himself. He told Rosa, "Begging your pardon, Captain, I know crew assignments are your prerogative. But I assume I'm leading the mission down there...."

"A good assumption," Rosa said.

"And I'm not going with someone who's demonstrated her inexperience on so many levels."

"Agreed," Rosa said, "Besides, you'll have a baby to nurse pretty soon. He'll be coming out of that artificial uterine fluid as soon as we can manage it."

"She's right," Mike said. "Your first responsibility is to your child."

"You just don't want me with you," Teresa said.

"Thank goodness," Mike told her. "You finally figured it out."

Rosa said, "That's enough." She told Teresa," Go back to your quarters. I'll send Lauren there to search for that Cetronen link."

"I protest this, Captain Sandage."

"Protest away -- if it weren't for your child, I'd as soon let you take a walk outside without a lifesuit."

Teresa held her head up high and left the bridge.

Alice said, "Captain -- look at *Cerenam* -- near the tops of the mushroom."

They all looked, and Mike was heartened to see that a large hatch on the side of the Cetronen craft was opening, though very slowly. "I bet that's a manual hatch," Mike said.

Rosa squinted at the viewscreen. "Which means Natai will be on his way in mere moments, after all." She spoke to Mike in a quieter voice. "You don't have to go down there. Codari -- and, I'm sure, Natai -- are obsessed with this idea of finding another paired, sentient species. But his obsession isn't ours."

"It's what Captain Codari wants," Mike said. "He's calling the shots."

"He's in charge of the mission. He doesn't make crew decisions for my ship."

"He assumed I was going, though."

"Yeah."

"I have the most experience making first contacts. And he came to trust me at Moruteb."

"I know he did," Rosa said.

"He made it clear he wants us to scout this world for a more extensive mission led by the Cetronen later on. So I'm going. The sooner I get us there and back, the sooner we leave." He started for the exit.

Rosa's voice was barely audible. "You've got to..." Mike paused as the door slid open. His captain's features were torn with grief. "You're the best, Mike. But you had Linna to help you for a long time. You've got to think of how she would react. What she would tell you."

Mike's throat felt as if it were about to close, and he cleared it with a quiet cough. "I've barely been able to think of anything else," he said, and went through the doorway and toward the hangar deck.

CHAPTER TWENTY

The shuttlecraft *Cosmic Egg* hurtled through the planet Vuraso's atmosphere, entering thick cloud cover at about five thousand meters above the surface. Mike piloted and Georges Remy sat in the right-hand seat, the co-pilot's position. Behind them sat Rishona Kwan and, squeezed into a seat made for Humans, the Cetronen paired symbiont Natai. Luther Kindred and Katarina Diop sat behind them in jump seats next to the cargo bay.

Mike leveled off about two thousand meters above Vuraso's surface. Georges kept track of their surroundings with constant sensor readings. "About to break out of cloud cover," he said. Sure enough, the *Egg* burst from beneath the clouds. The jungle less than a thousand meters below stood thick and lush, a blur of countless shades of green and blue, reflecting the fact that Vuraso's primary shone brighter than Sol, and the local foliage reflected most yellow and red shades.

Mike slowed the shuttle as they approached the landing spot they'd picked from orbit, and the jungle resolved into more detail. He glimpsed slim trees thirty or forty meters tall. *They meet my criteria for defining themselves as trees*, he thought. *They're tall plants. A biologist might disagree.*

The trees reached thirty or forty meters and formed thick canopies over much of the landscape. But in alternating patterns, broad-leafed plant species had captured wide swaths of the landscape for themselves, extruding vines that strangled any treelings that might attempt to encroach upon their territory, creating clearings among the forested areas. Mike wondered what the ecological advantage to that arrangement might be.

Natai's minor asked, "Do you see any lifeforms? I have to know if they're pairs."

Georges said, "I can detect some beings -- possibly animals, about a meter long, warm-blooded -- but I don't see anything. The noise from the shuttle might've scared them into hiding, though." He asked Natai, "Why does this business of the pairs mean so much to you, anyway?"

"This is a crucial part of Cetronen psychology," Natai said. According to mythology, the desert god Itherin split us in two, making us more than -- begging your pardon -- mere singletons, which are all animals on our world."

Mike took a quick glance at Georges, and it was plain he wished he'd never asked the question. "Final approach," Mike said. He eased the *Egg* onto Vuraso's surface beneath the morning sun.

Mike powered down the shuttle and collected his gear -- stunner in a holster on his right hip, and medical equipment, water bottles, and rations in a small backpack. They'd count on their lifesuits to activate and protect them against anything from animal attacks to enemy fire. Sensors had already told them the air was breathable.

"Everyone ready?" Mike asked. Several of them shared glances, then nodded toward Mike. "Let's go then -- I'm out first, Luther right behind checking our perimeter. Natai does sensor sweeps on possible threats from animal life, Rishona does plant life, Georges scans for any beings who might be intelligent or mechanisms that might have detected us. Got it?"

Again, nods all around. As everyone else gathered around the airlock, Katarina moved toward the pilot's position. She would remain on the *Cosmic Egg*, ready to lift off and snatch them out of danger if needed, back to *Asaph Hall*.

Mike cycled through the *Cosmic Egg*'s airlock. He made himself pause. *I've got to focus on what I'm doing, like it or not, he thought. If I get careless, someone else could die.*

He opened the outer airlock. With Mike's first breaths of Vuraso's air and first steps upon its soil, the planet instantly evoked much of its nature: he perceived an impressive complexity of smells, glimpsed dozens of different plant species, and walked across rich black soil in a grav field about a quarter higher than Earth's -- just enough to make their journey tiring and laborious. But like Earth's rain forests, this was an ecologist's dream, a place you could spend decades studying and still have more questions than answers.

Georges came up to Mike and said, "No threats, far as I can tell, from anything intelligent or created by intelligence."

Rishona was next up. "Plant life's generally benign -- that's not to say we shouldn't be careful. That means don't touch anything without checking it out, and certainly don't eat anything just because it looks tasty. And the usual, you know, being careful of thorns, that kind of thing."

Natai spoke up: "The same would apply for animal life -- taking care. Large animals that could be predators are within several hundreds of meters of our position, although most of them are headed away from us."

"The shuttle spooked them, then," Mike said.

"Part of that did not translate, but I believe I take your meaning. Also, I suspect some smaller animals could be masters of camouflage. And life chemistry here on Vuraso seems such that its animals could find nourishment from either Humans or Cetronen."

"Well," Mike said. "That's reassuring."

Natai said, "On the positive side, our stunners should be effective here, as well."

Mike touched behind his left ear as he waved toward Katarina, who was at the *Egg*'s pilot's position. "Mike Christopher to Katarina. Go to secure mode."

An energy dome instantly encased the shuttle. It would keep away any threats from plant or animal life and could probably withstand a couple of energy bolts if necessary. On the other hand, it was set to allow Humans and Cetronen free access. That was in case they had to make it back to the shuttle on the run. Over their datalinks, Katarina said, "See you soon."

Another wave to Katarina, a confident smile, but Mike's thought was, *I hope.*

Luther said, "I'll take the lead if you like -- clear the way for the rest of us."

"Sounds great," Mike said, knowing that Luther was the best bet to forge a trail, with his broad, solid shoulders and his hands that looked as if they could crush a bulkhead. Mike said, "I'll take the rear," waited for Georges, Rishona, and Natai to walk ahead of him, and followed them.

Luther's job in creating a path for them was easy at first; they stepped around the broad leaves of blue ground-hugging plants and over the intertwined vines of various shades of green that filled the spaces between. Within the first kilometer, the going became rougher, and Luther resorted to pulling aside clumps of vines that reached to waist-level as he cleared a path.

Another half a click on, and Luther led the way beneath their first tree canopy -- one so thick it took a moment for Mike's eyes to adjust to the lower light, and he guessed the temperature dropped by three or four degrees. Rishona kept making constant scans, which Mike felt was becoming distracting.

Sunlight was diffused through the canopy, giving their surroundings an aura of mystery. The very shapes of the trees, which Mike thought should have been thicker and more low-set than Earthly ones, but which turned out to be thinner, yet barely moved in the occasional breeze, hinted at wonders waiting, secrets unspoken.

A sudden movement right in front of Mike's face, and he squinted and waved his left hand in front of him. A cloud of insects, each about the size of a thumbnail, hovered in front of him. In turn, they reacted much less randomly to Mike's attempts to swat them than Earthly insects would -- they backed away from him as a clearly defined group, forming and re-forming themselves as if by thoughtful strategy.

Then one landed on his left hand.

He made himself hold that hand steady, and not give in to the instinct to flick it off or smash it with his other hand.

The insect had five legs, with the "extra" one apparently touching down first on approach, feeling the way for the rear legs, then the front legs, to set down. It had a bulbous torso and a pointy head with two eyes -- eyes which not only weren't compound, but stared right at him and blinked. Mike blinked back, especially when a closer look told him the tiny creature's torso wasn't as bulbous as he'd thought. That realization came when an even tinier head rose up from the other side of the insect, followed by a distinctly separate body.

This insect was a paired creature -- just what Natai was looking for!

Mike realized everyone else had stopped and was looking at him. The rest of the insects were gone. "Natai," he said, and the Cetronen started slowly toward Mike, clearly not wanting to frighten the insect away.

Suddenly the insect made a quick move as if to sting him, and Mike flinched even as his lifesuit nano generated a tiny patch of armor to protect him. The insect was gone in an instant.

"Why did you do that?" Natai's minor asked.

"That rear leg turned out to be a stinger, too."

"Are you hurt?"

"No, my lifesuit kept it from stinging me."

"Was that insect a pair?"

"It was."

"That is exciting, Mike! Please tell me you share that excitement!"

"What I can share is the desire to find out what you need to know, then get on our way. Besides, I thought animals were singletons on your world."

"They are. So if even the animals are paired here, imagine what truly sentient beings must be like."

Mike knew better than to protest that Natai's conclusion didn't follow. "Let's keep going."

They formed their line in the same order as before and began their trek once again. Mike had just gotten into the rhythm of walking, so important in a higher-grav world, when Rishona reacted in surprise to one of her readings. *That damn scanner*, he thought. *Someday she's going to be making a long-distance scan and fall into a pit right in front of her.*

Mike saw her pass up Georges to catch up to Luther, who stopped to talk to her. As everyone else gathered around, Mike asked, "What's the problem?"

"Another native lifeform. In that stand of trees just ahead. Bigger."

"Define 'bigger,'" Mike said.

"About half again as tall as you."

Natai's minor spoke up: "Can you tell if it's a pair?"

Mike couldn't think when he'd been more exasperated. "Enough of that. Let's see what we can find out."

Luther said, "I'll move that way."

"Just be careful." To Natai, he said, "Pay more attention to what we're doing than to whether something's a pair."

Luther started forward without looking to see whether Natai followed. He did. Rishona and Georges fell into line, with Mike bringing up the rear again.

A few steps into the stand of trees, and Mike only caught glimpses of Luther and Natai as they made their way deeper into the foliage, the only sound the occasional crackling sound of dried vegetation beneath their feet. The higher grav made it more difficult to proceed with stealth -- heavier footsteps, swifter-falling debris.

Mike lost sight of them as they continued into a thicker region of the forest. He became aware of sounds he hadn't noticed earlier -- trees swaying slowly back and forth in the far distance under stronger winds than earlier, what sounded like the cawing of a bird overhead. *I wonder*, he thought, *if those sounds were there all along and I simply hadn't noticed, or if some of them are caused by animals making their way back to their accustomed habitats after the* Egg *scared them off.* He looked ahead -- Georges and Rishona were still in front of him.

Then -- a commotion just ahead, a rapid rustling between the trees, footsteps approaching rapidly.

Instinctively, Mike drew his stunner. If something had attacked Luther and Natai before they could shout an alarm --

Then over his datalink, Mike heard Natai's minor's breathless voice: "Help -- we've been attacked."

Adrenaline rushing, heart furiously pumping, Mike rushed forward. He squeezed through an especially tight mass of vines and saw Natai's minor, separated from his major, running toward him through the woods.

Under different circumstances it may have been a comic sight, this thin, wiry being barely a meter tall running a zig-zag course between trees and over clusters of vines, his thin tail flipping back and forth as if acting like a rudder.

The minor reached Mike, caught his breath, and pointed back the way he'd come. "They attacked...both of us," he said, and nearly collapsed against Mike, his arms barely reaching Mike's waist.

Mike reached down and lifted the minor as he would have a seven-year-old Human child. He handed him over to Georges, saying, "Stay with him, see if he needs medical help. Rishona, you're with me." He touched behind his left ear to activate his datalink. "Luther, do you copy?"

No response. Mike proceeded quickly past another thicket, and saw a large form lying between two trees. *The major*, he realized. A quick check with his wrist sensor, and he saw the larger of the Cetronen pair was alive. *But if something here could take him down*, he thought, *then Luther could be in extreme danger.*

Not to mention the rest of us.

Mike halted, looked all around, looked overhead, and realized he was only seconds away from panic. He forced that feeling down and lifted his left arm to keep his implanted wrist scanner in sight as he swept 360 degrees with his stunner. "Directly east," he told Rishona. "About forty meters. Human lifesigns -- and something else."

Rishona got her portable scanner out for a more detailed reading as Mike kept his stunner pointed in that direction. All he could see was more of the strange trees, bushes, and vines -- no Luther.

Rishona didn't say anything for a moment that seemed to hang indefinitely. "Com'on," Mike said. "What've you got? We won't be helping Luther if we walk right into the same danger he did."

She looked up from the scanner. "Here he comes," she said.

Sure enough, in the distance, it *was* Luther. Mike started forward, but Rishona grabbed his arm and held on tight. "*No*," she said.

Mike started to protest, but Rishona's expression made him stop. "What is it?" he asked.

Rishona released Mike's arm and worked her scanner furiously. "Something's wrong -- the Human readings and the...the *other* readings -- they're all mixed together."

"Other readings? What other readings?"

Rishona's expression held an urgency he'd never seen from her before. "Another kind of being -- perhaps native -- mixed in with Luther's."

Mike didn't know what any of that meant, but knew only one way to find out. "OK, enough with the scanner, put it away. Keep your stunner on Luther." Mike hung his own stunner back on his belt.

"But -- why would I shoot Luther -- ?"

"I hope you don't have to."

Rishona raised the stunner and steadied herself. "I'm ready," she said.

"Good job," Mike said, and stepped forward. As he advanced toward Luther, more of the large insects he'd seen earlier swarmed around his face. He swatted them away -- *god*dam *those things*, he thought -- and kept going.

Luther was within twenty meters now, still walking methodically forward. *Something* had happened to him -- blood smeared his face, his clothing was ripped in several places, and he was walking with an odd, hesitant gait, like a toddler taking his first steps.

Mike called out, "Luther! Are you hurt?" Mike wanted to believe that Luther couldn't really have been harmed -- his lifesuit, after all, should've snapped on and protected him from any attack.

But Luther didn't reply, and his expression didn't change. In fact, his eyes didn't even appear to be looking in the direction he was walking.

Mike took a couple more steps forward. *Luther's eyes,* he realized, *are staring in different directions.*

Only ten meters separated them now. And Mike realized now something even odder about Luther's gait. *His legs aren't bending at the knees,* he thought. *His arms aren't bending, either. It's as if his body is...draped over something else.*

Mike pulled his stunner again and moved quickly to his left. Luther pivoted around, more quickly than Mike would've expected, given his methodical movements so far.

Rishona exclaimed, "Oh, my God!"

Without thinking, Mike looked toward Rishona, saw her anguished expression -- and saw her bringing her stunner up to bear on Luther.

Suddenly Luther's body was cast aside like a paper in the wind and from behind it a being that somehow was half again his height rushed at Mike with unbelievable speed.

Mike was just bringing his own stunner to bear and had a quick impression of onrushing body, teeth, and tail, when Rishona's stunner flashed.

The creature, no longer propelled by his own thick, muscular legs but only by his own inertia, knocked Mike flat onto his back. Now he had an even more visceral impression, one of giant jaws filled with teeth as long as his hand, and of breath that came from a centuries-old sewer. As for the rest of the creature's body, he was mostly aware that it was damn heavy.

Mike got his hands beneath the predator's body and pushed. Rishona leaned over them both and pulled. Together they rolled the stunned creature off him. Somehow it really was larger than Luther, complete with a ridge of bone along its back and a tail, apparently for balance, nearly a meter long. Its skin was gray, smooth, and slick.

"You OK?" Rishona asked.

Mike couldn't help but grin. "Surprised I'm not dead, mostly. Thanks for taking him out."

Rishona put away her pistol and pointed back the way the creature had come.

Toward Luther. Mike's grin faded and he couldn't help dreading every step that brought them closer to their friend.

Or what was left of him. Now he understood Rishona's exclamation before she fired.

All that was remained of Luther was the front of his body, lying before them like the mutilated remains of a rag doll. The creature had ripped Luther's face and hair from his skull to create a mask, eviscerated him from behind, and worn his arms, legs, and the front of his body like a macabre Halloween disguise.

Mike told Rishona, "I'm amazed that thing fooled us even for a second."

"We saw what we wanted to see," Rishona said. "Uh, Mike, here's one thing I'm not sure I want to know, but...where's the rest of Luther?"

Mike indicated the stunned creature. "Inside this one, I suspect."

"There's something similar on Earth," Rishona said, and got out her scanner again, set it to library function, made a quick search. "Here we go," she said. "It's like a crab spider. Found in South America."

"They do something like this?"

"On a much smaller scale. They, well, eat the insides of an ant's body, then wear it. That way it looks and even smells like its prey -- attracting even more of it."

"Goddam it," Mike said. So many emotions swirled within him -- guilt, regret, an undercurrent of fear -- that for a moment he didn't feel he could cope with all of them.

But his next thought -- *Linna always did.* She coped with her own emotions and everyone else's. Mike clamped down on his feelings so they faded to a mere distraction, something to be dealt with later, at whatever cost.

Georges and a reunited Natai headed toward them. *The major must've just been knocked out for a moment*, Mike thought.

Georges' eyes went wide with horror when he saw the limp pile of flesh next to Mike and Rishona that represented Luther's remains. Natai's minor took that in, but the major quickly moved on, carrying the minor toward the creature that had killed Luther. As far as Mike could tell, the major was completely recovered. *Though, underneath that fur*, he thought, *he could be pretty banged up. And a major's expression seldom varies, anyway.*

Georges asked, "How did that...*thing* penetrate Luther's lifesuit?"

"Don't know," Mike said. "That isn't a capability this kind of being should have. Anyone with a tech solution to that wouldn't have to forage for game."

Natai was kneeling down and examining the creature that had killed Luther. Mike went to Natai as the major stood. The minor's deep-set eyes were wide with excitement. "This is so exciting. This being is a pair!"

CHAPTER TWENTY-ONE

Mike swallowed his anger and said as gently as he could, "I'm sorry, Natai. I understand this is important to you. But...."

"No, I must ask you to forgive me," Natai's minor said. "You've lost a dear friend. I meant no disrespect."

"None taken," Mike said, but he was lying. He looked down at the creature. "How do you know it's a pair?"

Natai's major kneeled again and the minor leaned forward and indicated two orifices on the being's back, one on either side of the top of its ridge of bone. "These are very similar to structures we Cetronen minors have on our backsides. You seldom see them because of our fur." The minor stood up on the major's hump and started to turn around.

Mike said, "I'll take your word for it. I think our first priority is to get back to the shuttle. But isn't this being much too large to be a minor?"

"That's correct, Mike. This is, indeed, the major. But this species carries the minor on its back."

Georges asked, "Then where's the minor?"

"An interesting question," Natai's minor said. "I suspect somewhere close by. If he's anything like a Cetronen minor, he's bound emotionally with the major -- and knows the major is only stunned, not dead."

"I don't care about any of that. We need to head back."

Rishona, in the middle of one of her eternal scans, said, "I think...he's right behind me -- no, *don't look*. About thirty meters."

Without shifting posture or changing tone of voice, Mike said, "Let's get ready, then. We'll be safer going on the offense.

I'll go left, Georges, go right. Rishona and Natai, up the middle. Ready?"

Nods all around, except for Natai, but Mike assumed he understood, as well. Mike said, "*Go.*"

Mike ran to the left of the spot Rishona said should be the minor's hiding place. He was aware out of the corner of his eye that the others were running in their assigned directions.

There -- a being barely taller than Natai's minor dove from beneath a clump of bushes and bounded away from them in a series of leaps powered by thin but obviously strong legs. He also used his tail to push off in the same instant his legs did, adding both speed and distance to each leap.

In the higher grav, Mike was already breathing hard and his side was starting to hurt. *Damn*, he thought, *I didn't want to do this*. He got out his stunner, set it on wide beam, and fired.

The being went limp and tumbled to the ground.

Natai was first to reach this part of the Vurasoan pair. Mike thought, *I don't know if Natai's a spiritual being, but this has to be close to a religious experience for him.*

When Mike caught up to Natai, he leaned over and stood with hands on his knees, catching his breath. As Georges and Rishona came up to them, he said, "Georges, I'd like you to go back to that major -- feel free to walk -- and keep an eye on him. If he looks like he's waking up, stun him again."

Georges asked, "Then what?"

"Just wait for us. We'll bring the minor in a few minutes." Georges nodded and left.

"What about me?" Rishona asked.

"You're doing a great job with the scanner. Keep it up, I suppose."

Rishona's face reddened. "I think it...makes me feel secure."

"Well, make sure we *are* secure. Gimme a long-range scan for more beings like these or anything else that might be dangerous."

"I'll get right to it," Rishona said.

Mike turned his attention to the Vurasoan minor. He was surprised to see that Natai's minor had jumped down from his major -- a rarity, seen twice in one day! -- and was examining the being.

As with Cetronen paired symbionts, the Vurasoan was a smaller version of his major -- slick gray skin with that ridge of bone along the back, but only about a meter tall. Natai's minor said, "Look at these hands." The being had six fingers spread equidistantly around the palm of his hand. Mike supposed various combinations of those fingers fit into the orifices on the major's back.

Natai's minor continued: "An ingenious way for evolution to construct a pair. Imagine if primitive Cetronen enjoyed such capabilities -- accompanying your major on reconnaissance missions, leading him into battle -- the possibilities are endless! Mike, you look skeptical."

"There are disadvantages, too. A predator who's able to sneak up from behind could kill the minor more easily."

Natai's minor said, "There are certainly advantages to both biological systems."

Mike hesitated -- *Should I pursue this?* he wondered. *It may be like casting doubt on someone's religion or politics. What the hell -- forge ahead.* "Natai, don't sell your own people short."

"Failure to translate?"

"Uh...be glad for who you are and what you are, and don't worry about other Galactic species. We are what evolution made us, in every case."

"A fine thought, Mike. For now, though, I will be happy to know there are others like us in Galactic society."

Enough philosophy, I guess, Mike thought. "Let's take this minor back over to be near his major when he wakes up. I don't want to leave Georges alone for long, and we're *got* to get out of here."

Natai's major picked up the native minor and effortlessly slung him over his shoulder. Natai's minor scrambled back into his accustomed spot on his major's hump.

Mike touched behind his left ear. "Georges, you OK?"

"Just fine," came the response. "I've been scanning pretty regularly. Rishona's got nothing on me."

"How's that major?"

"Still asleep. You're just coming into sight."

"Keep alert." Mike pressed on through the woods, skirting more thick clumps of foliage. *Each step's a struggle*, he thought. *This planet's higher grav is wearing me down.*

And besides the physical exertion, I have to wonder how much I can bear emotionally. Linna dies. Luther dies. Who's next? My only consolation is that I'm more worried about the others than about myself. I'm at a point where I'd gladly place myself in danger to save any of them, and death would almost be a relief.

Nothing brave about it. Linna would understand. She'd look right at me and tell me I was too much of a coward to want to live. Not if it meant living with so much death and grief.

Even exploration -- and I suppose this mission counts -- isn't bringing me any satisfaction. And that's what I've always lived for, even as starcraft crews became my only family. What if I never get that back?

For a moment, he fought to keep images of Linna's gentle hands, the freshly showered smell of her skin, the sight of her body propelled toward a ravaged world, in that safe place where all such memories were walled off.

Then he realized he was nearing the spot where Luther had died. He walked past Georges without speaking and looked down again on Luther's pitiful remains.

Georges asked, "What about this being?"

Mike said, "By the time it wakes up, we should be long gone."

Georges looked Mike in the eye. "What if it starts stalking us again?"

"Do you intend to kill it just like that?"

"That might feel pretty good," Georges said. "And wherever Luther is, it might give him some comfort."

"Luther's dead. He's past comfort. This is a native of this planet just trying to feed or defend himself, and we're intruding upon him. I'm willing to kill to defend myself or others, but not in cold blood. At least not yet."

Natai asked Mike, "Do you believe this is an intelligent being or a mere animal?"

"I don't know about your people, Natai, but mine have concluded the difference between sentience and 'mere animals' is more a matter of degree than of kind."

Natai looked down at the unconscious bodies of the Vurasoan paired symbiont. "I want to take this specimen back with us."

"Absolutely not," Mike said. As Natai started to object, he said, "Either we would be taking a dangerous being back on board with us, or we'd have to kill it. You and Rishona should take as many readings as you can, and I can rationalize a couple tissue samples. But that's it. I'm calling Katarina, and she'll pick us up."

That's when Mike felt something touch his shoulder.

And Rishona pulled out her stunner and shot him.

CHAPTER TWENTY-TWO

Mike was impressed with how much of a role instinct still played in Human responses. Of course you can't dodge an energy bolt flashing toward you at the speed of light. Of course it was only a stunner.

Of course his lifesuit snapped on even before the stunner blast could strike his body.

He still ducked.

And in ducking, lost his balance, especially since *something* was behind him, grabbing onto him and pulling him to the ground.

Then it let go.

Still encased in the lifesuit, Mike pulled himself up and turned to see what had grabbed him.

Rishona said, "I *had* to shoot -- "

Then he saw.

The "crab spider," reunited and unconscious once again.

"Rishona..." Mike realized he was speaking through the lifesuit comm. A touch of his left middle finger to his palm, and the suit snapped off. A glance downward at that hand, and he saw it was shaking. He balled it into a fist, willing it to stop. He told Rishona, "You saved my life. If you hadn't shot it...."

"It just came up right behind you, out of nowhere. I never saw it move. I knew your lifesuit would protect you from the stunner."

"At least now we know how it killed Luther. It moved toward me slowly enough that the lifesuit didn't perceive it as a threat. I felt it touch my shoulder just before you shot it -- and me. "

Natai's minor pulled out his stunner. The weapon was tiny in his hands, like a child's plaything. He made an adjustment to its settings, fired and the "crab spider" disintegrated, becoming dust that the breeze blew into a fine mist. "Humans are too sentimental," the minor said. He told Mike, "I suppose you will object."

Mike stood with his hands at his sides, in part because they were still shaking and he didn't want to draw attention to them. "No. I won't." Mike heard a low rumbling to the west. "Uh-oh." The noise grew louder and he could feel the ground vibrating.

Rishona was checking her scanner again. "Lifeforms -- *lots* of them."

Mike said, "Define 'lots.'"

"Maybe a hundred or more -- and *big*."

"*Rishona* -- "

"I know! Big means about three meters long -- all headed this way."

Mike took a deep breath and touched behind his ear. "Katarina -- we need a pickup *now*!"

"Lifting!" came the response from the *Egg* as Mike looked up a gentle slope ahead of them. "Let's get as high up as we can," he said. "We have to hope they'll take the path of least resistance."

Everyone gathered next to Mike, who placed himself behind one of the wider trees at the top of the hill. *This would be comical if it weren't so dangerous*, he thought. *The four of us -- or, with Natai, would that be five? -- lined up like we're going to a cube show.*

The trees farthest to the west began to shake, then sway from side to side. The vibrations traveling through the earth became a visceral force in themselves, as if threatening to toss them off the planet.

The trees parted, and Rishona's hand clasped his shoulder, *hard*, but he barely noticed.

The approaching creatures were quadrupeds, brown-furred on top, tan on the bottom, thick-bodied and about the size of a Cetronen major. Their slender heads were topped with a swept back crown of bone, and their tapered tails sported stripes of black and orange fur as well as the brown and tan. *They're almost cute*, Mike thought, incongruously. *They've got their little striped tails, and little bony crowns.*

Vegetation flew all around as the quadrupedal beings roared past, and a cloud of dust obscured much of the landscape. Many of the larger beings, however, forced smaller ones into one another, and that quickly resulted in a pileup. Several twisted their heads around in anger to slam their crests into one another.

Mike saw more than one of the creatures raise their tails straight up and wave them around. *Like semaphores*, Mike thought. Those with their tails held high quickly gathered others around them, and with sharp-toothed snarls they diverted the path of the rest of the herd around the pileup.

The pounding of hooves faded, slowly. Rishona looked up from her sensorpac. "What about those tails going back and forth? And those bright colors -- I never expected something like that. I suppose it's to get the other creatures' attention."

In the sudden silence, Mike was aware once again of very sound, every movement. Out of the corner of his eye he saw something that gained his immediate attention.

As that something slammed against the back of his head and he fell to the ground.

All around him was cacophony -- screaming, stunner fire, the whistling of projectiles whipping through the air.

He looked up and saw Georges firing his stunner. Rishona was right next to him, apparently trying to find a clear shot.

Natai's major fought hand-to-hand with a being -- the same kind of Vurasoan lifeform they'd just seen, the same thick hide, the same dinosaur-like shield of bone, even the "cute" tail. But it fought as a biped, not a quadruped.

Mike raised himself to hands and knees, then touched behind his ear even as he saw two more such bipedal beings approaching. He pulled out his stunner as another Vurasoan rushed toward him, this one definitely a quadruped. He squeezed the trigger.

His shot struck the Vurasoan on the bony shield, and Mike was surprised to see it had little effect. The Vurasoan stopped about five meters away, stood on his hind legs, reached into a pouch at his waist, and tossed a fist-sized stone at Mike. The accuracy of that throw was extraordinary -- the stone struck Mike's hand and his stunner went flying as Mike groaned in pain. He scrambled across the ground to retrieve the stunner as the stone bounced a couple of times and rolled to a halt.

Two tiny eyes on the stone opened and stared at him for just an instant, before it sprouted short, thin legs and ran back in the direction of the Vurasoan who'd thrown it.

"The hell?" was all Mike managed to say before another living stone struck him in the side. He ignored that sharp pain, grabbed his stunner from the ground, and got to his feet even as he heard the Vurasoan charging him again.

This time the being was on all fours again, so close Mike could hear the *huffing* of his breath and the pounding of his broad feet. Mike got the stunner up and fired in the instant before he would've been run down.

The shot struck the Vurasoan in his left shoulder just as Mike did a quick sidestep. The Vurasoan's body plowed into the ground, its bony shield cutting a furrow in the dirt.

As Mike was just getting his bearings, another stunner blast made him duck. He saw Rishona standing over the apparently stunned body of one of the "living stones," confirming that it was organic rather than some form of rock.

Mike took in his surroundings. Natai's major stood at the center of a circle about five meters across that he'd apparently cleared for himself -- the prone forms of three Vurasoans testified to that.

Georges and Rishona were standing with their backs to one another, stunners at the ready, in case more of these beings charged them. As for the remaining "living stones" lying on the ground, they'd become dormant, giving the impression of truly being cold, hard rocks rather than lifeforms.

The Vurasoan Mike had shot began to stand up. *I've never seen anyone recover so quickly from a stunner bolt,* he thought as the being took his quadrupedal stance. *He was pretty impressive earlier coming at me on all fours, too, just as all those others were during their stampede. It gave the impression of them being animals. A stupid assumption. You'd think I'd never made a first contact before. I've gotten spoiled dealing with known species whose languages are in my datalink.*

Though perhaps the thought that I was seconds away from death distracted me.

The Vurasoan's legs tensed, and Mike took aim again.

A new voice rang out, just behind the crouching Vurasoan. That being spun around to face the new arrival.

He wasn't as tall as the other Vurasoans, but was no less a commanding presence. Mike had no idea what this being was saying, but he had all the other Vurasoans' undivided attention.

The native who had charged Mike went biped now to confront the newcomer face-to-face, protesting in a loud voice and waving his arms. *Looks like some kind of power struggle,* Mike thought. *If we could only understand what they're saying, we might be able to take advantage of it.*

Finally it looked as if the newcomer had successfully stood his ground -- his challenger backed off, and went to stand next to some of his comrades who were still recovering from being repulsed by Natai.

The newcomer Vurasoan approached slowly. He was shorter and thinner than the one who'd attacked Mike. His small eyes stared directly at him as if taking his measure. His face was flat by Human standards; his mouth was a mere slit, without lips. He had no nose and no external ears, only small openings just in front of the shield of bone. Mike wondered if that shield also helped reflect sound into those openings. In all, his facial features were virtually immobile, giving the being a strange sense of reticence.

The Vurasoan looked into the sky.

Katarina, Mike thought. *'Bout time the Egg got here. And this being heard it before I did.*

A touch behind his ear, and Mike said, "Katarina, we're next to a group of locals. They were trying to fight us, but it looks like they're more curious than anything else just now. Land close as you can, without being on top of them, and stand by."

"Understood," came Katarina's response. All five Vurasoans stared in apparent disbelief as the shuttle settled into a clearing about fifty meters distant, its gravitic drive easing from a high-pitched whine to silence within moments.

The newest Vurasoan turned away from that sight, then looked toward Mike and made a series of gestures, accompanied by much head-tilting and swaying back and forth. This went on for the better part of a minute, then the Vurasoan paused and glanced around at his colleagues. Whatever their injuries, those others stood taller now, as if their leader had accomplished something grand.

Mike purposely didn't respond right away. Rishona, in a quiet voice, asked, "What are you waiting for?"

"To see and hear more. Go too fast, and I'm liable to make a gesture or give them a look they find offensive."

Natai said, "Let me try to communicate. After all, I'm the one who's a paired symbiont."

"Uh, Natai," Mike said, "it doesn't look as if these beings *are* pairs."

"Nonsense. Their minors must simply be hidden on their bodies somewhere, or were waiting at a safe distance while these majors fought us." Before Mike could stop him, the Natai major stepped past Mike as the minor held out both his little arms in greeting.

The Vurasoan leader grabbed Natai's major by his broad shoulders and started to push him aside. *As if the major were an unruly child*, Mike thought.

As he watched the Cetronen struggle to break the Vurasoan's grip, though, came the realization: *Or as if I'm a master who can't control his pet!*

"Natai," Mike said. "I suggest you stand still for a moment."

Natai's major whirled around to face Mike. The minor waggled his ears, a sign of confusion. "Why?" the minor asked.

You don't want to know, Mike thought. "Just let me try to communicate for now. You have to trust me."

The minor sat taller in the major's grasp. "Then I will."

Thank a hypothetical God for small favors, Mike thought. He drew toward the Vurasoan leader, close enough to get a good look at the bone shield and marvel at how it gradually altered to become rough skin at the being's long forehead. He took another look into those slit-like eyes. *I've encountered enough intelligent species*, he thought, *that I have a good idea when I'm face-to-face with sentien*ce.

I hope this Vurasoan perceives the same in me. Because he doesn't in Natai. And that could mean a big problem if Natai makes the wrong noise or does the wrong thing.

The Vurasoan produced a new stone from a pouch. This one, however, rather than being dull and rough, was smooth and gave off a reddish glow. The Vurasoan held it out toward Mike, who said, "Well, here's a dilemma. Does he expect me to take hold of this?"

From behind him, Georges said, "Don't touch it. You don't know what it'll do."

Rishona spoke up. "He's right. They've already attacked us once."

Mike glanced back at them. "So their backup if they can't manage a fair fight is they hand you a deadly rock?"

Georges' hand clapped onto Mike's shoulder, making him jump, then feel foolish. Georges said, "We've already lost too many of us. Luther just now. Before that -- "

" -- I *know*." *Linna was alive, but falling into the incandescent fury of a star*. Mike held out his right hand and the Vurasoan leader lowered the glowing stone toward Mike's palm. The stone's touch was, if anything, anticlimactic -- cool and smooth, no more. *I guess*, Mike thought, *I was expecting it to pierce my skin or transmit an electrical shock or something.*

The Vurasoan kept his own hand on top of the stone, while not touching Mike's. The being's eyes closed and he lifted his head toward the skies. *What's he looking for?* Mike wondered. Divine inspiration?

But in that instant, Mike realized he was feeling more predisposed toward the Vurasoan. He leaned forward while keeping his hand placed directly beneath the stone. The Vurasoan, in turn, opened his eyes and stared directly at Mike.

I can trust him, Mike thought. *I know it. I can feel his sincerity. He never meant any harm --*

Mike gasped and jerked his hand away from the stone as the Vurasoan caught it in midair. "What the hell?"

Rishona: "What is it? Are you hurt?"

Mike kept staring at the Vurasoan. "No. But he just communicated to me. Or -- maybe the stone did."

Natai's major took a step toward the Vurasoan. "Mike, if I can just have the opportunity -- "

"Stand still!" Mike told the Cetronen. "They think you're an animal."

Natai's major halted. His minor stood up on the major's hump and folded his arms. "I refuse to stand here and be insulted."

"Then just stand there. That stone transmitted an impression from this Vurasoan. What I always imagined...Linna's empathy felt like for her. It made me feel that he was trustworthy, that the attack on us was just a big mistake."

Georges said, "Don't trust it -- we have no way of telling whether it's trying to deceive us. It could've been some kind of pheromone transfer, anything."

Natai's minor sat again. "A Cetronen pair -- an animal? How could such an idea endure?"

"Here it's the animals who are pairs," Mike said.

Rishona said, "The shuttle's here. These mysteries can wait."

"We're the ones who initiated this contact."

Georges said, "Which turned violent from the start."

"All the more reason to fix it. It's our responsibility. But if any of you want to go to the shuttle and wait, fine. I'll be along quick as I can."

Natai's major said, "Perhaps these stones are themselves the pairs!"

Georges traded glances with Rishona, then said, "I'll stay."

Rishona examined her scanner's readout yet again. She said, "Each of us is responsible for all the others. I'll stick here." To Natai, she said, "They're not pairs. Even a superficial reading tells me the stones are a different species."

Mike grinned at them both, then turned back to the Vurasoan leader, still standing passively before him. *You have a lot of patience*, Mike thought. *Perhaps more than I've been capable of during this mission.*

Natai's minor emitted a very Human-sounding sigh and said, "Mike, when might I -- "

Mike said, "Shush!"

Another ear-waggle. "Failure to translate?"

"Just...be quiet another moment. Please." *Damn Cetronen single-mindedness*, he thought.

To the Vurasoan, Mike spread his arms wide, hoping that small gesture of openness would signal his desire to avoid further conflict. *Although*, he thought, *I also have to be ready to grab my stunner again if these Vurasoans have other ideas.*

The Vurasoan leader leaned his head back slightly, tilting his head and his bony shield back and forth slowly. Mike realized some of the small openings just in front of the shield that he associated with the being's ears might also represent his sense of smell.

He's literally sniffing me out, Mike thought. Without taking his eyes off the Vurasoan, he told the others, "These beings rely a lot on sense of smell to communicate. That, and they use these stones as intermediaries to convey emotions."

Georges said, "But they've been talking to one another, too."

"Sure," Rishona said. "To *one another*. But to someone from another tribe -- "

" -- Or another species -- " Mike said.

" -- they use other methods. Just as we send purely mathematical messages to advanced Galactic species during first contacts, even though we don't speak that way."

Natai's minor stood on his major's hump again. "I *must* insist, as a member of the species that initiated this mission, that I take part in this contact effort."

Mike sneaked a glance at the Vurasoan leader again, wondering how long his patience might endure. *It's clear, though*, he thought, *that Natai's patience is about at an end.*

Mike pointed at the stone in the Vurasoan's two-thumbed hand. Then he pointed to Natai. When the Vurasoan didn't react at first, he pointed again to the stone, and back to Natai.

When the Vurasoan turned away from him, Mike's heart jumped -- he feared the being was about to walk away. But then the leader raised his arms and addressed the other Vurasoans in a rapid-fire, guttural tongue.

Asking their advice, Mike wondered, *or calling them to arms again?*

The other four Vurasoans responded at once to their leader's speech, but their facial structure allowed for so little movement that Mike had no sense of whether they were shouting approval or rejection. *It's like staring into a cat's face*, he thought. *It's easy to lay our own emotions over their expressions, to read too much into a slight widening of the eyes or a turn of the head.*

A sharp gesture from their leader, and the other Vurasoans fell silent instantly, as if they were an orchestra that had reached a musical conclusion. Then the leader turned back toward Mike. *Here it comes*, he thought.

The Vurasoan gestured toward Natai with one hand while holding the stone in the other. Natai's minor told Mike, "You see? This is the time in which I learn about these beings. You cannot know how I've waited for this moment."

But the next moments were obviously confusing ones for the Vurasoan, who kept trying to make eye contact with the major, and was clearly waiting for that larger being of the Cetronen pair to hold out his hand. Natai's minor was reduced to frantic hand-waving to draw the Vurasoan's attention to him.

The Vurasoan finally held the stone out toward the minor, who held out both hands to accept it. *The Vurasoan isn't looking toward the skies this time*, Mike thought. *And considering what little expression his facial features allow, and the way his head and bone shield are tilted -- is he somehow amused by all this? Dammit, I should know better than to try to interpret an unfamiliar species' body language, but that's what it looks like.*

For Natai's part, the minor seemed to be taking everything in stride, as he held onto the stone much longer than Mike did. *Maybe*, Mike thought, *there's something to this after all. Maybe these two species share a bond Humans can't. For Natai's sake, I hope so.*

But suddenly the Vurasoan leader's stance stiffened, and he snatched the stone away from Natai's minor, who yelped in surprise. A quick shout to the other Vurasoans, and he and the four others stretched out their forelimbs, fell forward, and were quadrupeds again.

"Uh-oh," Mike said, pulling his stunner. "Back off, Natai."

The major took a couple steps backward, and Mike had the distinct impression that was the major's doing, in a rare moment of initiative, because the minor was standing on his hump, saying, "I cannot understand this -- he believes I'm an animal!"

Mike stepped backwards, stunner at the ready as he waved Georges and Rishona back, as well. "Fire at the slightest movement toward any of us," he said. "Highest stun setting."

Georges muttered, "That might not be enough."

The Natai minor scrambled over the major's chest and onto his shoulder even as the major rushed forward, went low, and slammed into the Vurasoan leader. The major's powerful fists hammered the Vurasoan's chest repeatedly as the Vurasoan tried to leverage his bony shield around to strike at the major's face and shoulders.

Goddam it, Mike thought, and fired a stunner bolt at the Vurasoan leader. To either side of him, Georges and Rishona targeted a series of bolts at the other Vurasoans, who were trying to rush to their leader's aid.

The Vurasoan leader was the first to fall, whether from the major's blows or the stunner blasts, Mike couldn't tell. Then everyone turned their firepower to the other Vurasoans, who didn't quite make it to Natai.

As the final Vurasoan crashed to the ground, Mike touched behind his ear. "Katarina, we're on our way. Keep the lock open." He told Georges and Rishona, "*Go!* Before someone or something else comes along." *Luther*, he thought. *I'm so sorry*.

As Georges and Rishona ran toward the *Cosmic Egg*, Mike turned back toward the fallen Vurasoans and did a quick scan with his wrist sensor. The Vurasoan leader, the one Natai's major had taken on, was badly injured but should survive. The others, only stunned, would have bruises and plenty of aches, but nothing more.

Natai's minor was resuming his usual position on the major's hump, his tail whipping back and forth like an angry cat's. "You were right, Mike. Why did you have to be right?"

"What do you -- oh, you mean about...them not being pairs."

"The animals on this planet *are* pairs. It's the sentient beings who are...singletons."

"Natai -- you risked all our lives on what turned out just to be accidents of biology. There's no master plan deciding all this. We've got to *go*."

Natai's major turned and began to lumber toward the *Cosmic Egg*, and once again the minor seemed taken by surprise, and stood on the major's hump and looked directly at him. For a moment Mike thought the minor would protest the major's insistence upon leaving. Then the major looked down and Mike could tell a silent communication passed between them. By all accounts, Cetronen didn't have empathic or telepathic abilities -- perhaps the slightest change in expression, the eyes moving beneath that jutting brow, or the ears tilting just so, something Humans couldn't recognize, held the key to understanding.

Either way, Natai's minor turned slowly around and took its accustomed position on the major's hump, hands folded as if resigned. Natai proceeded at an impressive trot toward *Cosmic Egg*, with Mike rushing to keep up.

Within half a minute Mike was through the shuttle's outer airlock door, close on Natai's footsteps. Rishona sat mutely, make a brave show of holding back tears, Georges only muttered, "No more of this...no more," and Katarina lifted them away from Vuraso as if the world itself was repelling them away from its surface and back toward the stars.

CHAPTER TWENTY-THREE

As the *Egg* neared its matching orbit with *Asaph Hall*, *Cerenam* also came into view. The Natai minor, who was sitting in the co-pilot's position next to Katarina, jumped up and down on its major's hump. "I can already see that our raider is beginning to heal itself," he said. "Its biological systems are working better than I would've imagined."

Mike, sitting right behind the Cetronen, said, "About time something went right for us."

The minor asked, "May I try to contact my captain over your comm so all of you may hear?"

Katarina opened a channel. "Go ahead."

"Captain Codari? Can you hear me? How are repairs proceeding?"

Codari's answer was audio-only. "We are quite well. I'm grateful that you've returned safely. I was worried when you did not report in right away."

"Our mission was quite busy...sometimes terrifying."

"I see. But all are safe now?"

Mike leaned forward so Codari could hear him over the shuttle's comm. "Luther Kindred -- one of my crew -- didn't make it."

A silent moment, then Codari said, "I wish I had been given the opportunity to know him. We will honor him as we would one of our own. But forgive me, Mike, I must ask Natai -- was your mission fruitful?"

Natai's minor said, "Fruitful, yes. But we did not learn what we wished. In fact, quite the opposite."

A longer silence this time, which had Mike fighting to hold back anger. *Of course*, he thought, *Codari will grieve more over his own species' lost hopes than he would over a Human he'd never met.* Then the Cetronen captain said, "I'll require a full report, of course, Natai. Mike, I'm grateful to you and the other *Asaph Hall* crewmembers who helped Natai with his discovery -- even though we did not learn what we'd hoped for."

Join the club, Mike thought. *For every wonder we've seen, every bit of knowledge we've gained, we've all paid a terrible price.*

*****

Another funeral gathering on the hangar deck, this time for Luther. More solemn words and remembrances. Mike was ashamed that he knew so little about the man he'd worked with for so many years. He'd thought of him mostly as a quiet man, responsible, genetically engineered to be physically strong. *And he loved our roast beef sandwiches here on the Hall,* Mike recalled. *He tried to explain to me once why they were so good -- something about an individual replicator setting he'd come up with.*

But during the remembrance ceremony, Rosa mentioned his six brothers, about whom Mike knew nothing. They were all groundlings, had never been in space, not even to the Moon for a vacation. Luther was the wild one of the family, the risk-taker.

Chief Engineer Molly Hakata revealed that she'd been Luther's shipmate for years -- he preferred to be discreet about such matters, she said, although apparently the time for that was over, since Molly went on to describe some of their lovemaking in such detail that Mike could've sworn he *heard* people blushing.

Molly saw their reaction and started laughing, covering her face with her hand. Then the hand moved up to her eyes and Mike heard her sobbing, saw her shoulders shaking. Rosa went to comfort her and then the casket was launched just as Linna's had been, except Luther's destination was the more traditional one of Vuraso's sun.

Alice's voice over ship's comm interrupted the final moments of the ceremony: "Stations, everyone. This isn't a drill. The *Meradeus* just popped out of stardrive, and it's bearing down on us pretty quickly."

Mike looked toward where he thought Rosa was standing, didn't see her, then rushed toward the bridge.

*****

When Mike stepped onto the *Asaph Hall*'s bridge, he found Rosa had gotten there ahead of him and was standing at the center of the chaos, directing the crew's response as if conducting a symphony. To Darwin, at the con, she said, "I want an immediate stardrive solution out of here if necessary."

Darwin responded, "We're pretty close to Vuraso's gravity well for that."

"Only way I'm using it is if our only other choice is let *Meradeus* blast us out of space. Georges -- any response from the Drodusarel?"

Georges, next to Darwin at nav and comm, said, "None. Continuing to send."

"Katarina? Weapons?"

"Ready. For all the -- "

" -- good they'll do against a Sobrenian ship. I know."

Mike asked, "Can Govanek let us know about any weaknesses the ship has?"

"I already tried that," Rosa said. "She's a geologist, not a weapons specialist. She touched behind her ear. "Lauren?"

"Infirmary's ready. If there's anyone left alive to treat afterwards."

Damn," Rosa said. "I'd really rather not go out on such a pessimistic note."

Mike told her, "We play the notes in the score we're given."

Rosa let go a deep breath and told Darwin, "Ready with that jump?"

"Ready," Darwin said, but doubt made itself obvious in his voice.

Mike asked, "What about *Cerenam*?"

"I already talked to Codari. He says do whatever we have to -- fight or run. *Cerenam* still isn't up to doing either one."

Georges said, "Captain, the *Meradeus* -- it's coming in pretty hot."

"Let's see," Rosa said, and took a close look at the main viewscreen, which displayed a graphic of the captured Sobrenian ship's trajectory. "You're right. A pretty good fraction of lightspeed."

Mike went to a sensor console, made a quick check, and said, "They won't be able to stop here at Vuraso. Not without tearing their ship apart."

Darwin said, "Maybe they're looking to make an attack run on *Cerenam* and us -- then come back and pick up the pieces."

Mike took a closer look at the sensor readout. "Nope -- weapons not fired up. I'm trying to get a reading on lifesigns -- maybe something happened."

Rosa took a long look at the display on the main viewscreen, as if she were confronting an interesting scientific mystery rather than a potential danger to herself and her crew. "What *are* they doing?"

Darwin says, "Their trajectory and speed haven't changed since they dropped out of stardrive, No course corrections. And they're about to skim Vuraso's atmosphere."

Mike looked up from the sensors. He had the report on lifesigns he'd been looking for. Despite everything the Drodusarel had done, he could barely bring himself to say the words. "They're all dead."

The bridge became still. It took Rosa to break the silence. "What happened?"

"No way of knowing," Mike said. "There's a lot of damage inside the ship, as far as I can tell."

Rosa stared at the receding ship. "Maybe some of the Sobrenians survived and tried to fight back. Unless someone wants to overtake that ship someday and get on board, that's going to stay a mystery."

Meradeus grazed Vuraso's outer atmosphere, its automatic shields flaring red, then white, the ship bouncing off that atmosphere, now off on a new tangent, the glow of its shields fading, and the *Meradeus*, crewed only by its Sobrenian and Drodusarel dead, bursting outward into open space again, destination unknown.

*****

Not quite an hour later, Mike and Rosa were floating within the viewing sphere. On the all-encompassing display, the area of Vuraso Mike and the others had explored remained hidden on the opposite side of the planet. In the southern hemisphere, storm systems raged over much of the major continent. Far to the north, a canyon formed a harsh slash worthy of Mars's Valles Marineris. Near the equator, lava from a volcano on Vuraso's nightside marked a winding course into the ocean.

"A world as complex and unknowable as any other," Mike said.

Rosa didn't take her eyes from the display. "Philosophy? Not like you."

Mike smiled, realizing in that instant it represented his first unforced smile in some time. "Just after Linna died, I thought I'd never smile again."

"Hmmph. I knew you would. And I would. But maybe we'll never be young again."

"Forty-five doesn't seem so old." He told Rosa, "Neither should fifty-five."

"Hardly middle-aged. With luck, we still have more days ahead of us than behind."

"I thought I was ready to give up everything," Mike said. "This ship, exploration -- all of it."

"What changed?"

Mike stared away from the planet and out toward the stars.

"I found myself...I don't want to say enjoying the mission, exactly. I mean, Luther's death on top of Linna's -- I was ready to leave. I guess you'd say...I ended up *engaged*. I met a fascinating species. One of them handed me something that let me catch a glimpse of what Linna might have felt with her empathy."

"It's why we take the risk. It could easily have been you as Luther that died. Imagine what Syradok's going through."

"How'd he take what happened to *Meradeus*?"

"Lots of bluster, just what you'd expect from a Sobrenian captain. But I know it hurt. Species doesn't matter. Codari's right. A captain's place is on his ship."

"He could've been dead now, too."

"None of which is the point. He's a captain. Just as you're an explorer, Mike. Just as I'm both. We look backward only to cherish our best memories, never to let them rule us. Forward, always forward for us."

"Not for Georges. He decided he's heading back to Earth."

"Yeah. He did well for a long time, from what I understand of his family situation. But they're deeply committed to their past -- their traditions -- and they've drawn him back to them."

Mike said, "Maybe it's just temporary. Maybe he'll head back out one day. Either way, he's been farther and done more things than most people have."

"You know Alice is leaving, too. Transferring to *Sagdeyev*. So still exploring. Just not with us."

"I didn't know that. I'll...miss her."

"If you don't mind me saying, it looked to me like the two of you had become close in the past few days."

"We had," Mike said. "And I'll miss her. But if she wants to leave, maybe that's best."

"Hmm. I won't pry further. Then there's Teresa. Who knows what she's going to do?"

"I really don't care."

"Honestly, I don't, either. I can't imagine she'll be kept on as an ambassador."

"She's the last person I want to talk about."

"I hesitate to ask, Mike -- you're staying with us, aren't you?"

"What else would I do?"

"I'd hoped for a more enthusiastic answer."

"I'm sorry, I didn't mean it that way. But if I didn't stay here, what would I do? Go back to Earth? Sit around immersed in virts all day? Find a little village, putter around, say 'hi' to people I pass on the street?"

"Maybe someday," Rosa said, smiling. "When that's all we can manage."

Mike looked out toward the planet below, and beyond, toward the infinite stars. "But not just yet."

*****

Later, as Mike eased himself into bed, and let his breathing slow, he hoped part of his consciousness would remain aware, would allow him to try to touch Linna this time in his dream.

And in those final restless moments before he let sleep take him, he smiled, confident in the knowledge that he *would* touch her, first just a finger, then his hand, grasping her and sweeping her away from that star's incandescent fury and into that safe place where the best memories of her, her gentle hands, her skin's aroma, resided, secure in the knowledge that she was forever traveling, forever headed outward, exploring.

222

About the Author

Dave Creek's books include two short story collections – *A Glimpse of Splendor* and *The Human Equations*. His most recent book is *The Silent Sentinels*, a novella.

He's also a regular contributor to *Analog Science Fiction and Fact,* where many of his short stories first appeared.

Find out more about Dave's work at www.davecreek.net, on Facebook at Fans of Dave Creek, and on Twitter, @DaveCreek

In the "real world," Dave is a retired television news producer.

Dave lives in Louisville with his wife Dana, son Andy, a floppy-eared Corgi named Peggy, and two sleepy cats -- Hedwig and Hemingway.

www.ingramcontent.com/pod-product-compliance
Lightning Source LLC
Chambersburg PA
CBHW071150180726

48291CB00007B/2395